THE FOXE & THE HOUND

USA TODAY BESTSELLING AUTHOR
R.S. GREY

The Foxe & the Hound
Copyright © 2017 R.S. Grey
All rights reserved. No part of this book may be reproduced or transmitted in any form, including electronic or mechanical, without written permission from the publisher, except in the case of brief quotations embodied in critical articles or reviews.

This book is a piece of fiction. Names, characters, places, and incidents are the product of the author's imagination or are used fictitiously. Any resemblance to actual events, locales, or persons, living or dead, is coincidental.

This book is licensed for your personal enjoyment only. This book may not be re-sold or given away to other people. If you are reading this book and did not purchase it, or it was not purchased for your use only, then you should return it to the seller and purchase your own copy. Thank you for respecting the author's work.

Published: R.S. Grey 2017
authorrsgrey@gmail.com
Editing: Editing by C. Marie
Proofreading: JaVa Editing & Red Leaf Proofing
Cover Design: R.S. Grey
ISBN: 1546496726
ISBN-13: 978-1546496724

CHAPTER ONE

Madeleine

THE LOVE BETWEEN him and me isn't right. Some would even say it's unnatural...*wrong*. All they see is his size, and it intimidates them. He is massive, too big for his own good, really, but he's also handsome—*so handsome*—with chocolate brown eyes I can't resist. I won't sugarcoat it though—he's not without his flaws. He's a terrible listener, and frankly, independent to a fault. He's a sloppy kisser, and he leaves his things everywhere. But every time I come home and run my fingers through those luscious locks, I forget all of his faults. And when that hair falls out and gets all over the couch, and the bed, and my clothes, and the rug, I don't fret. I always know I'm just one lint-roller away from everlasting love.

Because he's the love of my life.

And he's my dog.

Well, technically he's my puppy.

Barely a few months old and already he's the size of a

small horse. Apparently, he's going to get pretty big, but I didn't know that when I adopted him. At the shelter, I walked past a tiny black and brown fur ball sitting in a cage all alone, barely a few weeks old. He sat there quietly, not begging to be petted or whining about his accommodations. He stared up at me quietly, studying me with those deep brown semisweets and I was head over heels.

Just like all the other schmucks filling out adoption papers, I'd walked into that shelter fully intending to leave just as dog-less as when I arrived. I'd even texted my best friend, Daisy for affirmation.

Madeleine: I'm just going to look. That's all.
Daisy: Oh, sure...Text me a picture of the dog you take home because you are NOT leaving there empty-handed.

I wanted to prove her wrong, but then I stumbled upon that little floof.

He's really cute, I told the shelter volunteer.

I agree. Unfortunately, he's too energetic, she lamented. *He's an owner surrender. The man who dropped him off yesterday—I think he was a firefighter—couldn't handle him.* I laughed and had her bring him into a little playpen so I could judge for myself. We played fetch and he acted like puppies do—energetic and happy for the attention—but then ten minutes in, he stumbled into my lap, curled up into a little ball, and promptly fell asleep. I was a goner.

"What kind of dog is he?" I asked, already imagining where he would sleep at my apartment. I'd get a small, cushioned bed and put it right at the foot of mine. I'd try to keep him off the furniture at first, but I knew I'd inevitably cave and give him couch privileges—who can say no to those doe-eyes?

The volunteer, who I now suspect moonlights as a used car salesman, shrugged and told me he was *of mixed heritage.*

"Do you mean like, a mutt? So how big do you think he'll get?"

She pretended to study his front paw, on which he'd rested his adorable little snout. "Oh, with those tiny little things? He probably won't get any bigger than a small golden retriever."

I chuckle thinking back on that exchange now. His paws—those "tiny little things"—seem to double in size every night. They are now big enough to carry the both of us down the sidewalk at breakneck speeds, even as I tug on his leash, trying to get him to slow down.

"Heel, Mouse! Heel!"

Yes, his name is Mouse, and when people hear it, they think I'm being so funny. *A massive dog named Mouse?! How clever.* I smile and nod, and I definitely do not tell them I named him Mouse when he *was* the size of an actual field mouse.

"Mouse, I have organic salmon treats!" I try again, and finally my voice seems to break through his thick skull. He slows his gait until he's right beside me on the sidewalk, staring up at me with those dopey eyes. His tongue lolls around, and if dogs can smile, Mouse grins ear to ear. He really is a dapper thing.

I feed him a treat and then hold another one in my closed palm so he knows it's coming. I've discovered that while I may not be the best trainer, I am fairly adept at canine bribery. And that will have to suffice for now, considering I'm already in my work clothes.

It's Monday morning and we're on our way to the vet. We've been multiple times in the last few months—another thing the volunteer conveniently forgot to mention. Puppies apparently need more shots than babies. I seriously think that he has better healthcare than I do.

This morning I formulated the questionable plan of walking Mouse to his appointment before work. Ever the optimist, I dreamed of a nice leisurely stroll, in which he'd finally heed the training I'd inconsistently applied. Mouse, however, is more of a realist. He wants to sniff and tangle himself in his leash. He wants to run and fulfill his destiny as a squirrel hunter. I consider aborting the mission and turning back, but I don't think I even could at this point. I have a crude understanding of anatomy, and wonder if it's possible for my arm to pop out of its socket like a fought-over Barbie doll.

He starts to pull again, having locked onto some kind of woodland creature up ahead. I panic and shove the salmon treat in front of his nose.

"Wild-caught Atlantic salmon treats, Mouse! *Remember*?!"

He doesn't remember. He doesn't give a shit about my stinky salmon treats, because whatever is up ahead is *wild and uncaught*. I guess that like a character in a cartoon, squirrels probably morph into bacon-wrapped filets in his eyes. He starts to pull and I trot after him, trying desperately to hang on to his leash. He is encouraged by the resistance and starts picking up speed. Suddenly I'm at a full sprint, and I'm convinced I see sparks flying from my high heels.

"No! Mouse! NO. HEEL!" I'm shouting at the top of my lungs, but he's not listening.

He's running and I'm tripping over my feet, trying hard

to keep up.

"SIT! DOWN! NO! *DO YOU WANT A TREAT*?!" I'm shouting nonsense at this point, hoping something will stick, but all he hears is the roar of the adoring crowd. He's gaining speed and I lose my footing. I nearly go down, but I catch myself in the nick of time.

I realize I look and sound hysterical at this point, but I have no choice. I remember seeing news stories about 90 pound teenagers summoning superhuman strength to lift entire cars off of their fathers, so I close my eyes and tug hard on his leash. Unbelievably, the message registers, and for a moment he stops, turns and faces me.

"Good…boy…Mouse…" I whisper, fearful of breaking whatever spell I'd cast. Though he rarely acknowledges my commands, his eyes light up at the sound of praise. He finally notices the homemade treats in my left hand.

"That's right, Mouse," I huff, trying to catch my breath. "All of this can be yours, and more, if you just—no, no, don't look at that squirrel—"

Mouse resumes course, leaping and jerking the leash out of my hand. I go down, limbs flying, and am greeted by the sharp sting of asphalt digging into my left knee and palm. I wince and squeeze my eyes closed, aware of the tears trying to escape down my cheeks. *I will not cry. I will not cry over a dog.*

"MOUSE!"

I sound bloodthirsty, irate—and I am. As soon as I catch up to him, I am going to surgically attach his leash to my hand, and then I am going to shove the rest of the salmon treats in the trash because the days of salmon treats are over. No more of the good shit—he can eat the store-bought crap like every other mangy mutt.

"Jesus! What the—" a masculine voice says from

around the corner.

I whip my head up and the blood drains from my face. That's where Mouse has gone. He pulled out of my hold and whipped around the corner. I push to my feet and hurry to follow after him, petrified of what I will find on the other side. He's a friendly dog, but he can be overzealous at times. Like an escaped mental patient that just wants to lick all of the faces in the entire world.

"Mouse!" I try again as I round the corner and find the most horrifying scene imaginable.

The pieces are easy to put together. There is a man sitting on the sidewalk. Mouse is on top of him, licking his face, and maybe that wouldn't be so bad if not for the mud. I cringe as I stare down at the massive puddle at my feet. I can imagine it now: Mouse rounding the corner, bounding right through the puddle, and then leaping on this stranger with enough force to knock him off his feet. His suit is completely covered in mud—his *designer* suit from the cut of it.

Shit. Shit. Shit.

I cannot afford to buy this stranger a new suit, so I only have one option. I will kill Mouse. I will kill him like Cruella de Vil and make him into a beautiful new fur suit.

"I am *so* sorry," I say, but then I realize he can't hear me because my hand is still covering my mouth, as I'm completely shocked at the audacity of my puppy.

"*Are you kidding me?*"

That's what the stranger says.

Though his words aren't nasty, the tone he uses definitely is.

I leap into action, realizing it's been nearly a minute and Mouse is still on him, licking his face. I grab ahold of his collar and yank him off.

"Bad dog!" I reprimand, hoping to convey my anger into dog-speak.

Mouse stares up at me, happy and oblivious. To him, it's been a splendid morning. It's not yet noon and he's had a walk, leapt through mud, and mauled a perfect stranger.

The stranger.

I'm reminded that he's still there as he gets to his feet and wipes at his suit, trying in vain to clear off most of the mud. It's no use. There are massive, muddy paw prints covering the entire front of his pressed white shirt and blue jacket.

"Are you hu—"

I have every intention of asking him if he's hurt, I do, but then I finally look up at his face for the first time and I am utterly speechless. Mouse didn't just maul a stranger. He mauled what Daisy and I would call *a perfect male specimen.* If Mouse had killed him, I could have stuck a pin in his body and mailed him to the Smithsonian. *Homo sapien perfectus.*

Even muddy, he gives most of Hollywood a run for their money in the looks department. And if he weren't currently scowling at me, I'd swoon. Hell, even with the scowl, I swoon a little bit. It's that perfect combination of piercing green eyes and strong jaw. He's clean-shaven, and his brown hair has been tousled by careful hands. He's tall, and even with his suit on, I can tell he's in formidable shape. It takes all of three seconds to confirm that he's the best-looking man I've ever seen in real life, and he's currently telling me to get my dog under control. He says I shouldn't have a dog like that if he's not properly trained. He is the preacher and I am the choir.

I can hardly do more than nod dumbly.

"He's a puppy," I say. Like that explains everything.

"Puppies aren't immune to training," he says, narrowing his eyes on me like *I'm* the problem—*me*, not the hellhound now sitting contentedly at my feet.

I think he's going to continue berating me, but he shakes his head and turns in the opposite direction down the sidewalk.

No! He can't leave. The last time a man that handsome stopped in this tiny town was back when Marlon Brando's car broke down on the nearby interstate in 1954. The chamber of commerce had a plaque made up and everything.

"Hey wait! Could I, umm...let me cover your dry-cleaning bill!" I shout after him. "Or maybe a chiropractor's appointment? Are you hurt?!"

He waves away my offer and heads back down the street, clearly in a hurry to distance himself from me. I stand there, frozen, admiring his retreating backside. It's incredibly depressing. I haven't come across a man who's elicited that immediate stomach-churning, hands-shaking, brain-short-circuiting reaction in years—maybe ever—and this stranger did. *He sure did*, and now he's walking away, retreating into the distance, and I know I'll probably never see him again.

I sigh and look down at Mouse. He's watching me with his head tilted to the side.

"You little monster. You could have at least kept him pinned a little longer, maybe given me a chance to win him over with my dazzling personality."

Mouse barks in response.

I remember that I'm currently bleeding *and* running late for my vet appointment. I sigh, regretting this latest episode in The Life of Madeleine Thatcher—one in which the stranger in the blue suit will likely have nothing more than a brief cameo.

CHAPTER TWO

I HATE TEXAS. I'm a northerner at heart. In Chicago, I could walk down a crowded city street and not have to make eye contact with a single person. Apparently in rural Texas, I can't even make it to work without getting mauled by a stranger's dog.

I still can't believe it.

I'm pissed.

And I'm late for work.

I left the frazzled brunette on the sidewalk yelling something about dry-cleaning—as if a bit of starch could fix the problems she has. Her time would be much better spent training that puppy, which is only going to keep getting bigger. What if I'd been elderly? Injured? Not in the mood to deal with mud on my suit?

I tear it off and toss it aside. There are a half dozen identical ones lined up in my closet, but I convince myself that one was my favorite. *She ruined my favorite suit* sounds much more dramatic than *she ruined my suit.*

I'm good at holding a grudge.

I brought that with me from Chicago too. That city knows how to really hang on to something. Just take the weather—eight months of winter just to spite the other four. Here in Texas, it's late spring and it's sunny and I wanted to enjoy a nice stroll to work, but she ruined that too.

I add that to my growing grudge as I finish changing and head back out the door. I've already notified the staff that I'll be running late, but it's still going to throw off the entire day. I wish I could have told that to the brunette, but I settled on berating her about dog training instead—not my most dignified moment, but it's hard to stay composed when a dog is trying to play hockey with your tonsils. I managed to suppress the obscenities that were filling my head. Just because I'm from Chicago doesn't mean I have to be a stereotype.

My car is waiting for me outside, so black and shiny. I apologize for thinking I could leave it behind. I learned my lesson the hard way.

The parking lot at work is full when I pull in, which means I'm running even later than I thought I was. I whip into my reserved spot and run through the back entrance. I hate tardiness, and I hate being behind on my schedule. I'll have to work fast to catch up.

My white coat is hanging on the back of my desk chair; I snatch it as I nod to a few of the office staff and offer up my lame apologies for being late. It's only my third week on the job, so I haven't been here long enough to prove how timely I am. I have the brunette to thank for that as well. I swear, if I ever see her again, I'll let her have it.

"Dr. Foxe, you have quite a few patients lined up this

morning," one of the assistants says when I step out into the hallway. I'm adjusting the collar on my white coat before she hands me the first file.

I nod. "Right, well, I don't want to keep them waiting any longer. Who's the first up?"

"Looks like it's Ms. Thatcher and her dog," she squints at the scribbled paperwork. "Moose, I think."

A half step later, I turn the corner to find the infamous brunette standing at the reception desk, regaling half the office staff with a story.

About me.

She's telling them about the incident and they're all laughing, enraptured by her words. Her dog—the one I am now intimately acquainted with—has his front paws up on the counter, begging for a treat.

"And you guys, I wish you could have seen the mud. I mean, I really did feel bad for the guy, but he just took off—*poof*—and now I swear to god, somewhere in Hamilton, there's some hot guy tromping around with my dog's paw prints all over his fancy suit."

Everyone erupts in laughter.

"Did you catch who he was?" my receptionist asks as she passes over a Band-Aid to the brunette. Apparently my suit wasn't the only casualty of the morning.

She shakes her head, her back still facing me. "He definitely isn't from around here. I'd have recognized him."

"Maybe he's traveling for business?" the receptionist offers.

"Yeah, he had that look about him."

"That has to be it. I haven't heard of any newcomers in town. Well, except for—"

I clear my throat. "Madeleine Thatcher and...*Mouse*."

What kind of dog name is Mouse? Moose would have

been more appropriate. No wonder he didn't listen to her earlier when she was trying to rein him in.

She turns at the sound of her name and when she zeroes in on me, her jaw drops and her brown eyes widen in shock.

"*You.*"

Mouse whines and tugs on the leash, trying desperately to get to me. Round two is seconds away from happening. I walk up to Madeleine and extract the leash from her hand while she still tries to recover from shock. She probably thought she'd never see me again. I expected the same, but somehow this is better. I'll get the last word, just the way I like it.

I hold Mouse's collar close by my side and walk him into the first exam room. He tolerates having to heel, but I can tell his energy is simmering just below the surface. He's spring-loaded, and if Madeleine isn't careful, he'll grow even more out of hand.

"You're my vet?" Madeleine asks, trailing after me. "What happened to Katherine?"

"She moved."

"You've got to be kidding me," she whispers under her breath.

"I take it you liked Katherine?"

"She was a few years above me in school. I've known her my whole life." She shrugs and continues, "And she gave me a fat discount."

I close the exam door behind us, but I don't let go of Mouse's leash. He's lost roaming privileges.

"He's a good dog once he settles down and gets to know you," Madeleine says, trying to vouch for him.

"I'd say we were pretty well acquainted this morning."

She crosses her arms and leans against the wall,

nibbling on her lip nervously.

"How long have you had Mouse?" I ask, changing the subject. Although I could easily find the information in the chart, I want to learn it from her.

"A few weeks."

I nod and force myself to look back at the chart.

"I got him from the shelter as a puppy. Well, more of a puppy than now."

She says it like that will win her sympathy.

"What breed of dog did they tell you he was?"

"I believe the word they used was *multinational*. Something like that."

I smile. "He's a Bernese Mountain Dog."

"*No*. They said he was a small lab mix."

"And you trusted them," I reply with a flat tone. "Now you're the proud owner of an untrained dog that will weigh more than you. Your *small lab mix* is going to easily be 120 pounds by next month."

"First of all, thank you for the compliment. Secondly, I don't care what he'll weigh—I just didn't want him to get *killed*." She pushes off the wall and yanks Mouse's leash away from me. "I'm sorry, do you interrogate all of your patients? Or is this some kind of special treatment?"

I look down at Mouse, who's staring up at me fondly. I like him much more than his owner. "You're not my patient, *he is*."

"Right, well, if you're finished, he just needs his next round of shots." She checks the watch on her slender wrist. "And I really need to get to work."

An assistant comes into the room with Mouse's shots, and it takes no time at all to administer them. He's docile and sweet, especially when I hold a treat out for him while I stick him with the needle.

"There. All set."

Madeleine is looking at her phone and shaking her head. "No. No. No."

"What?"

"Are you 100% positive about his breed?"

I'm guessing she's been doing some Googling.

Now, I have to laugh. "Yes. I'm positive. We can send off a DNA sample if you'd like."

She turns her phone around and shows me a photo of an adult male Bernese Mountain Dog. "He's going to be...well, a mountain!"

Though I shouldn't seek retribution, seeing her shock slightly makes up for the ordeal this morning. I feel much better when I walk out of that exam room. I'm scanning the next chart when I let myself dwell on her for a second. Even with the annoying first impression, it's obvious she's beautiful. I studied her surreptitiously during the exam, mainly because she was being so quiet—I wanted to make sure she wasn't doing anything nefarious. Still, it seemed like a waste not to take in the details. She was dressed for work in a cream sheath dress that was tight and cut perfectly for her long legs. Her hair was a rich brown, long, and curled softly down her back. The fact that she was in great shape probably has something to do with lugging Mouse around all day. Maybe on another day, I'd find her irresistible—but here, today, there are too many reasons to push her to the back of my mind and move on to the next customer.

And I do. I forget all about her.

Right up until I walk into my bedroom that evening and trip over my crumpled, dirty suit.

CHAPTER THREE

Madeleine

TODAY, I THINK I finally see why my mother adoringly refers to me as her "lost cause". For years I fought the nickname, arguing that my generation actually tries hard to cultivate the hipster image of not having one's life together. But my ruse falls apart when I line up next to my older brother. He's a doctor. Married. Good hair. You know the type. The fact that he's a wonderful big brother only makes matters worse. He's never missed a birthday. He always makes a point to call me at least once a week, even now that he's back in Hamilton, though I mostly ignore these phone calls because he's married to my best friend, Daisy. I don't have time to talk to them both, and anything I tell her, she can pass along to him.

Not to mention, lately I feel like he's been operating as a spy for our mom during these weekly chats. He can't help but ask about my job, my future, my investment holdings, my love life—can't we just argue politics or religion like a normal dysfunctional family?

Even now, there's a voicemail from him waiting for me on my cell phone, telling me about a housewarming party, but I have no time to call him back because I'm currently circling the toilet bowl of life. I'm late for work *again*, and I'm tripping into my heels as I rush out the door. My coffee is in one hand. My keys and cell phone balance precariously in the other. A banana is wedged in my mouth and a granola bar tucks into the front of my bra. I bolt out of my apartment, lock up, and turn just in time to find my landlord, Mr. Hall, pruning his herb garden across the covered pathway. He looks so innocent with those tiny shears, but I know better. Those damn herbs have already been trimmed to perfection. He's outside, pretending to garden for another reason.

"Ah, Madeleine, there you are," he says, removing his protective eyewear. As if stray rosemary clippings are the most underreported causes of gardening death in America.

I rush past him, waving as I go. After all, with my banana in place, I can hardly carry on a conversation.

"I need to talk to you about rent!" he shouts after me.

I wave again and then add a thumbs up just for good measure. I hold out hope that he means *Rent* the musical, but I'm reasonably sure it's about money. I'm not sure why he bothers. Mr. Hall and I have a very healthy arrangement going where he asks for rent on the first of the month and I pay him piecewise on the subsequent days of the month. But what I lack in timely payment, I make up for in baked goods. Mr. Hall hasn't wanted for banana bread in the three years I've lived here. Muffins, cookies, and cakes have rained down on him like some sort of delicious plague from the Book of Revelations.

I do recognize, however, that I'm pushing it more than

normal this month. I'm majorly overdue, but I have every intention of paying him—just as soon as I make it to work and earn a commission. That's just what I intend to do, if only my car would start. It likes to pretend it's going to fail on me once or twice a month. I slide onto the faded seat and twist the key, and it putters morosely.

"Come onnnnn," I groan, twisting the key again.

There's a low clicking noise, like it wants to start as desperately as I want it to.

I mimic the people in movies and TV, pumping the lifeless gas pedal before twisting the key once more, nearly hard enough to break it in two. The starter clicks pathetically and then, by some miracle, my car sputters to life.

"YES. THANK YOU!" I shout to myself, banging my hands against the steering wheel.

I do not have time for car issues this morning. I look at the bright red clock on my dashboard; I'm already five minutes late for our staff meeting. By the time I pull into the last available spot at the agency, I'm nearing the dreaded ten-minute mark. By that point, I should just feign illness and go home. But, as it is now, I skate into the room by the skin of my teeth and a half-dozen pairs of eyes snap up to look at me.

My boss, Helen, sits at the head of the conference table wearing an ill-fitting chartreuse dress. The rest of planet Earth has agreed to stop making chartreuse happen, but Helen isn't quite ready to give up. The color makes her look ill, but I would never tell her that. Fanned out on either side of her are my fellow real estate agents, all women, all carbon copies of one another. There's a leader, of course—*Lori Gleland.* She's positioned on Helen's right side and she watches me enter the room with a thin, arched brow carefully raised.

"Is this your third late arrival this quarter?" Lori asks, feigning concern. "I do hope everything is going okay for you at home."

I want to take Mr. Hall's pruning sheers to Lori's face, but instead I am a picture of stoic professionalism as I pull out the very last chair at the conference table: my reserved spot. So what if it also happens to be the spot meant for the lowest agent on the totem pole.

"Car trouble," I offer lamely when it's clear Helen isn't going to continue until I speak up.

The agent beside me, Sandra, leans closer and whispers so everyone in the room can hear, "I think you have something stuck in your bra, sweetie. It looks really...lumpy."

"Ah, of course."

I unsheathe the forgotten granola bar from my bra with grace and dignity then tear it open. I'm still hungry, after all.

Sandra rolls her eyes and I smile warmly. Sandra is Lori's minion. What Lori does, Sandra mimics, down to the chunky brown and blonde highlights streaked through short bobs. I take such delight in those chunky highlights. They are the visual manifestation of a request to speak with a manager at Applebee's.

"All right, that's enough of a distraction," Helen cuts in. "Madeleine, I'd like you to stay after the meeting so we can chat."

The room might as well break out in a chorus of *um-mum-mums* because Helen has never once asked me to stay after a meeting. Fortunately, Helen pulls the attention away from me a moment later by announcing with a sing-songy voice that "Lori was our top-selling agent last month!"

Sandra breaks out in staccato solo applause, but it fades slowly as no one moves to join her. "What is that, the fifth month in a row?"

Lori bats away Sandra's compliment. "Six, actually—but who's counting?"

Everyone titters at her terrible joke, and then Helen plays right into her ego by asking Lori to define her selling technique for the rest of us. If there's one thing Lori doesn't need, it's an audience. I predict her selling technique has something to do with showing the most cleavage possible, considering we're all a millimeter away from an eyeful of areola in that tank top of hers. Instead, she unveils what she calls *The Five Ss.*

"Smile, Suck Up, and Sell! Sell! Sell!"

Groundbreaking stuff here.

"Copyright Lori Gleland, all rights reserved," she adds with a laugh. "No, but really," she says, her tone turning deathly serious. "I am thinking about copyrighting that phrase."

"You would trademark it."

All eyes jump to me. I hardly ever speak up in meetings.

"What?" Lori asks.

I sit up a little straighter, already regretting my choice to leap into the conversation.

"You don't copyright a phrase, you trademark it, and that's the worst phrase I've ever heard, so there's no point in trademarking it."

I leave off the second half of my advice since I'd prefer to leave this conference room with my eyes still inside my skull.

Lori laughs awkwardly. "Right, well, the *point* is, selling real estate is about more than just a pretty face,

Madeleine."

I want to ask her why she's taken an hour to pile on so much makeup then, and bright blue eye shadow no less. What a treat.

"I think the *esses* sound great!" Sandra adds, trying to loop the conversation back to focus on her master's brilliance.

"The Five Ss," Lori corrects, adding air quotes this time. She really does intend on trademarking the thing.

The meeting is wrapped up shortly after that and I linger behind as I've been instructed. It's painful to know that five pairs of eyes are watching me as the rest of the agents leave the conference room, but I pretend to be enthralled by my notes from the meeting and act like I don't see them staring at me.

My notes read as follows:

- Take Mouse on a walk

- Let him loose so he's someone else's problem

- Maybe feed him double dinner and he won't wake you up at 4:30 AM whining??

- Buy snorkel, steal coins from fountain at the mall to pay rent

- Avoid Mr. Hall, but stealthily deliver double baked goods to his doorstep

"Madeleine." I jump when Helen says my name. "Did you find that meeting informative?"

I move to cover my notes, though she's still sitting at the head of the conference table so she can't see them anyway. I smile and nod, even tacking on a rambling compliment about how well she runs her meetings. I know she doesn't believe me because when she smiles, it doesn't meet her eyes.

She stands up out of her chair and walks closer to me. I

slide my notes onto my lap and she perches on the table right beside me. At this distance, her acrid yellow dress makes my eyes water, so I focus instead on her face—her sad, pitying face.

"Do you *like* working in real estate, Madeleine?"

"Of course!" I reply quickly.

"You can be honest with me. If this isn't the job you imagined it would be, I'd rather you tell me now than—"

"Helen, I really enjoy my job." It's the truth. "The days where I'm meeting with clients and showing them listings are my favorite. I enjoy the thrill of the chase, I just haven't found my stride yet."

"You've worked here for a year this month, Madeleine, and you've only closed on one listing."

She's merciful in leaving out the fact that the one listing I managed to close on was for my brother and Daisy's house. That was six months ago, and I've had no solid leads since.

"Because of that, I think it would be best if for the next two months, I put you on a probationary period."

"*What?*"

She holds up her hand to silence me. "Nothing too serious. I won't be breathing down your neck every second, but I think you need a bit more motivation."

"Don't you think the problem is with Hamilton? This town is growing, but *not* that quickly. There are just not enough people looking to buy property!"

She leans back and shakes her head. "See, that's where you're wrong. Hamilton is flourishing, and if you really put your nose to the grindstone, I know you could be one of my top sellers."

She really thinks it's possible for me to turn my embarrassing sales numbers (or complete lack thereof) around, and when I leave the conference room in a daze, I'm not sure if I'm upset that I'm on probation or inspired by her mini pep talk there at the end. I settle somewhere in the middle at neutral, glazed over. All the other agents are already in their cubicles, placing phone calls and returning emails. Lori has a full headset in place as I pass by her, a blue stress ball throbbing in her left hand. Her face resembles a trader on the stock-market floor as she jots down notes with her free hand.

"That house will set fast, Barney. The lot is oversized and it's only a block over from Main Street. Every client I've been in talks with has wanted to look at that house..." Her voice fades as I continue walking and then it explodes again out of nowhere. "Yes!" she shouts to the whole office. "I just sold Walnut Street!" Then she proceeds to ring the tiny bell that hangs on the corner of each of our cubicles. Helen wants us to ring them every time one of our clients buys or sells a property. If she had it her way, the office would sound like a handbell choir on Easter Sunday.

My bell has been rung exactly once, although I *have* bumped into it accidentally a few times. Lori hates that the most. I swear I heard her whisper *stolen valor* the last time.

"Whoop, there it is!"

"Raise the roof, Lori!"

"YOU GO GIRL!"

The other agents hurry to congratulate her with dated catchphrases and I mumble along with them. It's not fun being Bitter Betty. I'm not used to the role, and it leaves a bad taste in my mouth. Eventually, I will have to leave the agency or learn to put up with Lori in a healthier manner...like killing her with kindness, or murdering her with smiles, or disemboweling her with compliments. That sort of thing.

I drop my coffee and notepad on my desk and take a deep breath. It's time to get to work. My cubicle is clean, my inbox is empty, and I have one blinking red light on my office phone, indicating a voicemail. I smile as I take my seat, confident that it's Mr. Boggs getting back to me about one or more of the houses I showed him yesterday. Mr. Boggs has been a client of mine for as long as I've been working at Hamilton Realty. While he was passed on to me because no other agent could stand working with him, I feel like he and I share a sort of kinship with one another. He's old and grumpy and cynical, everything I aspire to be one day. Also, Helen makes us meet a weekly quota for showings, and I can always count on Mr. Boggs to fill up at least one of my days with aimless wanderings around Hamilton's real estate market.

Too bad the voicemail isn't from him.

It's from Daisy.

"Hey, just wanted to remind you about the housewarming party tonight. Lucas has completely gone insane with inviting people. I don't even know half the guests who are supposed to come, so if you don't show up, I'll kill you—before Mr. Boggs does." Daisy has said from the beginning that at best, ol' Boggsy is just wasting my time, and at worst, he's planning on abducting me. I disagree. "Anyway, come early and bring Mouse if you want to. Last week he chewed off a chunk of our living room rug, and Lucas might let me order a new one if he chews off a little bit more of it. Okay, Beth's calling my name about a patient, so I better go. Have fun dealing with Lore-the-Bore at work today and I'll see you tonight."

Just as the voicemail cuts off, Lori's bell chimes again, announcing another sale.

"I guess I'm just on fire today!" she exclaims.

"You're all that and a bag of chips!" someone shouts.

Though it's tempting, I don't skewer my eye with the nearest pen. Instead, I get to work.

CHAPTER FOUR

I DIDN'T PLAN to be this dysfunctional at 27, but dysfunctionality has a way of creeping up on you. One second, you're 22, wrapping up your undergraduate degree from a top business school, and then suddenly, you're sitting alone in your car at 27, wondering how five years slipped through your fingers without so much as a blink.

There are the obvious struggles—my bills are piling up, my rent is late, and my car is a clunker—but it's the other, more personal aspects of my life that keep me up at night. The fact that I am currently (and probably forever) single is a much harder pill to swallow than my overdue rent. Dealing with car troubles isn't so bad if you have someone there to commiserate with.

Worse, my single status is not from a lack of trying. I am signed up and active on no less than four dating apps. I've attended multiple Hamilton Singles events, and I'm never one to shy away from a blind date.

My mother has been relentless about it too. Just last week on the phone she babbled on about how when she was my age, she already had two kids. I told her I have Mouse, who is pound for pound worth about five kids, but she didn't seem to think that compared. Whatever. There's nothing more I can do. I want to be madly in love as much as she wants me to be, but unless she can wave a wand and magically produce Mr. Tall Dark & Handsome for me, I'm kind of screwed.

See, my lack of a love life doesn't really have anything to do with me. I mean, sure, I'm not *everyone's* cup of tea. I'm kind of sarcastic and crass at times, but Daisy assures me guys don't care about that because of my other more *prominent* features. I think her exact words were, "You're hot, you're in shape, and you've got nice boobs. I don't see the problem."

She might be lying to me to keep me from throwing myself off the nearest cliff, but I've lived in my body long enough to know it's not the problem.

Hamilton is the problem.

This town is small.

Most dating apps show you eligible men within a certain number of miles. I've widened my parameters to encompass the entire county, but the prospects are still abysmal. I scroll through Tinder now as I sit outside of Daisy's house, wondering if I'll see a new face pop up. I don't know why I bother; there are never new faces. I scroll past Jimmy, who was my boyfriend in elementary school for a week and a half. There's Martin, who is about a foot shorter than me on a good day, and Cale, the cowboy who lives on the outskirts of town who isn't half bad-looking once you've had three or four beers. Oh and look, it's Jared, the guy who owns Hamilton's only gym and who routinely updates his dating profile to include even more overly tanned, overly muscled bathroom mirror selfies. I swear if you ran a finger down his arm, you'd come away with spray tan goop.

I have zero new matches on all five of my dating apps, and though I'm tempted to let it get to me, I don't. This is nothing new. Hamilton is Hamilton, and unless I'm willing to pack up and move to a bigger city, I'll have to make the best of it—and I do. Right before I head inside, I RSVP to a Hamilton Singles event in two weeks. I haven't been to one in a month, and I'm optimistic that this one will be worth my time. *See Mother?! Contrary to what you think, I don't just sit at home wallowing in self-pity. I put myself out there.*

Daisy opens her front door when I'm not even a quarter of the way up her front path. She must have been parked at the window, waiting for me.

"Hey stalker."

She ignores me, rushes forward, and grabs my arm.

"I don't want you to get excited, but there's someone here I really think you should meet. Wait..." She scans the ground around my feet. "Where's Mouse?"

"At home. He got really dirty after I took him to the park and I didn't want him ruining your stuff."

She groans. "That's precisely what I *want* him to do. Your brother is so stubborn about hanging on to things. That rug in the family room is hideous, but he doesn't seem to think we need a new one unless the current one is ruined."

I laugh. "I'll try my best to spill my wine tonight."

"Thank you. Now, hurry, there's a new guy here that I've never met before and I *think* he's single!"

Though she seems excited, I'm not. Daisy only moved

back to Hamilton two years ago, and she's routinely confused by who's an actual newcomer and who just decided to grow a beard.

"If it's Kyle Parker again, I'll punch you. He's lived here his whole life Daisy—he just has a man bun now and I swear it confuses you every time."

She rolls her eyes and keeps dragging me after her, which is no simple feat considering the footwear she's decided on tonight. Her whole outfit is spot on and trendy: a simple red dress with nude pumps. Her blonde hair is loosely braided down her back, probably left over from work, and her makeup is just enough to make her already beautiful features stand out even more. I now regret changing into jeans, even if I did put on the pair that makes my ass look, in Daisy's words, "killer".

"Should I change into something of yours?" I ask as we pass through the foyer. "You're a lot fancier than I am."

She turns and gives me a onceover, breaking out in a slow smile. "No, you look hot. That shirt is just tight enough to show off your figure without being indecent, and I like when you wear your hair down like that. It drives guys insane."

I shrug, remembering the zero new matches waiting for me on my dating apps. I guess I'll have to take her word for it.

We pause in the kitchen for wine, and I can see most of their guests clustered out back on their wraparound porch. Surprisingly, it's a nice evening in Texas—not too hot, and the mosquitos have yet to invade for the summer. Everyone is sipping wine or beer and sort of hovering around in clusters. As far as parties go, this is extremely tame.

"No beer pong? No kegs?" I ask as Daisy pours me a glass of chilled white wine, my favorite.

She levels me with a glare. "Your brother wanted a low-key housewarming party."

"Yeah, about that—is it still considered a housewarming party if you guys have already lived here for six months?"

She shrugs as she finishes pouring herself a glass. "It's taken us that long just to furnish the place, so yes, it counts."

I nod and take in my surroundings. Their house is beautiful, one of the older Victorian-style houses that line the streets of downtown Hamilton. It was recently restored, but the original wood floors were left intact. Their dark stain juxtaposed with the white marble countertops and modern light fixtures make the home feel updated and fresh. In short, I'd cut off my right arm to own a house like this.

Honestly, I can't believe it's been six months since I sold it to them. I cringe thinking of how little of that commission check is left. I used a large chunk of it to pay off the last of my student loans, and I put some of it in savings. The rest might as well have floated away like sand for all the good it did me. A couple months of rent and I'm right back where I started: in desperate need of a new client, one who isn't Mr. Boggs.

"Ready to head outside?" Daisy asks me, her tone a little gentler than usual. She can probably sense I've had a hard day at work. There's no need to ramble on about Lori and the rest of her minions; Daisy has heard it all before, and she sympathizes as much as she can. She and Lucas own their own family practice and have the luxury of being their own bosses. I've daydreamed about quitting the agency and going to work for them, but working as an office coordinator in a small doctor's office doesn't really interest me. Besides, I like real estate, even if I'm not very good at it.

We head outside and Daisy sticks close to me as I nod to the guests I know, which is a good portion of them. Most of them are classmates I've kept in touch with over the years. In a small town, it's kind of impossible not to, especially with the assistance of Facebook. Susie Mathers is sitting on a rocking chair a few feet away with her feet up on a cooler as a makeshift ottoman—she's nine months pregnant and about ready to pop. Her husband, Dale, stands just to her left chatting with friends, and all the while, his hand sits on her shoulder. It's a sweet gesture, and it makes me guzzle my wine faster than I should.

I'm about to go refill my glass when Daisy yanks on my arm. "There's the guy!" she whispers. "Over there talking to your brother."

It's not hard to find Lucas. He's hovering on the porch stairs with a small group of guys, and I recognize all of them except the one with his back turned to me. He's wearing jeans and a black t-shirt. I tilt my head in his direction and Daisy nods in confirmation.

I narrow my eyes, trying to assess as much of him as possible from the back. His dark brown hair is mussed up and cute. His arms are toned, and though I don't think I've ever really been the type to notice, he has a great ass. Still, I highly doubt he's new to town. Daisy has steered me wrong too many times in the past.

Lucas sees us standing in the doorway staring and waves us over. The stranger turns and follows his gaze, and I have my answer.

My eyes widen in shock.

Oh, I know him all right.

"No. *No*. I know him," I hiss to Daisy, but it's already

too late. She doesn't hear me—she's too busy playing Cupid and pushing me toward the group. I have no choice but to follow along with her plan. If I plant my feet on the deck and resist her, I'll trip and fall on my face, and that's the only thing worse than actually giving in.

The guys watch us approach. I hug Lucas and nod to his friends, then I reluctantly force myself to glance toward the last man in the group.

Adam.

The asshole vet.

"Madeleine," he says, greeting me with a small nod.

"*Adam.*"

Everyone in the group is silent, staring between the two of us and trying to dissect our cold greeting.

"I hardly recognized you without Mouse," he quips.

I smile and it's fake and he knows it. "And I hardly recognized you without that scowl on your face."

The scowl in question now takes over his handsome features. There, now that's the Adam I know.

Daisy speaks up first. "Wait, you two already know each other?"

"He's Mouse's vet," I explain quickly.

Adam smiles, but it doesn't reach his green eyes. "We met before that though. I have the muddy suit to prove it."

I stare down at my wine, grateful that their back porch isn't lit with spotlights considering how red my cheeks are. "Oh, yeah. True. I guess Mouse mauled him or something the other morning, no big deal."

Lucas doesn't have the decency to keep his mouth shut. "What do you mean Mouse *mauled him*?"

I suddenly hate my brother.

Especially because now I have no choice but to regale the whole group with the story of how I'm the worst dog owner in the world. All the while, Adam stands across from me with one hand in his pocket and the other wrapped around a beer koozie. There's a small smile lingering on his lips and though I wish he would look away, he's watching me, curious—probably champing at the bit to cut me off and finish the story in his own words.

"I apologized and offered to pay for dry-cleaning. He didn't take me up on the offer, and here we are. Can I get anyone a drink?"

Everyone is staring at me like they're deer caught in headlights. It's as if they've never heard of the classic *girl's dog mauls stranger* story.

"Okay, I'll take that as a no," I say, turning to head back into the kitchen to refill my wine glass.

Daisy trails after me and barely manages to contain herself until we have the back door closed.

"That's the guy you emailed me about the other day!?"

It was the morning after the "mauling" incident and I had to tell someone. Now, I regret going into detail about how cute he was. She knows I'm interested.

"Yes." I nod simply. "That's him."

"He's really nice and really good-looking, Madeleine, AND he has a great career too. A veterinarian? How noble is that! He cares about animals."

I over-pour and have no choice but to sip the top of the wine from the glass so it doesn't spill over the edge when I pick it up. Oops.

"I don't see why any of this is relevant."

"Because you're single," she points out.

"Oh right, I'd forgotten."

"And Adam could definitely remedy that situation."

I laugh again. Apparently Daisy didn't read the email carefully enough or listen to my story outside. Her gears must have already been cranking underneath all that shiny hair of hers.

"Why did you invite him here anyway?" I ask, turning the table. "How do *you* know him?"

"Lucas invited him. He's renting the house across the street. Apparently he's only been in town for a few weeks."

I stop sucking the wine from the top of my glass and whip around.

"Excuse me, did you just say he's *renting* a house?"

She shrugs like it's not a big deal. "Yeah. It sounded like he just needed something temporary while he got settled."

So he might be in the market for a house.

Which means he might need a realtor.

He might need *me*.

"If you'll excuse me, I've got to see a man about a house."

"What? No! Daisy, you're supposed to date him, not *work* for him."

I stopped listening to her a while ago and I'm already halfway to the back door. Lori's Five Ss are running through my head. *Smile. Suck up. Sell, sell, sell.* Right. Easier said than done with a man like Adam. Fortunately, I have the foresight to snatch a cold beer from the ice bucket on the back porch just before I make my way back to the group on the stairs.

Smile, I remind myself.

I flash my pearly whites, and I'm confident my dimple is adorably visible. He assesses me as I approach. I try to stretch my smile even wider, and then his green eyes narrow and he frowns. FROWNS. Who frowns at people these days? You're supposed to hide your emotions behind a mask of polite indifference—that's what my mother always taught me.

"Here you go, Adam. A fresh beer for your, uh…koozie."

My hand is outstretched, the beer is there dripping with condensation, and he doesn't take it. He leaves me standing like that for a solid ten seconds, and everyone in the group is stunned into silence. It seems I'm pretty good at ruining the flow of conversation tonight.

"I just started on this one," he replies, holding up his still-full beer.

Lucas chimes in, "I'll take it, Maddie."

I snatch it out of my brother's reach. "You should stay sober, Lucas. What if there's a medical emergency?"

"What, is Mouse coming over later?" Adam quips.

Everybody laughs.

I resist the urge to sear him with my gaze and I think he can tell, because he defuses the situation with a small smile.

"Thank you for the beer." He takes the bottle from my hand, careful to keep our fingers from touching, and plops it down on the railing behind him. "I'll put it right here and when I'm done with this one, I'll drink it."

I grin. "Sounds good. So, Adam, you're new to town?"

He glances toward Lucas and then back to me, clearly confused by my shift in attitude. "Moved here about a month ago."

"He's renting the house across—"

I cut Lucas off before he can continue, my attention laser-focused on Adam. "Where did you move from?"

"Chicago."

He seems to be uncomfortable with my line of questioning, so I try to ease up and act a bit more natural. "Ahhh, Chicago. So you're into hot dogs, deep dishes, large reflective beans, that sort of thing? I've always wanted to visit."

Daisy laughs. "Bullshit, you hate the cold. I tried to get you to go two years ago and you said 'over my dead body'."

If we were sitting down at dinner, I'd kick her in the shin under the table. Since we're all hovering in an awkward circle, I have no choice but to smile and wave away her old, outdated information.

"Oh Daisy. I loooove cold weather now, especially in *Chicago*."

Adam nods. "Yeah, I'm not a fan myself. That was part of the reason why I wanted to move down here."

I scramble. "Oh, right, me too. I wouldn't really call myself a fan of cold weather per se..."

I'm aware that the other members of our group are starting to drop like flies. Two of Lucas' friends have already peeled off, and Lucas himself is inching away. I swear Adam keeps darting his gaze over my left shoulder, trying to find an escape. That can't be right, though. I'm usually an *excellent* conversationalist.

"Did you own property back in Chicago? A house? Condo maybe?"

"Maddie, you're being weird. Stop interrogating the guy," Lucas says, clapping Adam on the shoulder. "C'mon man, you want to see the garage? There's a ping pong table in there."

Adam doesn't even hesitate, fleeing with Lucas without so much as a backward glance in my direction.

I curse under my breath.

"What the hell was that?" Daisy asks, taking my glass and sniffing the wine suspiciously. "Has this gone bad? Did you just have some kind of mini stroke?"

I stomp my foot. "No! Dammit. I was trying to secure

him as my next client."

"By acting as if you have half a brain?"

"I don't know! Usually I don't have a problem talking to clients. Adam makes me nervous."

"Because he's so hot?"

"Because he looks at me like I'm the scum between his toes!"

"Yeah…I did notice that. Did you see his eyes though? They're green—super cute with his brown hair."

"You aren't helping."

"Oh right, sorry."

I scoot closer to her so I can see into the garage. Lucas and Adam are laughing as they set up the ping pong table, and Adam looks much more comfortable now that I'm no longer in his presence. Still, I need to convince him to be my client. "Do you think I should go in there and try to talk to him some more? Maybe grab him another beer?"

Daisy points to where the first beer I brought sits on the railing, lonely and forgotten. "I think you should take a break there, champ."

I suddenly feel like crying. Actual fat tears are seconds away from falling down my cheeks. "I really need a new client, Daisy."

"Do you want me to buy something? I can get a condo downtown, how's that?"

I laugh and a half-sob spills out with it. "You can't swoop in and fix all my problems. Helen put me on probation today."

"What?! You're the best realtor she has. It's not just about who can sell the most houses."

"I appreciate your support, but that's exactly what my job is."

"Yeah, well everyone else who works there looks like a

weird clone. My mom actually saw Sandra at the hair salon last week asking for 'the Lori'. How weird is that?!"

Usually that little snippet of gossip would have made me smile. Not tonight.

"I think I'm going to head home."

She's concerned. "Do you want me to come with you?"

"No. Stay here. Have fun with your guests."

She wraps me in a hug and I don't pull away. I'm not a hugger, but then again, neither is Daisy. "If I can, I'll put in a good word for you with Adam."

I cringe. "Don't bother. I'll find another client somewhere else. And hey, I'm showing Mr. Boggs some houses next week. Maybe he'll actually buy something."

"Hey! Maybe he will."

That's when I know Daisy really does pity me, because we both know Mr. Boggs isn't going to buy a damn thing.

CHAPTER FIVE

I'M IN HAMILTON, Texas, for my family. My brother and his wife live here with my two nieces. My mom moved down here a few years ago, and when shit hit the fan in Chicago, it made sense that I would pack up and join them. I had other options: Los Angeles, New York, Hawaii—*they need veterinarians in tropical paradises too.* My family won out though, and I moved to the Lone Star state. I've been here almost a month now, and I regret my choice every day. It's Saturday night. Yesterday, I was at that housewarming party for my neighbors, but now I'm grocery shopping, because that's the kind of sad turn my life has taken. Back in Chicago, my friends are at the opening of a five-star restaurant, sipping sake—I know because they accidentally included me on the group text about the event. I had to remind them, for the tenth time, that I moved to Texas. They booed and kicked me out of the group.

But I'm not bitter.

I'm here for family.

I weave through the frozen food section and remind myself again, *I'm not bitter*.

I could have plans if I wanted them, but I don't. I'm not in the dating game at the moment. I'm riding the bench, happily. There were a few women who showed interest last night at the party, and my sad, cold heart felt nothing for them. Well, that's not all true. I did feel something for Madeleine, but I think that had more to do with annoyance than anything else. She has an uncanny way of grating on my nerves, and the fact that she just keeps popping up is getting ridiculous. I wonder if it's a small town thing; I'm not used to it. I could go a year in Chicago without bumping into any of my friends unintentionally. By comparison, in the last few days, I've had the displeasure of crossing paths with Madeleine three times.

I laugh out loud.

Make that four times.

There she is standing in the medicine aisle of the grocery store, wearing a pair of short daisy dukes and a white tank top. She has on brown leather flip-flops, and even from my spot at the end of the aisle, I can see that she's painted each of her toenails a different color.

Who is this woman?

And why am I not pushing my cart away at this very moment?

She reaches forward and inspects a box of Band-Aids, and the movement gives me an opportunity to check out her insanely sexy legs...and the matching skinned knees she is undoubtedly here to treat. A gift from Mouse, I'm sure.

Half of me thinks it serves her right for adopting such an impractical dog, and the other half of me (the part still capable of human emotion) feels slightly bad that she's injured.

I glance away, toward the checkout. There's no one in line. I could pay for my shit and be gone in ten minutes, or...

"Adam?"

I whip my gaze back and see her eyeing me suspiciously. I realize I do look odd, hovering there at the end of the aisle, so I push my cart forward until I'm standing right in front of her. She briefly glances over my groceries. There's a ton of fruits and vegetables, a couple pounds of lean protein. By comparison, her basket is filled with apples, ramen, and what looks to be dusty Valentine's Day candy on clearance. Makes sense considering it's mid-May.

"Oh...I was just going to tell the manager that these are probably expired," she says, defending the heart-shaped Reese's.

I look away so she doesn't see my smile. "You don't have to defend your groceries against me."

She grunts under her breath, and it catches me by surprise. Every time I'm around this woman, she has a different personality. One second she's hot, the next she's cold. Last night when she brought me that beer, it almost seemed like she was trying to ingratiate herself to me. Now, she's back to being cold, aloof.

I should turn around and go checkout. After all, I'm not in the market for female companionship, friends or otherwise. Yes, I am aware of the fact that if I *were* looking for a woman, Madeleine would be my exact type. I've always had a thing for brunettes, and she wears her long hair down, loose and curly down her back, wild almost. Her skin tone is warm and inviting, and there are definitely freckles across the bridge of her nose and cheeks. Her bare legs keep drawing my attention, and for some absurd reason, I can't find fault with her mismatching toenail polish. It's kind of endearing.

More than all of that though, she has an air of unabashed confidence about her, like she's never spent a single day uncomfortable in her skin. It's sexy as hell.

"You're being weird."

I look away from her legs and stare up at the Band-Aids. "What?"

"First I see you hovering at the end of the aisle, frozen in place, and now you're here, completely silent. Are you about to have a breakdown or something?"

I frown. "No. I was just…thinking."

She puts the carton of bandages back on the shelf and instead reaches for the generic box sitting beside it.

"I take it my suit wasn't Mouse's only victim?"

I glance up and see her eyeing me with barely contained disdain.

"Listen, can you please spare me the lecture about what a terrible mistake it was to adopt him? I would do it again without a second thought."

I cringe. I suppose I have been a little tough on her, especially considering her intentions came from the right place.

"You're right, no lecture," I begin, offering an olive branch. "You clearly love him, so there's no point in trying to convince you to give him up." Her eyes widen at the absurdity of that idea, so I continue, "He's your dog."

She nods. "Yes. Exactly." Then she glances down at her knees and sighs. "And yes, I've tried to train him to heel, but as soon as he sees a squirrel or a—"

"Well-dressed stranger," I supply, and am pleasantly

surprised when she shoots me a wide smile.

"Yes, exactly. Once he spots something he *likes*, he just takes off with no regard for the human he's dragging behind him."

I nod. "It's not unusual. All puppies are going to do that. It just wouldn't be as much of a problem if he wasn't so big."

She frowns and drops the bandages into her basket. "I swear he doubles in size every night."

"It's not completely hopeless. There's a puppy training class starting at the YMCA tomorrow night."

The words are out before I have time to consider them. Do I want her in my training class? Before tonight, I would have said no, but something about her sad skinned knees plays on my heartstrings—the few I have left.

Her brows shoot up in surprise. "Really? Do you think they'd have room for one more addition?"

Tell her no.

Nothing good will come from this.

You think she's sexy, that's why you care about her skinned knees.

"Yeah." I nod, starting to back away. "It should be fine."

Apparently my mouth isn't connected to my brain anymore.

She nods, her smile doing something weird to my insides.

"Well thanks. I really appreciate it. I know we didn't exactly start out on the right foot—"

I'm scared she's about to go down a road I don't want her to, so I nod and cut her off. "That's why we have two of 'em. See you around."

I hightail it out of that grocery store before she can get

another word in. I hate Texas. From now on, I'm driving one town over for my groceries. No more random run-ins with Madeleine Thatcher—though I guess random run-ins won't matter anymore because I've just ensured that I'll see her every week at puppy training class. *Bravo, Adam.*

I wonder if it's too late to move to Hawaii.

CHAPTER SIX

Madeleine

"**MR. BOGGS, I** assure you this house is up to code." I rifle through my paperwork just to confirm. "Yes, see here, it was just inspected last month."

He shakes his head. "Inspections mean nothing. Inspectors are crooks, the whole lot of them. If we're gonna start trusting inspectors, you might as well start showing me open caskets instead of open houses."

I barely manage to stifle a groan. *Boggsy certainly has a way with words.*

He taps on the wall, trying to find a stud, and when he does, he looks none too pleased about it. "That doesn't seem like sixteen inches apart. Shoddy construction, if you ask me."

I'm not shocked by Mr. Boggs' assessment of this house. Over the last year, I've shown him no less than fifty properties, and he has found fault with all of them.

"Perhaps if you shared your budget, we could narrow

down our—"

He waves away my question, as he does every time I ask it. Mr. Boggs isn't concerned about budgets—he always says they're like crabs in your craw. I haven't quite figured out what any of that means.

"I've told you, if it's the right house, I'll buy it," he repeats for what has to be the hundredth time since our first meeting. Call me a pessimist, but it's hard to believe him. He's not the sort of dapper gentleman you'd find living in the nicer area of Hamilton. His jeans are worn. His cane—which he uses to favor his left leg—is peeling away at the handle, and I can't be certain, but I swear the scent of Cream of Wheat trails after him like a bad shadow.

I'm not just judging him by his appearance either. Mr. Boggs and I have sat down for *many* lunches to discuss housing options, and I can't recall him ever picking up the tab. I have a growing suspicion that he's either lonely, or just using me for free bacon and eggs at Pam's Diner. But I refuse to give in. Without Mr. Boggs, I'd have no clients, and that's too sad, even for me.

"And you double-checked that this place hasn't been constructed on an Comanche burial ground? No arrowheads or funeral mounds?"

He's being serious.

I shake my head.

"I searched through the old city building records at the library," I repeat for the hundredth time—it feels like a personal mantra at this point. "The only thing notable about this plot was a big oak tree they had to cut down to build the house."

"Hmm, that's obviously a bad omen," he grumbles under his breath. "Trees are like—"

"—like the Earth's hats," I say, finishing a bizarre

sentiment I'd heard a half dozen times before. He nods approvingly before wandering off down the hallway. I chance a passing glance around the small bungalow I'm showing him today. It's beautiful, originally constructed in the 1920s but completely remodeled in recent years. The previous owners had to get approval from the Hamilton Historical Society before beginning renovations, which means the bones of the house are still there, detailed and ornate. However, they're not Mr. Boggs' taste.

"Not the right one," he concludes with a thump of his cane on the hardwood floor. "Not even close this time."

I don't want to be dramatic, but I swear I see my savings account dwindle just a *little* more in this moment. I haven't had the heart to check its balance in a while; I think it would give me a heart attack if I did. Besides, it's not Mr. Boggs' problem I'm so strapped for cash. If he wants to look at a million homes and waste my time, that's his prerogative. It's up to me to find a new client though, one who will actually buy something.

• • •

I nearly forget about puppy training class. I stayed at the office late, cold-calling various leads around town. It's my least favorite part of the job, but sometimes it can produce real results. In all, I set up three meetings for later in the week. Loretta Rae is looking to sell her modest townhome, Greg Van wants to upgrade to a bit more land, and Cameron Carr thinks he's finally ready to "escape the rent trap and find an equitable investment property". In the beginning, I'd have gotten my hopes up about all three potential clients, but I know better now. Loretta Rae will find some reason to become suddenly attached to her house and won't want to sell for all the tea in China, Greg Van will see how expensive land prices are at the moment and suddenly find that he doesn't mind what little land he currently has, and Cameron Carr just likes to show off vocabulary words he learns from skimming The Wall Street Journal every few weeks.

Still, it's something, and I won't let my bubble burst just yet. I look at the small orange clock mounted in my cubicle and cringe when I see the time. It's already half past five, and according to the YMCA's website, the puppy training class starts at 6:00 PM. I have just enough time to run home, change, and grab Mouse and a granola bar on my way out the door. Dinner will have to wait.

I take it as a good sign when my car leaps to life on the first turn of the engine. I smile over at Mouse, who is currently perched on the passenger seat, the whole upper half of his body hanging out the window. He loves car rides, and I've learned it's best to just roll the window all the way down for him—otherwise I'm left with a whole mess of slobber to wipe off the glass afterward.

The YMCA is across town, but it still only takes me ten minutes to get there. I'm surprised by the number of cars I see in the parking lot, and even more surprised when I step into the small gymnasium where the training class will take place. There are twelve metal chairs arranged in a semicircle, and all of them are taken. The room is made up largely of women about my age. I recognize most of them, but there are a few that must be new to town. I nod to Jessica and Valerie as I pass, though most of my attention is focused on keeping Mouse at bay. With so many dogs in the vicinity, he's tugging on the leash and jumping, trying as hard as he can to get to them.

"It's not playtime, Mouse," I hiss under my breath. He's the largest dog in the room by a mile. Most of the attendees have brought in small poodle mixes, and though I'm hesitant to admit it, they look to be much easier to handle than Mouse.

I find a nice spot on the ground beside the last chair and place Mouse on my left side, away from the tiny Chihuahua currently cowering under his owner's chair. His eyes seem to be begging for dear life, but Mouse is lying on his side, trying to get as small as possible so the puppy might start to like him. Poor Mouse; it's hard being the size of a bear.

The Chihuahua's owner scoots her chair away from us.

"Oh, he's really friendly," I promise with a smile.

And he is. For all his faults, Mouse wouldn't hurt a fly—just his owner.

"I have no doubt," she replies haughtily, turning her attention to the woman on her right.

Well then.

For a few minutes, I focus on Mouse and try to get him to settle down. Once he realizes we're staying with all these other puppies for a while, he might not feel like he has to *OMG meet them all right this very second.* I can feel him begging me to let him go play. His big eyes stare up at me, and then he lets out a hilariously dramatic groan. I rub his belly as a consolation prize.

"Yeah, once I saw that flyer downtown, I knew I had to come to the class," Chihuahua girl says to her friend.

"Was that the one with his photo?"

"Yes!" she replies. "It was just there at the bottom, but I saw all I needed to see."

They both laugh, and I pretend I'm not eavesdropping.

"I heard from Cassie, who heard from Mary, that he just moved to town. Apparently he's the new vet."

"Oh really?" her friend asks. "Looks like I'll be taking Moxie in for monthly—*no*, weekly checkups."

Another round of annoying tittering follows, and for some reason I'm shocked that they're talking about Adam. When he mentioned the training class yesterday, he didn't mention he would be the one running it.

That changes things. I'm honestly not sure I would have shown up had I known, but it's too late now because Adam is walking through the gym doors with training supplies tucked in a bag over his shoulder.

"Oh my word, he's even better in real life," Chihuahua girl whispers under her breath.

I decide that as soon as it's not so obvious, I'm moving to sit at the other end of the half-circle. I can't take much more of their commentary.

Adam spots me right away, probably because I'm the only attendee parked on the floor. I half expect him to ignore my presence altogether, but he walks straight for me. Mouse takes notice and leaps to his feet. All my effort in calming him down is out the window now that his favorite target as of late has made an appearance. Mouse jumps and whines, desperate for Adam to step within the three-foot radius his leash allows. I try to get him to sit, but it's no use.

I'm aware of the entire room watching me try and fail to corral my dog, and yet all it takes from Adam is one deep command—"Mouse, *sit*."—and the dog actually listens. Only then does Adam reward him with a few pets.

"Is that part of the training class?" I laugh. "Learning how to alter our voices so they sound more commanding?"

It's meant to be a joke, but Adam looks up at me with an odd expression.

"Oh, I was kidding…"

He smiles. "I know. Here."

He tosses me something and I have to think fast to catch it before it falls to my feet. I hold it out and then realize it's two somethings: black kneepads like the kind I used to wear whenever I roller-skated as a kid.

"Oh ha-ha, looks like everyone's a comedian," I say, genuinely amused.

He's wearing an adorably crooked smile when I glance back up.

"I saw them in a shop earlier and thought of you."

Whoa.

I freeze, slightly taken aback by his admission. I guess he sees the shock on my face, because he shakes his head. "Y'know, only because of your skinned knees. Obviously you don't have to wear them."

The whole exchange is made a thousand times more awkward because we are still the center of the universe, AKA this small puppy training class. I don't have to look at the women sitting beside me to feel the death glares they're sending my way. Adam walked into class and talked to me first, *and* he gave me a gift, *and* he said he was thinking about me.

I'm almost tempted to put on the damn kneepads just to prove a point.

"Well thanks," I say, holding them up. "Maybe I'll go rollerblading with Mouse."

"I'll call the National Guard."

As soon as Adam walk away, Mouse leaps into the air, and snatches one of the kneepads out of my hand.

"No!" I rebuke. "Bad dog!"

He drops it instantly, coating my shoes in a nice bit of slobber.

"I guess *some* dogs need this class more than others,"

says the woman beside me. Her friend laughs, and Adam pretends he doesn't hear them. For that, I'm grateful.

After a nod in my direction, he walks to the center of the gymnasium and offers a small wave to everyone. "I guess it's as good a time as any to get started. We have one more attendee joining us in a bit, but we'll go on without her."

Oh good, another person to compete with for Adam's attention.

The thought is there, blaring in my brain before I can stop it. Since when am I competing for his attention? If anything, I want to do the opposite. I've made such a complete fool of myself the last few times I've been around him, there's no hope for anything but a nice, weird friendship to settle into place between us, and even that is probably asking a bit much. Still, he invited me to the training class, and he extended an olive branch in the form of kneepads, right?

"Sorry! I'm here! I'm here!"

Spiders crawl down my spine as a familiar voice drifts into the gym, and I glance up just in time to see my coworker Lori bobbing into the room, all but dragging an ancient-looking Pomeranian behind her.

Adam waves away her apologies. "No, you're just in time. Have a seat—" He remembers that all of the chairs have already been claimed and corrects himself, "Or stand, it doesn't matter. We'll be moving around here in a second anyway."

Lori sees me, narrows her eyes, and continues speed walking to the opposite end of the half-circle. I rarely see her outside of work, and the fact that she's here means I won't be enjoying this training class nearly as much as I'd hoped. Though, there is one bonus: Lori in civilian clothes.

I've had the pleasure of seeing her sport some truly heinous work clothes, but tonight she's gracing us with a hot pink Juicy Couture tracksuit *à la* early 2000s. Her dog, the decrepit white fluffball, is wearing a matching hot pink fur collar.

"Isn't your dog a little old to be in here?" someone asks, trying to edge out the competition.

"Yeah, isn't this a puppy class?" pipes in another.

Unfortunately, Adam quiets the rebellion before it really starts to spread. "In my experience, the whole can't-teach-old-dogs-new-tricks story is just an old wives' tale. I think everyone should be welcome here."

How very polite of him. Especially since he's mostly addressing old wives.

I glance over to find Lori beaming up at him like he's the second coming of Christ. She's probably imagining what he would look like in a matching pink tracksuit of his own, a perfect little velour family in the making.

After, Adam passes out a waiver form we all have to fill out before he jumps into training. I wasn't sure what I was expecting, but he really does know his stuff. We're all given a bag of dog treats and a training tool Adam calls a clicker. It's a small instrument he instructs us to wear around our wrist, and any time our dogs perform a desired behavior, we click the clicker and reward him with a treat. It's a very easy concept.

I tell Mouse to sit.

Mouse sits.

I click and then treat him.

Unfortunately, not everyone has such an easy time catching on—either that, or they're feigning confusion in exchange for an extra minute or two of Adam's time. Chihuahua girl, who I learned is named Beth, seems to have never heard of the concept of positive reinforcement in her entire life.

"So I click it before or after she does the trick?" she asks for the tenth time.

Adam nods patiently. "Always after. We're trying to connect the behavior to the sound of the click, and the click to the treat."

"Oooooh, I think I get it now!"

She doesn't.

Adam has to help her for ten more minutes. Meanwhile, Mouse and I are practicing our sitting—well, he's the one doing the sitting, but I'm asking him to do so, and he's doing an *excellent* job at it. The clicker seems to hold his attention, and he enjoys getting rewarded for the behavior. Best of all, he's not trying to tug on the leash and run for another dog. He seems to be content with training, and Adam takes notice.

"You're doing really well," he says when he has the time to stroll over to my corner of the gymnasium. I smile and tell Mouse to sit.

For once, he listens right when I need him to.

I click and treat.

"You can take the clicker with you on your walks with him," he points out. "Every time he looks up at you while he's by your side, click and treat. It'll encourage him to keep his attention on you instead of on squirrels or pedestrians who happen to catch his eye."

I beam. "Genius! I'm definitely trying that."

He nods and turns to head for another student, but I strike up a conversation first.

"You know, it's funny, I wouldn't have pegged you as the puppy training kind of guy."

He runs a hand through his hair and smiles. "Honestly,

I'm not. Apparently my predecessor at the clinic set this class up, and since there were a few students who'd already signed up, I didn't want to cancel the class. I guess it's a good way to drum up business."

I nod. "Well you're doing a good job."

His brows rise at my compliment. "Thanks."

And then I decide that if we're going to be friends, I can tell him the truth. "By the way, half the people in this class only signed up because they saw your face on the flyer."

I swear he blushes then. His green gaze meets the ground and he shakes his head, a rosy tinge coloring his cheeks. Adam the Vet saves puppies for a living *and* he blushes? Daisy is going to have a field day.

"I figured something was up. I've already been asked for my number four times."

"No way!" These women are ballsier than I thought.

He shrugs. "It's not a big deal. I'm just the new guy in town."

"Mhm, I bet you didn't get any attention *at all* back in Chicago."

He frowns like I've just said something to annoy him.

"It was just a joke." My turn to shrug.

He shakes his head. "Yeah, I just...for a second there, I forgot you knew I lived in Chicago. I should probably go help out some other students."

"Right. Yeah," I say, because nothing better comes to mind. Just when I think he and I are moving in the right direction, we careen into awkward, murky territory. I've never had this problem with a man before, and I don't like it. It makes me feel like I'm back in middle school, trying to impress the popular boy.

The remainder of class passes faster than I thought possible as Adam walks us through a few more basics of the clicker and explains how the class will run. At the end of the six weeks, our puppies will go through a training test, and if they pass, we'll be given a paper diploma we can show everyone in our life that cares to see it—i.e. no one. Still, I want that diploma.

I successfully avoided Lori the entire 60 minutes, but I can't help but seek her out as we're packing up. Her Pomeranian is splayed out on the floor, panting and exhausted from the class. Mouse, by comparison, could still run a marathon without batting an eyelash. Lori doesn't seem to realize how tired her dog is, though; she's busy schmoozing Adam and slightly dragging the limp creature along the gym floor. I can't hear her, but I can see that she's ass-deep into her Five Ss. She smiles, bats her eyelashes, and then reaches out to touch his arm. I sneer.

It's bad, but it gets worse when I see her withdraw a business card from her massive Louis Vuitton purse. She nods and presses the card into his hand, and I'm sure the color is completely drained from my face. My hands turn to fists at my side and I'm seconds away from drawing blood. Is she seriously trying to take him on as a client right now? *Here?* And then I'm horrified because the answer is obvious: Lori being in the puppy training class wasn't a coincidence. With Lori, it never is. She must have heard Adam's renting and run to unhook her dog from life support for one last training class. All just so they could meet "organically" and she could start "essing" all over him. What a diabolical asshole.

I've never liked her more.

But I can't let her get away with it. I knew Adam first, and if he's going to be anyone's client, he's going to be mine.

I wait another minute or two as a few more students

filter out of class, and then I make my move. I'm sure there are ways of being sly and polite about it, but I need to strike while the iron is hot.

"Dr. Foxe, can I steal you for a second?"

He finishes up his conversation with another attendee and then directs me to the side of the room. He seems pleased that I came to talk to him, which I take as a good sign.

"Did you have fun in class?" he asks, reaching down to pet Mouse. He knows just the spot to scratch behind Mouse's ear, and my dog is basically putty in his hands.

"Yeah, it was great. I already feel like Mouse has improved, and it was only one class."

"That's great." Adam looks up at me and I'm momentarily blinded by those green eyes. They really are something.

But I'm not here to ogle his eyes.

"Yeah, so listen…I know Lori probably just mentioned something about being a real estate agent…"

He laughs and pushes back to stand. "Yeah, she gave me the whole spiel."

"Ugh, how annoying for a realtor to assault you the first time meeting."

He shrugs and I continue while I still have the nerve.

"But since this is like, I dunno, the fifth or sixth time we've met, I figured I should let you know that Lori and I actually work at the same agency."

He nods slowly, probably putting the pieces together, but I can't assume anything. I need to make myself perfectly clear.

"And if you *were* looking to purchase a house here, I would love to represent you. I mean, Lori is great, but ughh, so tactless, am I right?"

I laugh then, but he doesn't join me.

"Is this what you wanted to talk about?" He tilts his head, studying me. "Selling me a house?"

"Oh, umm…yeah." I'm floundering. "Basically I just wanted you to know that I'd *love* to work with you."

He tugs his hand through his hair and backs up. "Jesus, you people are relentless. At least she had a business card."

Abort. ABORT.

"No! I just didn't want to let the opportunity pass without—"

He laughs and backs up. "Well you definitely didn't let the opportunity pass. Now your behavior at Lucas' housewarming party makes way more sense. I thought you were bipolar there for a second, but now I realize you were just being nice to me because you want my business."

Sort of…yes.

"No!" I lie. "Of course not. I'm not like that, I'm a nice person!"

"When it benefits you," he adds, and I feel my cheeks burn.

It's not true, not *really*.

I hold up my hands in defense. "Listen, let's forget I ever said anything. Clearly you're not looking for a real estate agent, and even if you were, it definitely wouldn't be *me*."

My self-deprecating humor completely deflects off him. His mouth is tugged into a sharp frown, and I just need to leave. There's no way I'll salvage the situation.

"Okay, well, I better get Mouse home. He needs his dinner."

I did too before this conversation completely stole my appetite. He doesn't offer anything more than a curt goodbye, and I'm left with a painful sensation in the pit of my stomach on the drive home. Mouse is hanging out the window, happy as can be, but it doesn't cheer me up. I arrive back at my lonely apartment, ignore the melodramatic *RENT OVERDUE* sign taped to my front door, and flip on the light.

Mouse's toys are strewn across the tacky brown carpet. My secondhand furniture is in desperate need of replacing, and sadly, the mess of dishes I left in the sink last night is still there, taunting me. I crack open the fridge, take in the pitiful fare, and slam the door closed again. There's no denying it: my life is crumbling. I'm days away from caving and moving back in with my parents—either that or just leaping into the Rio Grande and letting it carry me down to Mexico.

Hola, me llamo loser.

I slide down to the floor and don't even realize I'm crying until Mouse trots over and starts licking the tears from my cheeks. It's the saddest, sweetest moment of my day, and I don't fight his affection. I wrap my arms around his abundant fur and pull him closer.

He licks and licks, and I don't even mind his puppy breath. It's soothing, right up until I glance down and see the two kneepads sticking out of the top of my purse. They make me cry harder.

CHAPTER SEVEN

I'M IN A lousy mood the next morning and though I'd like to blame it on my packed schedule, deep down, I know that's not what's bothering me. I was too hard on Madeleine last night at the end of the training class. At the time, I was pissed, and maybe somewhat…embarrassed. I went out of my way to invite her to the training class and bring her a little peace-offering, and though I'm good at denying it, I'm attracted to her—yet every chance she gets, she reminds me that she doesn't see me that way. To her, I'm a potential client, nothing more.

That should make me happy. After all, I'm not looking for any kind of relationship, strings attached or otherwise, but in the heat of the moment, when she drew the line in the sand, I couldn't help but feel like it was a blow to my ego. *Sure, I don't want to date, but she doesn't know that.*

At the very least, she and I could have been friends, but now that seems out of the question too, considering how I acted last night. The hurt expression she wore as I berated her (for the second time) is going to be forever burned in my mind.

Maybe we just don't mix.

But I refuse to believe that.

I couldn't take my attention off her last night. She was working so diligently with Mouse, minding her own business in a corner of the gymnasium, and over the course of the hour, I caught myself watching her a dozen times. I'd tell myself to focus on another student and their dog, and yet my attention would wander right back to her.

She was good with Mouse, patient when he was learning and quick to reward him when he mastered a new trick. I saw a different side of her, one I wanted to get to know…up until she asked me if I was in the market for a real estate agent. That burst my bubble real quick.

"Dr. Foxe," calls Derek, one of the vet assistants, from outside my office door. "Your next patient is ready for you in exam room two."

I tell him I'll be right there, but there's no folder waiting for me outside the exam room. I knock on the door, assuming he left it inside on accident, but as soon as I see my mom perched in one of the chairs, I know I've been set up. Even now, I can hear my staff laughing out at reception.

She looks up at me, her short, gray bob accented by a pair of blue earrings that match her dress. On her lap is a stuffed animal bird, and even though I'm in the throes of a shitty mood, I can't help but crack a little smile.

"Mom, to what do I owe this pleasure?" I ask, closing the door behind me. "And did you actually make an appointment? I've been behind all morning."

She holds up the bird. "As a matter of fact, I did. Birdie here has an ear infection."

"Funny."

She sighs and sets the stuffed bird back on her lap. "It's the only way I can see you these days! You moved from Chicago a month ago and I've only seen you twice!"

"That's more than you used to see me."

She offers up a classic mom glare. "Well it's not *enough*."

"How are Samuel and the kids?"

"Good. They're planning a barbecue this weekend and I want you to come."

Barbecue I can get behind. Incessant nagging from every single one of my family members about my life, not so much.

"I'll have to look at my schedule," I say, unable to meet her eyes.

I might have lived halfway across the country from her for the last ten years, but she's still my mom, and she can see right through me.

"Fortunately, your schedule is right up front at reception, and I already looked. You're free Saturday afternoon."

"They don't have my social life penciled in up there," I point out, though it probably would have been best to keep my mouth shut.

Her green gaze—the one that matches mine to a T—lights up. "So you've got *social* plans this Saturday?"

If by plans she means driving one town over for groceries, then yes, I'm booked.

"Nothing worth mentioning," I reply, which seems just vague enough. I could be talking about a date; I could be talking about a drug-filled orgy. She can fill in the blanks herself.

She sighs, annoyed with me for not opening up more.

That's what she gets for having two sons though. If she wants to have a heart-to-heart, she has Samuel's wife. Kathy hasn't stopped talking since the day she joined the family.

"I just want you to move on and be happy. I know it's only been a few months but—"

"I am happy," I insist. "And I have moved on."

"Oh really? Have you been seeing someone?"

"Sure."

"Okay, then, what's her name?"

I forgot that she's been calling my bluffs since I was in diapers. I need to just make up the first name that comes to mind.

"Madeleine."

She squeals and I pinch my eyes closed. Giving her a name, even a false one, was a bad idea.

"Perfect, you'll bring her to the barbecue on Saturday."

"No can do," I say, rounding the small exam table and angling toward the exam door. I have other patients to see, a job to do.

"What, is she a convict or something? Y'know Adam, one day you won't have a mother to nag and pester you."

"I'm not so sure." I shake my head, deflecting her mom-guilt with an imaginary force field. "You're in perfect health. You walk two miles every day and during your last physical, your doctor said you had the heart of a thirty-year-old."

She waves away my facts. "Yes, but we could all go"—she snaps her fingers for emphasis—"just like that. What about runaway trains or lightning strikes?"

"Oh Jesus—"

"Yes, the good Lord could call me home at any time."

I massage my temples, trying to quell the impending

headache that seems to trail after every one of our conversations. "Let me get this straight: I have to come to the barbecue on Saturday because otherwise you might *violently perish*?"

She nods, smiling. "Yes, Adam, that is *exactly* what I'm saying."

"Wow. That's fuc—"

"*Adam!*"

"Messed up," I correct hastily. "You realize if I don't come and you do get hit by a train, I'll have to live with that guilt for the rest of my life."

She nods again, so damn pleased with herself.

"So I can expect you for a late lunch on Saturday at Sammy's?" she asks, standing and straightening her sundress. She just breached my defenses, and she doesn't even look ruffled.

I blink, completely at a loss. She's stooped to an all-new low, and at the moment, I can't think of a single way to get out of going on Saturday.

"I'll be there," I say with a dazed tone.

"With Madeleine?"

"We'll see. She could be busy."

My mom steps closer and fixes the lapels on my white coat, though they were already laying perfectly. "Sweetie, she won't be, not if you're asking her out. If I know women, she'll rearrange her whole schedule to be there with you."

I wish that were the case, but with Madeleine, it couldn't be further from the truth. After last night, there's no way she'll accept my invitation.

"It might just be me."

She flinches and presses her hand over her heart. "Oh, my *heart*, suddenly it hurts so badly…"

"Are you seriously feigning a heart attack right now? Do you have no morals?"

She steps back, drops her hand, and smiles. "Not when it comes to my children, my dear. I'll do just about anything for you."

I shake my head. "You need therapy."

"And *you* need to bring Madeleine on Saturday. I cannot *wait* to meet her!" She heads for the door, her stuffed bird tucked beneath her arm. Just before she leaves, she glances back over her shoulder. "Oh, and she's not a vegetarian is she?"

"I honestly have no clue."

She laughs and waves away my answer. "Well you two have probably been too busy doing other things to worry about food."

I laugh.

Yeah...not exactly.

CHAPTER EIGHT

IT'S THURSDAY MORNING and I have hope. Even though I had to pull money from my savings account this morning to cover rent. Even though Mouse chewed up another pair of my work shoes. Even though I haven't gone on a date in two months, and the closest I've been to a climax recently is when my beat up car starts vibrating at about 35 miles per hour. But I do have hope—either that, or I'm way over-caffeinated, I don't know. Does hope make your hands shake?

I'm at work and Lady Helen has invited me into her office for tea this morning. I hate tea and am suffering through an Earl Grey just to please her. I think with another ten tablespoons of sugar and honey, it would taste good, but I'm too nervous to keep adding to my cup. It's already nearing overflow level because I refuse to take another retched sip.

"So Madeleine, I'm sure you know why I've asked you

in here this morning."

"Oh, umm...yes."

I spill a bit of tea on my pencil skirt when I attempt to set it back down on her desk. Fortunately, the hardy cotton-blend material is black and conceals everything—I learned that lesson a week into owning Mouse.

She smiles at me from her throne—a gaudy cheetah print tufted chair that reaches a foot past her head—and then she leans forward to drop her chin on her hands.

"You've been on this little probation for a week now and I'd like to hear what changes you've implemented."

"Oh yes. Absolutely." I scramble through the papers on my lap, as if the answer will be found on one of them. Then I laugh awkwardly and force myself to smile and sit up straight. "Umm, since last week, I've gathered a few leads. As you might have heard, Greg Van wants to sell his property and purchase a bit more land. I've already gathered up quite a few lots with good acreage, and we have a time set for tomorrow so I can show them to him."

She nods, seemingly pleased. "Good. What else?"

What else?

"Oh, um, Loretta Rae mentioned to me last week that she'd like to sell her townhouse downtown. She's owned the property for years and—"

Her smile tightens as she shakes her head. "Loretta won't sell. Lori was in contact with her earlier this year."

I glance down at my lap. Sitting right on top of my stack of papers is a list of creative ways to show Loretta's house when we put it on the market. It's now obviously worthless. I stuff the paper at the back of the pile and then remember my last potential client.

"Cameron Carr spoke with me last week about purchasing an investment property."

"Good. Have you had contact with him since?"

"Err, well, he's been a bit difficult to nail down this week. I've left him two voicemails and sent him an email. I could try to call him again today, but I don't want to spook him or anything."

She leans back and steeples her fingers. "You can never be too aggressive. For instance, it's not out of the question for Lori to create seemingly happenstance moments for her to run into her more stubborn clients."

I grunt, thinking back to her attendance at the puppy training class. "Yes, I know."

"I take it you aren't comfortable with that?"

"Oh, I didn't say that!" I scurry to cover my tracks. Helen loves Lori. In Helen's eyes, Lori can do no wrong. Meanwhile, *I'm* the agent on probation. If Lori stalks her clients until they give in and work with her, then maybe it's not such a bad idea. It's clearly working for her—her bell has chimed three times this week while mine has collected another layer of dust, much like my love life.

I open my mouth, prepared to tell Helen I'm fully prepared to go into stalker mode, but right then, my cell phone starts to ring. Unlike most work environments, we're encouraged to have our phones on us at all times in case a client is calling. Helen wants us available 24/7, and that includes now. She waves for me to answer it and I glance down at the unknown number.

Unknown numbers are good. While 50% of them are scam calls from Nigerian princes or credit card companies, some of them (okay, there's only been one) are clients trying to get ahold of me. My heart soars with the possibility that it's the latter. I excuse myself from Helen's office and swipe my screen to answer the call.

"Hello, Madeleine Thatcher speaking."

"Madeleine, hey. It's Adam."

I rack my brain trying to think of an Adam I've been in contact with at the agency lately. I usually only have a handful of clients, but I like to treat each of them as if they're my only client. I like to be up to date with every email, every phone call. If I've been in talks with an Adam lately, it does not ring a bell. Still, I play it cool.

"Mr. Adam! Of course, nice to hear from you."

It's a good, neutral greeting.

"Um, right. Can you talk for a second? I'm sure you're at work."

I frown, confused.

"Yes, I'm at the agency, but I'm definitely available to chat."

Then he laughs and I freeze. Have I said something wrong? Usually clients find me courteous and professional.

"You have no clue who this is, do you?"

I laugh, if only to join him and make it less awkward. "*Of course I do*. It's Adam!"

Meanwhile, I'm sprinting to my cubicle so I can pull up my recent email history. *Adam. Adam.* There's an Adam Keller I tried to work with last year, but that can't be—

And then it clicks.

"Ohhhhh, the vet! The puppy man!"

He laughs again. "Yeah, most people just call me Adam."

I blush. "Of course. Sorry. I'm just a little surprised you called. How did you get this number?"

My work phone number is listed on our agency's website, but he called my cell phone.

"I might have found it on the puppy training waiver."

I relax in my chair. "Wow."

"Sorry for the breach in privacy."

I shake my head, though he can't see me through the phone. "No, it's not that. I'm just surprised to hear from you." He seems remarkably happy to be chatting with me on the phone now considering the last time I was around him he wanted nothing more to do with me, except to maybe—

"Oh god, are you kicking me out of the training class because of what I did last week? I know that was out of line, but I swear I won't pester you about real estate anymore. You have my word."

"No, it's not that. Actually, I'd like to apologize for how I handled that situation. I shouldn't have snapped at you like that."

My eyebrows hit the ceiling. "Oh. Wow. Okay." Then I think for a second. "Is that why you're calling? To...um, apologize?"

There's a pause, and for a second, I think the call cut off. I move it away from my face and see the call time ticking away. By the time I press it back to my ear, I catch the tail end of a sigh.

"Actually, no. I have a proposition of sorts."

A proposition?

Why does that sound like the start of a sex contract or something? Oh god, it's not that. My mind is jumping to conclusions because I *wish* it were a sex contract. Hell, at this point, *any* contract might get Helen off my back.

"Oh?" I ask, hoping to sound only mildly curious.

"Yeah. I'll just cut to the chase. Basically, I'll let you sell me a house, but you have to do something for me first."

Sex.

He wants lots and lots of blowjobs. Oh god, I'm starring in a low-rent porno.

Or worse...

He wants my organs.

That's fine. He can harvest all of them if he'll let me sell him a house. I imagine it now: in a week I'll stroll into Helen's office and announce I've sold a huge house. She'll beam and ask me how I did it, and I'll lift up my shirt and show her the scar from which they took my kidney.

"Madeleine?" Adam asks. "Did I lose you?"

I laugh because he's done the exact opposite.

Without hesitation, I reply in earnest, "Adam Foxe, whatever you want, you have yourself a deal."

CHAPTER NINE

I FORGOT TO ask Adam what he needs me to do for him. I just accepted his proposal and hung up before he could go into details. Armed robbery, midnight séances, free tax preparation—I'm prepared for anything. I even consider for a moment that he might be asking for help at the veterinary practice, so I watched a cow birthing video on YouTube and only threw up in my mouth once. That's how badly I want to sell him a house.

Friday night, I'm sitting at Daisy's house with Mouse, watching old movies and scrolling through Tinder profiles. Daisy likes doing it with me since she never used dating apps herself.

"Oh, *God no!*" she says, swiping past yet another prospective mate.

"He wasn't half bad!" I snap, trying desperately to claw the phone out of her hand.

"He was posing in front of a cherry red Corvette in his

profile picture. What kind of guy does that?"

Sure, his picture screamed *insecure douchebag*, but if I swiped past every guy who didn't perfectly meet my specifications, it would just be me and Mouse growing old together.

Daisy doesn't believe me.

"There are going to be better prospects, you just wait."

My phone buzzes in her hand with an incoming text and from the look on her face, I know it's not from my mom. Since I'm currently with her, I know it's not from Daisy, and that rules out the only two people who text me on a regular basis.

"One new text from *Adam Foxe*?!" she exclaims.

I try, yet again, to snatch the phone away from her, but she holds it over her head. Mouse leaps to his feet and starts to bark, assuming this is all some spontaneous game.

"Hand over the phone, Daisy," I snap in a very authoritative, very no-nonsense tone.

It only makes her laugh as she starts to read the text aloud.

"Hey Madeleine, it's Adam. I'll pick you up at your place tomorrow around 11:30 AM."

I pretend not to care, sitting very still with my arms crossed on the other end of the couch. She can read all the text messages she wants; she's not going to get any information out of me.

"Adam is texting you."

"Yes."

"Adam the vet?"

I shrug.

"Why is he texting you? And why is he picking you up tomorrow?"

I'm very good at the silent game—being the younger

sister to a brother as annoying as mine meant it was an absolute necessity as a child.

"And why did he put a kissy-face and heart-eyes emoji?"

"*Really?*"

"Ha! That was a trick. So is he taking you out on a date or what?"

I pretend to pick dirt out from beneath my nails. Then I shine them on my shoulder.

"You're not being funny," she says, finally tossing my phone back to me.

"Ha!" I snap as I open the text again and read it for myself. It reads exactly as she'd recited, sans kissy-faces. I'm slightly disappointed that he isn't revealing more information.

I decide to push my luck and text him back.

Madeleine: What if I'm busy tomorrow afternoon?

Daisy leaps off the couch and leans over my shoulder so she can try to read what I'm typing. I block her view just as my phone vibrates again. He replied quickly, faster than most guys usually do. Normally I have to sit and stare at my phone for at least thirty minutes before guys get around to texting me back, usually more. It's torture, and I'm glad Adam doesn't try to play those stupid games. Then it hits me that maybe he does play those games with girls he's actually interested in. It's not like we're texting about an actual date after all.

Adam: Then unfortunately, there's no deal.
Madeleine: Wow. Is this like a Chicago mobster

thing? Are we sinking a body into Lake Michigan?
Adam: No. Sorry, I just really need your help.
Madeleine: Care to elaborate on it then?

Daisy shakes my shoulders, trying to get me to show her what we're saying. Naturally, she makes me send Adam a string of gibberish by accident.

Madeleine: weoy9873568hekrthJEHW@#
Adam: What?
Madeleine: Ignore that.
Adam: I can't go into much detail. It might scare you away.

The cow birth video plays through my mind again and my stomach turns over. It's definitely that. I'm going to have to put my arms up a cow's vagina tomorrow just so I can sell him a house. Do other agents have to go to these same lengths to earn a commission?

Madeleine: Okay fine. I'll send over my address.
Adam: Great, see you then.
Madeleine: WAIT. What should I wear? A dress? Jeans? Hazmat suit?
Adam: Just something casual that you wouldn't mind getting a little dirty.

Oh sweet Jesus.

Adam: Oh, and Mouse is invited too.

"Ha!" Daisy shouts just as she tears my phone out of

my hand. She also takes the top layer of skin off my thumb. Very polite.

"Have you ever heard of a little privacy?!" I shout, but it's no use. She's already reading our text exchange, no doubt inserting feelings and double meanings where none belong.

"Did he ask you out on a surprise date or something?" she asks, tossing me back my phone once she's finished.

I shouldn't reward her terrible best friend behavior, but there's no point in being stubborn. Daisy will wear me down eventually, just like she did with my brother.

"No, as a matter of fact, it's not a date."

"So…you two are hanging out as friends?"

I narrow my gaze on her, taking in her perfect skin and bright blonde hair. Sure, *now* she's in pajamas, but normally she's put together in fancy business clothes underneath her crisp white coat. Daisy has her life together. She's a doctor and she's married. She has her own house, and pretty soon she'll probably start popping out my nieces and nephews. It's because of this that I can't tell her the honest truth—that I, Madeleine Thatcher, have hit an all-new low. I am all but prostituting myself in the name of real estate. Daisy won't understand. She'll tell me to quit, to get a new job. She thinks I'm talented and "going places". She doesn't seem to understand that the only place I'm headed is the poorhouse if I don't earn a commission soon.

"It's nothing," I say, standing and finding Mouse's leash. "Can we just drop it?"

"Yeah, of course."

I'm surprised she's willing to cooperate—my expression must look particularly desperate. On my way to the door, she can't help but ask one more time, "You'd tell me if it was a date, right?"

Fortunately, she can't see me pinch my eyes closed in distress. "It's definitely *not* a date."

CHAPTER TEN

AT 11:25 AM the next morning, I'm standing on the curb outside my apartment, waiting for Adam. I've selected a pair of worn jeans that are flattering, but not *too* nice, and a white blouse I can easily swap out for the vintage t-shirt I packed if we end up knee-deep in some sort of bovine-birthing activity. Mouse is lounging at my feet, the brown, black, and white pattern of fur on his face even more cute than usual thanks to the brushing I gave him this morning. He's grown in the last few days, already surpassing the size of a large Labrador. I resist the urge to give in to my anxiety about his size and instead do an inventory of the tote bag hanging on my shoulder. I've come prepared for whatever the day will bring. Inside, I've packed one Tupperware full of homemade oatmeal chocolate chip cookies, a water bottle, my vintage t-shirt, sneakers, a few granola bars, a rain jacket, and treats for Mouse. It's nearly filled to max capacity, but I have no other choice. I still

don't actually know where Adam is dragging me, and I wanted to come prepared for any situation.

I'm actively debating breaking into the cookies early when a black, sporty Audi pulls up to the curb and draws my attention. I spot Adam behind the sleek tinted windows and can't help but laugh. He's definitely not from Texas. If he were, he'd be driving a truck or some kind of rugged SUV. This shiny thing looks expensive and easy to destroy, and I know Mouse will make short work of it.

"Morning," he says, sliding out of the driver's seat and rounding the back of the car.

Mouse leaps to his feet and goes wild, but Adam uses his authoritative tone and instructs him to sit before getting close enough to pet him. Mouse responds to his command, but his whole body still shakes with excitement as he sits, patiently waiting. As Adam pets Mouse, I take a step closer to his car and inspect the pristine the interior. Everything is clean and gleaming; it looks like he just got it detailed this week.

"We should take my car," I declare, stepping back before the intoxicating concept of plush leather and power-lock windows can draw me in.

"What? Why?" He pushes to stand and I turn.

It's then that I realize he's dressed in a pair of jeans, brown leather boots, and a gray long-sleeved t-shirt pushed up to his elbows. The material is thick and well-made. He looks adorable with his tousled brown hair and bright green eyes. I swear he's even a little tanner than the last time I saw him, not to mention his bone structure; it's strong and intimidating, the stuff dreams are made of.

While all of that might have been important if we were going on a date, the only thing I truly care about is that he's not dressed for manual labor. I take that as a good sign.

"Why should we take your car?" he asks again, snapping my attention away from his clean-shaven jaw.

"Oh." I point to my old clunker parked a few spots away, glistening like a murky, chipped diamond in the sunlight. "Because Mouse is a terror and I would hate for him to ruin your upholstery or get hair everywhere."

Adam shrugs. "I really don't mind."

I look down at Mouse and see a hint of mischief in his light brown eyes.

"Yeah, still, it's probably for the best."

I instruct Adam to take the free parking spot beside mine and then we're both sliding into my car at the same time. I try to see the car through his eyes. He just stepped out of the latest and greatest Audi on the market, and my upholstery is thin and ripped in a few spots. The air conditioning craps out every now and then, and a few buttons on the dashboard have disappeared in the last month or so, thanks to Mouse. Then there's the lovely sound it makes as I try to start her up.

"Bad starter," I say with a weak smile.

He frowns. "Are you sure?"

No, I'm not sure. I haven't taken it in to a mechanic because that is something that people with money do. For now, I pretend it's just a bad starter and go about my day blissfully ignorant.

After an awkward number of attempts and failures, it finally jumps to life and I toss Adam another smile. "See? She's just a little stubborn."

He hums, too gentlemanly to argue with me.

I hear rustling in the back seat and turn to see Mouse with his snout stuck halfway into my tote bag.

"No! Mouse, those aren't for you!" I snap, reaching back for the bag.

"Did you pack food?" he asks before the bag comes into full view and his eyes widen. "Correction, did you pack your entire pantry?"

I blush and try to hide it. "*No*, just a few necessities."

He relieves me of the bag and stows it on the floorboard at his feet. The oatmeal chocolate chip cookies are poking out right up top and he notices them right away.

"Cookies?"

"Homemade cookies," I correct, putting the car in reverse. "Where should I head?"

He points out to the left. "Toward town. Why'd you pack cookies?"

"Because you wouldn't tell me what we were doing, and I wanted to be prepared for anything."

"In what situation exactly would you need homemade cookies?"

I frown. "Au contraire—*you tell me* one situation that isn't made better by cookies. Besides, there's other stuff in there too. Sneakers and a t-shirt, that sort of thing."

"I like what you have on."

It's a nice thing for him to say. The white blouse belongs to Daisy, and her chest is a little smaller than mine so I wasn't sure if I could pull it off as well as she does.

"Why do you have gardening gloves in here?"

I was too focused on driving to notice him rifling through the bag.

"Oh, yeah, those are for the calf-birthing."

"*The what?*"

I laugh. "Like I said, I wanted to be prepared."

"We're just going to my family's barbecue."

I swerve into oncoming traffic and Mouse flies across the back seat just as a passing car lays on their horn. I straighten out the wheel and return to my lane. When there's a clearing, I pull off to the side of the road.

With the car in park, I turn to Adam to find him eyeing me warily.

"We're going *where*?!"

He holds up his hands in defense. "Just a small barbecue, nothing serious."

"No. *No*. A *family* barbecue is serious! This was not part of the deal."

He tips his head and smiles. It's adorable, but I refuse to notice. "Technically, you agreed to do anything I needed you to do."

"That's when I thought you'd be asking me for a lung or something!"

"So you were prepared to donate an organ, but a family barbecue is suddenly too much pressure?"

He's mocking me.

I narrow my eyes. "Don't try to be cute."

He rakes a hand through his hair and turns his green gaze on me. I feel it melting my cold, hardened heart even as I try to resist. "My mom insisted I show up with a date. She can be…persistent, and I thought it would be easier to give in than to keep trying to fend her off."

My knuckles have turned white on the steering wheel. My heart is still hammering in my chest.

"So then why didn't you bring a date?"

"I did," he replies, very matter-of-fact.

I snort. "No. You could have asked any female in Hamilton, *literally* any one of them, and they would have gone with you."

"Well, I asked you."

I work up the courage to look at him, and I realize the mistake quickly. In my small car, he's too close to me. I can smell his body wash—*mountain fresh*. I can see the dark green circle that rims his irises. I can almost pretend he's a living, breathing human and not a robot cyborg programmed to rescue puppies and make women swoon.

"You didn't ask me, you presented a proposition I couldn't refuse."

He scrunches his brows in thought. "I thought it was sort of the same thing."

My head falls against my seat and I pinch my eyes closed. "They're going to ask us questions and it's going to become glaringly obvious how little we know about each other."

"We know enough."

He sounds so confident, so prepared to follow through with the ruse.

"Okay, well did you let them know that I have a child?"

"*What*?!"

"See?!" I say, turning to face him. "You believed that because you hardly know me!"

He laughs then. It starts out slow, just a smile stretching across his face, and then his head is thrown back against the seat and he's laughing hard, pressing his hand to his chest. I sit in silence, watching him, helpless to prevent a matching smile from developing on my lips.

"You think this is all some kind of game, don't you?"

When he can finally catch his breath, he replies, "It can be if we let it."

I roll my eyes.

"C'mon," he continues. "It's just an hour or two spent in the company of nice strangers. At the very least, you'll get a good meal out of it."

"And the commission from selling you a house," I point out, trying to read how serious he is about holding up his end of the bargain.

He nods in confirmation. "And that."

I sigh and put the car back in drive, slowly merging with traffic. He directs me toward his brother's house in downtown Hamilton and just before we park, I smile at my preparedness.

"By the way, this is the perfect situation for homemade cookies."

• • •

We decide it's best if I walk in with the cookies and Adam takes charge of Mouse. I've been practicing walking him with the clicker, but he's too excited by the prospect of being in a new place to heed his new training. I step out of the car and straighten my blouse, trying to surreptitiously inspect his brother's house without being obvious.

It's a large two-story ranch-style home on a large lot. There are old, massive oak trees scattered around the front yard, and a boxwood wreath hangs on the front door. As we head up the path, I can hear voices filtering out from the back yard, and the front door is whipped open before we even get the chance to knock.

A fashionable older woman stands in the doorway wearing a sleeveless pink sundress paired with a colorful spring scarf. Her fingers are covered in rings, and gold bracelets clink on her wrist as she raises her hand to wave us inside.

"Come in, come in. You two are just in time!"

I smile and step into the house, grateful when Adam introduces me quickly.

"Mom, this is Madeleine, the woman I told you about."

The woman I told you about?

My eyebrows betray my shock before I realize his mom is watching me. I quickly replace my expression with a smile. "It's a pleasure to meet you, Mrs. Foxe."

I hold out my hand, but she pulls me in for a quick hug instead. When she's done, she holds me out at arm's length and beams. "You can call me Diane."

"Oh." I smile. "Of course."

"You're quite a stunner," she says, glancing down my outfit. "And I love what you're wearing." I should feel uncomfortable, but it's been a long time since I've been objectified like that and I'm more than happy to accept the compliment.

"Thank you. I hope I'm dressed okay. I wasn't sure what I was in store for."

It's the understatement of the century, but Diane doesn't know that, up until a few minutes ago, I thought I was going to be part of some kind of illuminati sacrifice ritual.

She waves away my concern and locks her elbow with mine, dragging me out of the entryway.

"And you brought cookies?" she asks, eyeing the Tupperware in my hand.

"Freshly baked this morning," I brag.

She turns over her shoulder to Adam, who's following us into the house with Mouse by his side. "I love her already!"

I bask in her praise. After the months from hell I've had recently, this is a much-needed reprieve. Hell, if all else fails, maybe I'll date Adam's mom?

She continues leading me through the house, pointing out rooms as we pass them. We eventually make it to the kitchen and she releases me so she can take the cookies and display them artfully on a platter. I'm happy I had the forethought to add extra chocolate chips. They'll be a hit for sure.

"I've met Beauty, now who's this beast?" Diane asks, finally acknowledging Mouse, who is (thankfully) sitting at Adam's side. If I had control of his leash, he'd be jumping all over, trying desperately to get Diane's attention.

"This is Madeleine's dog, Mouse," Adam supplies, reaching down to scratch behind his ears. Mouse looks up at him affectionately and for a second, I forget that this is all a game of make-believe.

"Adam said it would be okay if we brought him," I say, laying the blame on him just in case.

"Of course. We're dog people!"

She steps closer to pet him and I feel I owe her a warning. "Oh! He just started puppy training, so he doesn't have all of his manners down pat quite yet."

As if on cue, he jumps up to lick her face. Diane laughs and bends down to get on his level, and Mouse naturally takes full advantage of this unwise move. He launches a slobber assault on her and I cringe, but she doesn't seem to mind.

"I used to have a Bernese when I was younger," she says wistfully.

"You did?" Adam asks before I can.

She nods and rubs Mouse's ears. "She looked just like this when she was a puppy. Such a good dog."

After Mouse has had enough pets to last him a lifetime, the voices outside catch Diane's attention.

"Oh, we should head out. Everyone will want to meet Madeleine and Mouse."

My stomach churns at the idea of meeting more family members, but then I remind myself that this doesn't matter. There's no pressure to impress anyone. I can be myself and relax, eat as much barbecue as the button on these jeans will allow.

"Do you want some wine before we head out, Madeleine?"

It's early afternoon, but Diane already has a glass, so I don't hesitate. "I'd love some."

With wine in my hand and a beer in Adam's, the three of us head out into the back yard. Fortunately, my fear isn't realized—it's not filled to the brim with family members. It's an intimate group, just a couple sitting near a grill and two little brunette girls jumping on a trampoline. They look to be the exact same age, and even from a distance, it's not hard to confirm that they're twins.

"Those are my nieces," Adam fills in. "Allie and Payton."

"ADAM!" they squeal in unison, clamoring to get off the trampoline and run to hug their uncle. It's an adorable sight, and then they pull back and look from me to Mouse, unsure of who they want to attack first.

The dog wins out, and I don't really blame them. Mouse is pretty cute.

"A dog!" one of them exclaims.

"Can we pet him?" the other begs, her hands clasped in prayer. "Oh please! Can we pet him?"

"You'll have to ask Madeleine," Adam says, pointing to me.

They turn their gazes on me and I find green eyes the same shade as Adam's staring up at me from pudgy-cheeked faces.

"Madeleine, *may* we please pet him?!"

I smile and nod. "Of course, but be careful. He gets really excited and I don't want him to accidentally hurt you."

They stop listening to me after 'of course', but Adam

has enough sense to make sure nothing happens. After they've made their short introductions, he finally unleashes Mouse and the dog takes off, running around the massive back yard like a bat out of hell. The girls squeal and run after him, and it's hard to tell who is more entertained by the game, the girls or Mouse.

"Well, I think we've found a way to keep the girls occupied for the next few hours," Adam says, glancing over to me with a smile.

"Madeleine!" Diane calls from near the grill. "Come meet Kathy and Samuel!"

I look to Adam for backup as we head over and he steps closer, placing a possessive hand around my shoulders. It's the first time he's touched me. I'm hyperaware of that fact, and though my first instinct is to pull away, I don't. Instead, I settle into the closeness as he tucks me into his side. He has just enough height on me that we fit perfectly. I feel small and delicate, cherished.

"That's my brother and his wife," he whispers under his breath. "Samuel and Kathy."

I glance up at him, and he tightens his hold on my shoulder.

"Are they going to bite me?"

He smiles, and up this close, it's torture. "No, but Kathy will think something is off if we aren't affectionate."

"Ohh, gotcha."

His reminder of the proposition is like a bucket of cold water being dumped on my head, and now I want to step away and put some distance between us even more. The second I'm reminded it's only a well-crafted lie, the fit no longer feels organic.

"Madeleine! It's so good to meet you!"

Adam's sister-in-law rushes forward to greet me, and I

use the excuse to step away from him.

"Hi. Kathy, right?"

She beams and glances between Adam and me, probably sizing us up as a couple. When her smile widens another inch, I assume she's pleased with what she sees.

"Yup, and that's my husband, Samuel, Adam's brother," she says, pointing over her shoulder to the guy manning the grill. Adam has a few inches on him and his waistline is a little trimmer, but I can definitely tell they're brothers. He tips his spatula my way like an army salute and I laugh.

Adam joins his brother and Kathy grabs her empty wine glass before tilting her head to the back door. "Want to come inside for a second?"

Oh God. This is interrogation rule number one: don't let them split you up.

"Oh yes!" Adam's mom says just before she takes a seat in a lawn chair. "I forgot to check on the potato salad."

Kathy flashes me a playful glare just before she pushes me back inside. "I didn't realize potato salad needed to be watched."

"I heard that!" Diane calls out after us.

Kathy grabs my arm, laughing. "Run before she throws her wine at us!"

I've been around Adam's family for less than five minutes and I already know they're one of those families that actually enjoy being around one another. There's no pretense, no strained formalities. Even now, as I finally get a good look at Kathy, I can see why. She's beautiful and relaxed. Her red hair is thrown together in a messy bun and she's wearing overalls—OVERALLS—and she's really pulling them off. They're fitted down her legs and rolled up at the ankle. She's paired them with a tight white top and bare feet, and the overall effect is adorable. I immediately decide to purchase a pair as soon as I have, well, any income at all.

"I really like your outfit."

She pulls the white wine out of the refrigerator and tosses me a lazy smile. "Thanks. Samuel calls me a farmer when I wear these overalls, but I bought them at J. Crew, so what does he know?"

"No way! That's why they're so cute."

"Want me to top you off?" she asks, nodding toward my wine glass with the bottle in her hand.

I've barely touched my glass, but I don't want to be rude. I wink and step closer. "Maybe just a bit."

She laughs. "God, I've been around you for five minutes and I already think you're better than Olivia. When I first met her, she wouldn't shut up about some heirloom bone china she was getting restored. Who gives a shit about plates? Honestly."

"I'm actually a fine china expert. I work on the Antiques Roadshow," I reply, completely deadpan.

Kathy pauses pouring my wine, looks up, and then laughs. "You really had me there for a second."

"Most of my plates at home are of the plastic or paper variety," I admit with a shrug.

"Mine were too until we registered for our wedding. Now we at least have a semi-matching set from Pottery Barn, but the girls have done their best to break every last one."

I laugh. "They're so cute, but I bet they're a handful. How old are they?"

"They just turned six."

"Wow." I turn to spot them outside, lying on the grass beside Mouse. It appears their game of chase is on a temporary hiatus. "Do twins run in your family?"

She comes to stand beside me, following my gaze past the glass window. "No. Samuel and I had trouble conceiving. People harp about adoption and how many children need good homes, but I just…couldn't give up, I guess. Samuel and I agreed that if Clomid didn't work, we'd change course and try for adoption."

One of the twins reaches out and pats Mouse on the head. He takes advantage of her kindness and scoots closer, resting his chin on her chest.

"But it worked," I say, turning to Kathy.

She beams and clinks her wine glass with mine. "That it did."

Our mission in the kitchen is finished, but neither of us makes a move to head back outside. Spring is fading into summer quickly which means we aren't yet melting to the pavement when we step outside, but still, the kitchen is cool and quiet.

"Do you want children, Madeleine?"

I don't have to consider her question. "Of course."

"Sorry, I probably shouldn't ask someone that within ten minutes of meeting them."

I shrug. "I don't mind."

"Olivia didn't want kids."

It's the second time she's mentioned this mysterious Olivia, and I have to resist asking her to elaborate. If Adam and I were dating as we've claimed we are, I'd likely know about her by now. My curiosity will have to take the back seat for a few more hours.

Diane comes in the back door and sees us standing there, propped up against the kitchen island.

"Kathy, Samuel is asking about barbecue sauce."

"It's out there."

Diane holds up her hands in surrender. "That's what I told him, but he swears you didn't bring it out yet."

Kathy murmurs something under her tone that sounds suspiciously close to *I'm going to murder my husband* right before she heads out the back door. Diane catches my eyes and we exchange a knowing smile.

"They've been married for twelve years," Diane says, opening the refrigerator wide enough to pull out a massive bowl of potato salad.

"Wow, that's quite the achievement. They must have been young when they got married."

"Twenty-two," she confirms, placing the bowl on the island and rooting around in the drawers for something. "I told Samuel he needed to wait. They'd barely finished college—what did they know about marriage?"

I prop my elbows on the island just as she finds what she's looking for: paprika.

"I suppose they didn't listen?"

She laughs as she sprinkles the spice on the top of the dish. My mouth salivates. "My kids rarely do."

My stomach churns as I realize how quickly this charade is going to crumble. I didn't expect Adam's family to be so open and welcoming. Standing across from Adam's mom while she opens up to me about her children cuts me to my core. She's so nice, and I'm standing in her son's kitchen lying to her.

"What do you do for work, Madeleine?"

"I'm a real estate agent."

She nods, seemingly impressed, and I don't rush to correct her. If a tree falls in a forest and has only sold one house, it's still a tree, right?

"I'm a kindergarten teacher down at Hamilton elementary," she says with a proud smile.

"Oh! I must have gone before your time. I would have remembered you."

"No. I moved down here after Kathy and Samuel got married."

"From Chicago?"

She nods. "So how long have you and Adam been seeing each other?"

"Oh, um…" I stare out the back window and spot Mouse sporting a brand new hot pink headband. The girls are dressing him up, and he's happy to let them as long as they keep the scratches flowing.

"Must not be that long," she supplies for me.

I laugh and it sounds tight and awkward even to me. "No, not long."

"Has he taken you out on dates, or is that too formal these days? When Samuel and Kathy were first dating, they used to just go hang out with friends and study. How's that for romance?"

I mentally scroll through the activities Adam and I have done together: a vet visit, puppy training, a random run-in at the grocery store. None of them can be twisted into something romantic.

"We haven't done any serious dates," I reply, confident I'm not really telling a lie. "Just little things."

She hums, and I finally work up the courage to glance up her way. She's eyeing me with suspicion; of course she is. She can probably sniff a lie from a mile away after spending all day, every day with kindergarteners.

"Adam was hesitant about bringing you today," she continues. "I think he was worried we'd scare you off."

I bark out a laugh before I can help myself. This, of course, only makes her more suspicious, but I'm quick to cover my tracks. "No, it's not that. He probably just didn't want to introduce me to his family yet. Y'know, some women might read too much into it."

She tilts her head, her potato salad long forgotten. I'm her new project. "Something tells me you aren't one of those women."

I shake my head. "Definitely not."

"Something also tells me you and Adam aren't dating."

She says it just like that, like she's commenting on the color of the sky.

I feign utter shock. "What? Of course we are!"

She smiles, proud to have found her mark. "No. I was pestering Adam about moving on the other day and he thought he'd get one over on me if he brought someone to the barbecue."

"No. *No*, umm...he and I—we *have* been seeing each other." I'm a stammering mess and it's all Adam's fault. He dropped this mission on me this morning. I had no time to prepare, no time to wrap my head around my character. *What are her motives? Her likes? Dislikes?* I'm supposed to be playing his leading lady, and he'll probably renege on the agreement if I'm not convincing.

"It's all right, I won't let him know that I know."

I squeeze my eyes closed, willing the ground to open up at my feet. "I'm really sorry. I didn't feel comfortable with the plan, but he didn't give me much choice."

At that, she seems alarmed. "Did he threaten you?"

"No! No. He actually, um, agreed to be one of my clients at the agency if I pretended to be his girlfriend today."

His mom laughs—*cracks up*, in fact. She has to press her hand to her chest and I swear she's about to keel over from amusement. "Oh this is too good. *Too* good."

"Wh—What's too good?"

She finally gets ahold of her laughter and then she leans forward, whispering to me conspiratorially. "It's obvious, isn't it? If this is just one big act for him, we just have to flip the script."

CHAPTER ELEVEN

THE DAY IS going better than I could have imagined. Madeleine is playing her part to a T, my mom and sister-in-law are half in love with her already, and my nieces are completely enamored by Mouse. I sit back in my lawn chair, staring out at the scene before me, trying not to gloat. It's almost too easy. I'll be able to milk this barbecue for months. Every time my mom brings up moving on, I'll remind her that I have. *It's not my fault Madeleine and I didn't end up working out.*

She'll have no leg to stand on. I won't know what to do with all my free time—her constant pestering ate away whole chunks of my day. I could take up running again, maybe finally get around to reading the books stacked up on my nightstand.

My mom takes a seat in the lawn chair beside mine.

"Should be ready any second now," Samuel announces from his station at the grill.

Thank god. The smell of barbecue chicken has made my

stomach growl for the last half hour.

Kathy has the girls go in to wash their hands and gather up plates and dishes for the picnic table outside. Madeleine offers to help, and I smile. She fits in so well. No one would ever guess she's not really here by choice.

That's when I notice my mom staring at me.

I turn, and she smiles.

"I'm happy for you, son," she says, tilting her head toward Madeleine. "She is *quite* a catch."

I nod. "Isn't she?"

"Beautiful," she says.

"*Very.*"

"Smart."

"And funny," I add.

"How'd you manage to snag someone as good as her?"

I shrug and take a victorious sip of my beer. "Right place, right time I guess."

"Oh, you'll have to tell us the story over lunch."

"There's nothing to tell, really. Boy meets girl, falls for her, same ol', same ol'."

My mom shakes her head. "Nonsense. I bet it's a great story, and Madeleine says you've taken her on quite a few dates. She even told me about what you did for her last week."

I rack my brain, trying to think of what Madeleine could have told her. Was it about puppy training? The vet visit? Surely she didn't completely make up a story.

"C'mon, you remember...she went on and on about the hot..."

She waits for me to fill in the rest and the silence drags on so long that I finally have to give in.

"Dogs?" I supply.

She laughs and bats my arm. "*No!* The hot air balloon

ride you two took at sunrise!"

I take another sip of beer just in time to nearly spit it out all over the grass. Somehow, I manage to force it down and nod, playing along. "Of course, yeah…the hot air balloon. We've done so much that I forgot about that."

"Wow, must be some whirlwind romance. She told me about the camels too. Y'know, I've never even seen a camel in real life!"

What the fuck, Madeleine?

"Oh yeah. She loved the camels." I nod again.

"A camel ride through the park—so creative, Adam. Most men would have stuck with a horse-drawn carriage, but not you. Who taught you to be so romantic?"

I tug at my shirt's collar, trying to loosen the material just a bit. "*Ha*. Guess I got it from you."

"I swear when I look at her, I can see exactly what my future grandchildren will look like."

Alarm bells blare like sirens in my head. "Grandchildren? C'mon Mom, we've only been dating a few weeks."

She looks stricken. "Madeleine says it's been longer, that you two even talked about marriage sometime next spring."

"*Next spring*?!"

I should have known better than to leave Madeleine alone with my mother. I thought she would play along. Be nice, stay quiet—*that was the plan*.

"It does seem quick," she admits. "Was she lying?"

The mention of that word nearly forces me to break out in hives.

"No, of course not. I mean, she and I have entertained the idea. Nothing serious, obviously."

I thought my heart was dead—*gone*—after Olivia, but

Madeleine has proved it's alive and well, beating so hard I can barely see straight. She walks out of the house with plates stacked in her hands and I stalk her approach to the picnic table, waiting for her to look up at me so I can convey all my anger with one glance. She ignores me, and why wouldn't she? Between Kathy and my nieces, she barely has a spare minute. Allie has stolen her brown sandals and is tromping around the yard in them. Payton declares with a shout that she gets to sit by Madeleine during lunch. Then Allie chimes in, claiming the spot on the other side of her.

Even this annoys me now. She wasn't supposed to charm them; she was just supposed to be a warm body. I needed a living, breathing female to get my family off my back, and now she's wooed them all and probably made my life ten times worse. I won't hear the end of Madeleine and Mouse. Even the alliteration adds to my annoyance at this point.

"Adam, you coming over to join us?" Kathy asks with an amused smirk.

I realize then that everyone has taken a seat at the picnic table except me. I'm still sitting, stewing in my lawn chair.

"Girls, I'm sure Adam wants to sit by his girlfriend," my mom says, trying to convince Allie or Payton to give up their seat beside Madeleine.

Neither of them budge. Payton even grips the table with her tiny fingers, daring one of the adults to pry her from her seat.

"It's fine," I reply gruffly, heading around to the other side so I can sit directly across from her.

This is better.

I can skewer her with my gaze all through the meal.

She finally glances up at me, all smiles and butterflies.

The sunlight brings out the varying degrees of brown in her hair: chocolate, caramel, cinnamon—all edible. Even her eyes are beautiful. For the first time, I notice they're the color of coffee with a touch of cream, that gentle brown color that usually gets overlooked for flashier shades. She tilts her head, probably wondering why I'm glaring at her. I narrow my eyes.

"What's wrong?" she mouths.

Such beautiful innocence.

I don't reply. Instead, I accept the bowl of potato salad getting passed around the table and load my plate up with a heaping spoonful. I might not appreciate her meddling, but I do enjoy my mom's potato salad.

"Do you want to go get a drink with me?" Madeleine asks, her voice a little shaky.

"I'm all set," I reply, shoving the bowl in her direction so hard that it nearly spills in her lap.

"*Adam*! Jeez, what's up with you?" Kathy scolds.

"Madeleine doesn't mind, do you?"

She shakes her head, but her bare foot collides with my shin under the table. It's a warning shot, and I don't plan on heeding it.

My mom, meanwhile, is smiling like a fool at the head of the table. "Guess what I did while you all were setting the table."

I don't care to guess, but my nieces are too gullible to ignore their grandmother. They see her waving her cell phone like a pendulum and their little brains nearly explode.

"What?!"

"What is it Grandma?"

"Well, apparently there's this app that merges two people's faces so you can see what their baby will look like!"

My fork slips from my grip and falls to the grass. Mouse is on it within seconds, licking off what little potato salad is left. By the time I reach down for it and sit back up, my mom has turned the phone around to reveal the photo.

"Ahh!" I flinch.

She's merged my face with Madeleine's, and the result is nothing short of horrifying, a tiny gremlin thing that looks nothing like a human child.

Everyone cracks up, even the girls, but Madeleine sits silent across from me, obviously taken aback.

"I'm sorry, but no baby looks like that!" Kathy says, pressing her hand to her mouth to conceal her laughter. "Why did they give it Adam's full head of hair?! *And his stubble?*"

"The proportions are all off," Samuel adds. "What baby has a jawline like that?"

My mom tilts the phone so she can see the image again. I can tell she's barely containing her laughter as she replies, "I think she's cute, and the app was free, so what do you expect?"

When I peer back at Madeleine, her gaze is focused on her food, and beneath the spray of freckles on her cheeks, she's sporting a healthy blush. She's obviously embarrassed, and though I should, I don't feel bad. This is what she wanted. She fed my mom lies and now the woman has gone off the deep end, merging our faces and planning our future family.

"Let's hope she takes after Madeleine a bit more than that," Kathy says with a laugh.

"*She's not pregnant*," I point out, since the table seems to have forgotten this minor detail.

My mom waves away my bad attitude. "Oh c'mon

Adam, it's just a little fun."

"Maybe she doesn't even want kids," I point out.

"She does. She told me," Kathy says confidently.

I'm baffled. We've been here for less than an hour and she's talked to Kathy about kids and gone on about a wedding to my mom. Is she insane?

"Hypothetically," Madeleine chimes in, her voice growing weaker by the minute. "In the future…"

"Oh, don't let him spoil our fun," my mom says, reaching over to grab Madeleine's hand. "That app didn't get it right. You two will make beautiful babies."

I can't stand sitting here for another second. I push away from the table and head over to where Samuel stashed the beer in a cooler by the grill. I still have half a bottle, but I down it in one long swig and reach down for a fresh one.

When I return to the table, I hear faint murmurings about Olivia.

"I never did like that woman," Samuel says unabashedly.

If there's one topic I want to discuss even less than having children with Madeleine, it's my past relationship with Olivia.

"She was always a little cold in my opinion," Kathy says.

"Enough," I boom.

The table goes silent.

"She's not here to defend herself. Talk about something else."

Madeleine pushes to stand. "I think I better go."

Yes, I think you should.

"No!" Payton shouts, reaching for her hand. "We haven't even had dessert yet."

"And you still have half your food," Allie points out.

"I forgot Madeleine and I have other plans," I say, scrambling for some kind of excuse to get out of this situation. "We were only going to stop by for a second."

No one buys my excuse, but they're too polite to insist we stay. Kathy rushes inside to pack us some leftovers while Madeleine retrieves her shoes from Allie. The girls pout as they hug her goodbye, and so does my mother. Samuel is oblivious, eating his chicken and sipping his beer in silence. He's the only one I'm not angry with.

Once Mouse is back on his leash, we head for the front door. Madeleine trails behind me, and I don't have to look to know she's upset. I don't care. She made her bed and now she has to lie in it.

"Here. *Here*!" Kathy says.

I turn back in time to see my sister-in-law foist three large Tupperware containers into Madeleine's hands.

"The top one has two slices of apple cobbler in it. It's Adam's favorite."

Madeleine's bottom lip quakes when Kathy wraps her in a hug. "Thank you. That was sweet."

"It was really good to meet you. Next time you come, you'll have to stay longer, okay?"

Madeleine nods and turns away quickly, probably so Kathy won't see her expression start to crumble. I glance away, angry at the semblance of pity I'm starting to feel for her.

Kathy opens the door for us and we head for Madeleine's car in silence. I load Mouse in back, and Madeleine takes the driver's seat then passes me the Tupperware containers in silence. She starts the car and pulls away from the curb. We don't talk, don't even acknowledge one another's existence. I'm minutes away from freedom, minutes away from putting this shitty afternoon behind me, but then, of course, it gets worse.

We're out on a country road, halfway back to my house when smoke starts to rise from beneath the hood of Madeleine's car.

"No, no, no!" she says, slowing down and pulling to the side of the road.

"It's overheating."

"No shit!" she snaps, quickly turning off the ignition and stepping out of the car. I follow after her, popping the hood before she gets the chance. Steam rises in plumes and I push her back instinctively, knowing how easily she could get burned.

"It's my car," she points out, annoyed.

"Yeah, and yet you refuse to take care of it," I say under my breath.

I inspect her coolant reservoir, and as expected, there isn't any near the fill line.

"When's the last time you checked your fluid levels?"

She crosses her arms. "I assure you my fluid levels are just fine."

"You're out of antifreeze. Are there any gas stations nearby where we can get some?"

"Uhm, no, but I have some water bottles in the trunk."

"That'll work, but I can't unscrew your radiator cap until the car has cooled down, and that will take forever. Here, give me your phone."

"Why?" she asks, stepping away from me.

"Let's just call a tow."

She shakes her head vehemently. "No! That's expensive. You said it yourself, it just needs some water."

"That's probably just one of the *many* things wrong with this bucket. You need a mechanic," I say, walking back around the car to get my phone.

"Adam! We are NOT calling a tow truck!"

I turn back to see her glaring at me with murder in her gaze. "We're stuck in the middle of nowhere!"

"Downtown is that way," she says, pointing to the left. "Start walking if you want to get home so badly."

"I don't want to get home! I want to get away from you!"

"Well that makes two of us!" she snaps, throwing her hands in the air and turning to walk off down the road.

Mouse starts barking from the back seat, excited by the turn of events.

I watch Madeleine walk another few feet before sinking down on the edge of the road and resting her head on her knees. She looks so tiny, vulnerable.

"Will you get up?" I ask, my tone sounding barely a notch above bored. "A car is coming and they're going to hit you."

"I'm on the shoulder," she defends.

I'm left watching the car careening toward us in the distance—a massive red truck complete with a muddy cattle guard. I'm half-certain Madeleine is about to be road kill, and she doesn't care. I groan and run for her, hooking my hands beneath her arms and hauling her out of the way just before the truck tears past us. Her hair whips up and the air surrounding us is momentarily tainted with her fragrant shampoo.

It's lavender, and on another day, I would have liked the smell.

"Are you trying to get yourself killed?" I ask gruffly.

The truck technically didn't come close to hitting her, but I'm looking for any excuse to fight at this point.

She wiggles out of my hold and tugs down the front of her blouse. "After the afternoon I just had, MAYBE I

AM!"

"Oh, after the afternoon *you* had? *AFTER YOUR AFTERNOON*?!"

"Stop shouting at me!"

"What was that bullshit you fed my mom about elaborate dates! About marriage!"

She whips around and her brown eyes sear into me. "What are you *talking* about? What dates? *Marriage*? Is this a joke?"

I stalk toward her until I'm pointing my finger into her chest. "Don't play coy now. I never asked you to go for an academy award with your acting."

She pushes me and I stumble back. "Oh fuck off, your mom called your little charade the moment we stepped out of the car. She clearly wanted to have a little fun with you. I guess she went overboard."

"So, what, she asked if we were really dating and you just spilled the truth?"

Our voices carry out over the bleak landscape around us, but we don't care. There's no one around for miles, just Mouse, who has slithered into the front seat of Madeleine's car and is resting his head on the dashboard.

"She's a kindergarten teacher, Adam! They're basically human lie detectors. She got it out of me, and I figured it was better to tell her the truth than to keeping lying to her face."

I'm dragging my hands through my hair for the hundredth time today. Soon I won't have any left.

"So you're saying you're no better at lying than a 6 year old?"

She throws up her hands and stalks off. "I'm saying that maybe if you'd given me more than 5 minutes of warning, I might have been able to concoct a believable backstory."

"Speaking of that—did you tell my mom we were getting married?" I blurt after her.

"No!"

"Any made-up dates? Something about a *camel ride* in the park?"

"NO! *What* are you talking about? Do you think I'm a *complete* psychopath?" She doesn't even bother turning around to address me, just waves me off and walks away. "If you're angry, you need to take it up with your mom. She's the one who created that demon baby thing on her phone."

I shudder at the memory.

"To be fair, our kids would be cuter than that," I point out. Not that it matters.

I think I hear her laugh, but she could also be crying at this point. Either way, I give her space. For ten minutes, she stands off to the side of the road, cooling down and staring out at the rolling pastures. I head back to her car and sit beside Mouse, patting his head and wondering how in the world I got myself into this mess. My life was settled back in Chicago—*I* was settled there. Now I'm stuck on the side of the road in the middle of Texas with a hotheaded brunette who needs a mechanic yesterday.

I stare down at my phone and contemplate going over her head, but it wouldn't end favorably for me. Instead, I recline the chair and close my eyes. It doesn't take long for guilt to start to seep in and replace my anger. From the sound of it, Madeleine didn't really do anything wrong. My mom guessed we weren't dating because she's not an idiot, and I should have picked up on her little games sooner. Instead, I'd assumed Madeleine was crazy enough to concoct wild tales about hot air balloons and camels. I smile. Now that I've had a few minutes to think on it, none of it makes sense.

How many camels are there in Hamilton, Texas?

I'm going to have a word with my mom. She thinks she's so funny. Even now, she's probably gloating at how easy it was to dose me with my own medicine.

I realize I've shouted at Madeleine yet again for something that isn't really her fault. She probably thinks I need anger management. Hell, maybe I do. But for now, I just need to get this car running.

I reach across and pull the trunk release lever. Her eyes follow me curiously as I haul the 24-pack of water bottles up to the front of the car. I take off my button-down so that I'm left in my undershirt.

"Are you trying to pull the ol' stranded-stranger-will-do-*anything-for-a-ride* trick? Because it will probably work better if I start to strip," she says bitterly.

I stay quiet, and bunch the thick cotton material inside my right hand and place it over the warm radiator cap. I take a deep breath and turn my head, steeling myself before twisting the pressurized cap as quickly as possible. My skin prickles as the hot steam escapes through the fabric, and I release when I hear the characteristic pop.

"Start the engine."

Mesmerized, Madeleine obeys.

Her car starts on the first try, as if in gratitude for the modicum of attention being paid to it. I work quickly, emptying a disheartening number of water bottles into the radiator. Finally, the water overflows and I re-cap the line.

Much to Mouse's delight, we both hop back in the car and Madeleine starts driving. We're silent for a while, right up until I gather the courage to glance over and apologize.

"I overreacted and I'm sorry."

She grunts, her gaze never wavering from the road.

"I shouldn't have been so rude to you back there. I thought you'd lied to my mom about a marriage proposal and it pissed me off."

"Yeah, well, I didn't. I played nice with your family until your mom extracted the truth out of me. I'm sorry for telling her, but that was a stupid plan to begin with. Who brings a fake date to a family barbecue?"

When she says it like that, it sounds pathetic.

"A guy who's desperate to get his nagging mom off his back."

The tension in her expression lessons slightly. "Why didn't you just invite someone you're actually interested in instead of dragging me along?"

Simple.

"I don't want to date right now. I'm not *ready* to date, so there's no one I could have really asked except for you."

"Does she want you to be dating someone?"

"Desperately."

"Because of Olivia?"

I turn away. "Yes, because of Olivia."

"Is she an ex-girlfriend?"

It feels weird to talk about Olivia with Madeleine, mostly because I don't talk about Olivia with *anyone*, not since leaving Chicago.

"Ex-fiancée."

"Huh."

I glance back and she meets my gaze. The anger is gone, replaced with healthy curiosity.

"How long were you engaged?"

Five years, six months, and four days.

"A long time."

"How long is a long time?"

"Five years." My words are barely audible, but she

hears them anyway.

"*Five* years?!"

I shrug. "We didn't want to rush it."

"Did you get engaged after the first date or something?"

"We dated for three years."

"So eight years total. Yeah, I'd say that's the definition of 'not rushing it'."

I'd like to change the topic, but nothing comes to mind. I could bring up how poorly I behaved at the barbecue, but I don't want to go down that road again.

"May I ask who broke it off?" she asks gently.

The question should bring a wave of pain and residual feelings, but for the first time I can remember, the memory of Olivia has no effect on me.

"She did." I shrug. "By sleeping with my best friend."

The audible gasp that follows that revelation doesn't surprise me anymore. It's not a pleasant detail, but it's important.

"Well, that's a polite way of ending things."

I smile out the window.

There's a long pause before she asks her next question.

"Do you miss her?"

There's a longer pause before I reply.

"Honestly? No. I miss our dog. I used to run with her in the city."

"And she got to keep her?! After sleeping with your best friend?"

I know. I regret not fighting harder, but at the time I just wanted out. I wanted to pack my bags, cut my losses, and leave. I left Molly with Olivia because it was easier, and now...

"I wish I hadn't let her."

"Well, if you want a running companion, you can have

Mouse any time you want."

I glance into the back seat and Mouse is sitting with his tongue lolling out to the side, completely content. Then, I look back and study Madeleine's profile. She's focused on the road, her cheeks flushed from standing out in the sun and her hair wild from the wind. I'm aware of the guttural urge to reach out and touch it, to touch her, but then I remind myself that not twenty minutes ago, we were berating each other. Something tells me if I reached out and touched her now, she'd bite.

"Why are you being nice to me after what I just put you through?"

"I guess I feel bad for you," she shrugs, tossing me a lazy smile. "And now it looks like I owe you a suit *and* a shirt.

I laugh at her blunt delivery.

"And more selfishly, Mouse has a lot of energy." She glances in the rearview mirror. "It'd be pretty nice if someone took him on runs every now and then."

"So is this a truce, then?"

Her brown eyes meet mine and she smiles. "Somehow, I don't think a truce with you will last long."

Though I wish I could, I don't disagree.

CHAPTER TWELVE

Madeleine

I MADE A crucial mistake—I forgot to ask Adam about holding up his end of the bargain. To be fair, there wasn't really a good time for negotiations on Saturday. Between his mom planning our future family, us shouting at each other, and my car deciding to crap out, I somehow wasn't able to broach the subject of real estate. I have to be careful, especially after how he reacted at the puppy training class. It's a delicate matter, and one I need to handle with tact if I intend to actually convince him to let me sell him a house.

That's not to say it wasn't on my mind the entire day though. As we shouted at each other while plumes of steam billowed out of my car's hood, all I wanted to ask was, *Will you still let me sell you a house?*

Pathetic, I know, but I've come to terms with where I'm at in life. A person can only pretend to take a fake phone call when they walk by their landlord so many times before their self-worth and decorum fly right out the window.

My Sunday passes in a vaguely miserable state. I scrounge through my pantry and refrigerator and come up with the ingredients for blueberry muffins for Mr. Hall. I owe him rent again soon, but the muffins will fill his belly until I can make that happen.

After I finish baking and deliver the goods, I tidy up my apartment and rearrange the furniture, convincing myself the space looks bigger and brighter with the sofa facing the window. Unfortunately, my new feng shui technique reveals a pile of dirt and dog hair lurking beneath the old sofa spot. It's a metaphor for my life, no doubt, but I refuse to read into it. I sweep it up, toss out the trash, and then exercise Mouse.

Only when I'm back home in my clean apartment, sweaty from a healthy grown-up workout, do I allow myself to entertain the idea of calling Adam. If we were dating, I wouldn't dare. After yesterday, we both need a cooling off period—but we aren't dating, and I need him desperately. As such, I don't get to play the role of the cool, aloof woman. I get to play myself: desperate, awkward Madeleine. It's a slightly less glamorous role, but one I feel confident that I can nail.

Too bad he doesn't answer.

Not the first call I make at 2:00 PM or the second call I reluctantly dial at 7:20 PM.

I leave a voicemail both times, aware of how tight and strange my sing-songy voice sounds.

"Hey Adam, it's Madeleine. I was just calling to touch base with you concerning your end of the bargain. Also, do you do oil changes? Ha-ha-ha give me a call when you can. Bye."

Then—because, as my mom has told me since I was

five years old, I enjoy fixating on things—I spend every minute for the next five hours breaking down my first message and deciding it was too vague. I could have been talking about anything, and my stupid joke was distracting. So, in the second message, I clarify.

"Hey, it's Madeleine calling again. Just in case you weren't sure what I was talking about, I would still love to take you around Hamilton and show you some real estate. It's a buyer's market right now and there are quite a few properties that would be worth your time. We can take your car this time! Give me a call. Okay. Bye!"

There can be no confusion over why I've called or what my intentions are, and yet he doesn't bother getting back to me, not Monday, Tuesday, or Wednesday. I even have Daisy call me from her office phone and her cell phone to confirm it's not a problem on my end.

"Are you waiting on a call from a client or something?" she asks because she's nosy and doesn't seem to have enough patients at her clinic to take up her time. Sad.

"It's nothing. Thanks for your help."

She keeps rambling on before I can hang up, even as I tell her I'm about to be late for a company meeting.

"Hey, tomorrow night—do you want to hang out? It'll be you, me, Lucas—"

"Oh, sorry, I'm busy."

There's no point in letting her finish. Do I want to be the third wheel on another one of my brother and Daisy's dates? *Yeah, that's going to be a hard pass.*

"Doing what?" she asks, not quite believing me.

Too bad for her, I'm not lying—for once.

"I signed up for another Hamilton Singles thing. It's at the bowling alley."

"Romantic."

"Yeah, well, I always thought I'd meet my husband while dressed in clown shoes, so it looks like I'll finally get my chance."

Whatever Daisy's response is, I can't hear it because Lori leans into my cubicle on the way from the kitchen, a fresh cup of coffee in hand.

"Hey Madeleine, just wanted to remind you that the meeting starts in ten minutes."

Her constant droning could give the boss from *Office Space* a run for his money.

"Is that Lori?!" Daisy asks through the phone. "What is she wearing today? Describe her outfit in excruciating detail!"

My hand muffles her voice enough that Lori can't overhear. Meanwhile, I smile with every ounce of false congeniality I can muster. Honey is positively dripping from the sides of my mouth.

"Yes, I can't wait for it. I'm about to head over."

She doesn't relent. "Hmm, okay, it's just that you've already been late for multiple meetings this quarter, and I heard that you're on parole." She says the word like it's a slur, even glancing over her shoulder to confirm no one else has heard her. "Or was it probation? Either way, it's just probably best if you aren't late again."

I want to take a pair of scissors to her loud highlights, but I misplaced the scissors I usually keep in my top drawer a few months ago. Instead, I'm forced to stand, hang up on Daisy, and follow Lori over to the conference room with pen and paper in hand. We're the first two to arrive.

She takes her usual spot beside Helen's chair, and I pick a spot on the opposite end of the table. Her perfume is strong. *Chanel* number five, she told me once, bragging. *Oh really? On you it smells like a number two.*

"I think I'll be closing on two properties today," she announces to the mostly empty conference room. Gloating is her way of making small talk.

"Wow. Congrats," I say, trying to wring out just a few more ounces of artificial sweetness. I'm aware that my reserves are running low, and I need to ration if I'm going to have to endure alone time with Lori for the next few minutes.

"Yeah. One of the properties is downtown, in the historical district. It should bring in *quite* the commish."

I hum as though I'm interested, but really I'm texting Daisy S.O.S. under the table.

"What about you? Do you have any new clients? Helen mentioned something about you working with Adam Foxe last week, but I didn't believe it. When I approached him, he said he wasn't in the market for a house."

I should tell her the truth. I should explain that I probably won't be selling him anything—a house, a condo, a shoe. I should confirm that he isn't in the market, but then I'd have to endure her pitying gaze, and I just can't do it. Not after my weekend from hell. Not after Mr. Hall cornered me this morning and demanded I pay last month's rent before he logs on to LegalZoom and figures out how to serve an eviction notice.

"Yes, well." I shrug, not meeting her eyes. "It happened really naturally."

Nice and vague. Good, Madeleine.

"Has he signed anything yet? A contract to work with you?"

She's fishing, trying to pick apart my lies and force me to admit the truth.

"I sent it over to him today."

She nods as if impressed. "Right, well...we'll see if he

actually signs them."

And then because I have nothing productive to add to the conversation, I look down at my phone and busy myself by adding a pair of scissors to my Amazon cart. Snip snip.

• • •

I've been to a few Hamilton Singles events in my day. The organization has hosted them at buffets, bars, and parks, but this is the first one I've seen at a bowling alley. It's a massive space, and the coordinators have cordoned off half of the lanes specifically for the event. There are balloons and a bright purple banner hanging on the wall that says, *Get the Ball Rolling for Love!*

I'm half inclined to back up slowly and bolt, but my principles won't allow it. I've paid for the event—only $5, but still. For five bucks, I refuse to not at least get my fill of greasy nachos and stale beer.

When I check in, I'm handed a pair of size 8 bowling shoes (which of course look like size 13s) and a pin that is supposed to differentiate us from the normal Wednesday night bowling alley crowd. The pin is a two-inch hot pink circle that announces to everyone in big, bold letters that *I'M SINGLE AND READY TO MINGEL!* I think they meant *mingle*, but it appears no one caught the typo before the pins went to print, and I feel too bad pointing it out at this stage in the game.

"All right, so pin that onto your shirt and then head over to lane six to join your team!"

"Oh, we've already been assigned teams?"

The coordinator's smile falters slightly. "We thought it would be easier that way."

Easier for them, sure, but I've been stuck with Allen, Mitch, and Judith—my gym teacher from middle school who was painfully old even back then, a forty-year-old widower, and a woman who looks to have ten years on my mom, respectively. Allen pretends he doesn't remember teaching me middle school kickball, and Mitch is too busy downing his fourth beer of the night to be much of a conversationalist. Judith and I decide we'll be partners, and I try really hard not to let my disappointment show. These events are rarely worth my time, but I've met one or two guys over the years. At the very least, it feels like I'm being proactive about my love life. I'm throwing myself at fate and giving love a chance, but tonight, this team of mine is almost a slap in the face. When did my situation become so hopeless? When did my old gym teacher become an eligible bachelor for me?

"You okay, sweetie?" Judith asks when I don't respond to her question.

I try to shake myself out of my funk. "Oh, yeah. Fine. Just thinking."

"About love?"

Mostly wondering if I should run and slide headfirst down the lane, hoping that the pin-setting machinery will take me out of my misery. But I also think about packing my belongings, grabbing Mouse, and moving away from Hamilton. There have got to be better prospects outside of this tiny town—job-wise, love-wise, life-wise. Hamilton is slowly suffocating me and I worry if I don't get out soon, I never will. I'll be Judith—swinging five pound balls at fifty, "mingel-ing" with other single retirees. I glance down at my pin and am about to rip it out of my shirt when I hear a voice that makes my situation one hundred million times worse.

Adam is here.

Adam is here, close by, laughing and having a jolly ol' time.

I scan through the rest of the event attendees and then turn around to inspect the other lanes. I should never have looked, because four people I'd rather not have witness this fiasco are setting up their own bowling night at the lane right next to the one I'm assigned to. It's Daisy, Lucas, Adam, and a woman I recognize as one of the medical assistants from Hamilton Family Practice, the clinic Lucas and Daisy own. They set this up, this double date *thing*, and suddenly I'm furious.

"Sweetie, you're up," Judith says, trying to nudge me.

I push to my feet and tell her to skip my turn.

"You'll take a penalty if you do that!"

I couldn't care less.

Her name is Tori, the medical assistant. She looks young, maybe 22 at the most, which means I have about five years on her. Is that a lot? Too much? Does Adam want some fair, fresh-faced girl right out of college?

Why the hell do I care?

I stalk over to their group and Daisy spots me right away. This is her fault. She knew I would be here.

"Madeleine!" she exclaims, seemingly innocent and happy to see me. "What a co-inky-dink!"

When she comes over to hug me, I pinch her on the back of the arm as hard as I can.

"Why are you here?" I hiss as she jerks away and rubs her arm.

"OW! We wanted to do a bowling night. Lucas hasn't been in a while."

I don't even look at my brother. I know him, and this doesn't have his fingerprints anywhere near it. No, it's my best friend's handiwork all right.

Adam is watching me from behind Daisy, a curious little smile playing on his lips. His gaze takes me in and then it stops pointedly on the hot pink eyesore pinned to my top. He spots the typo, grins, and my cheeks turn another shade darker.

"Hey Madeleine," he says, meeting my gaze.

Even in this hazy bowling alley, his eyes twinkle.

"Oh, hello Adam. I'd assumed you'd died. I was about to write your obituary."

I don't include the second part, though I really want to. I want to call him out for ignoring all my voicemails, but it's too embarrassing to admit in front of all these people. Instead I smile and keep my lips zipped.

It's right then that Tori comes into view from stage left. She steps closer to Adam, like he *belongs* to her or something. Her skin is shiny and I don't see any pores on first glance. "Sorry, Madeleine, I just keyed in the names and I don't think it will let me add another."

I smile, but it feels more like a sneer. "No problem, I already have a partner anyway."

As if on cue, Judith *yoo-hoos* for me to come back and join their game.

"Do you play in a league or something?" Adam asks, furrowing his brow to take in the scene behind me.

Tori bursts out laughing. "Oh, it's the *singles* thing!" Then she drops her voice a little bit. "My grandma used to go to those after she retired."

Lucas and Daisy both throw Tori scolding glares, but it's Adam who speaks up first. "Oh, that sounds fun, and it's probably a good way to meet people."

My shoulders straighten a little more at his defense. "Yeah, it's okay. I mostly do it for the cheap food and drinks."

He grins, and for a second it feels like just the two of us standing here, smiling in our clunky bowling shoes...except while I probably look like a dweeb in my off-the-shoulder dress, Adam looks just as sexy as ever in his jeans and black Henley shirt.

"Adam," Tori says, her voice slicing through what would have been a perfect moment. "I really need something to drink."

"Oh, okay." He points to the left, still smiling at me. "The concession stand is right over there."

Tori huffs and walks off, and I'm left wondering why I can't move, why I'm hovering here, staring at a man who has proved time and time again that he wants nothing to do with me.

"Madeleine, you should join our game," Lucas says. "I'm sure we can reset the game."

It's tempting to take him up on the offer, but I don't want to leave Judith hanging even more than I already have. I wave away his invitation and promise to meet up with them later.

It's impossible to concentrate on my own bowling game with theirs taking place so close by. Tori's high-pitched baby voice seems to carry over to lane six no matter how hard I try to block it out.

"Oh my God, Adam!" she squeals just as I stand to take a turn. "You're so good!"

I slip my fingers into the holes, wind up, and then dispatch my third gutter ball of the night.

Dammit. Dammit. Dammit.

Bowling is definitely not my thing, but I didn't think I'd be *this* bad.

"It's okay, Madeleine! We can still catch the boys,"

Judith says cheerfully. As depressed as I am, I laugh at the notion of calling the geezers across from us "boys".

I turn to head back to my seat and notice Adam watching me. He's been doing it for the last thirty minutes, and each time I feel his attention on me, I look up and we do the awkward-eye-contact, look-away-quick thing. This time I don't give in to the urge to look his way. There's a chance he still has some semblance of respect for me, but after that third gutter ball, who knows.

I've barely reached my seat when loud salsa music starts to filter out of the speakers overhead. One of the coordinators of the singles event grabs the mic and after a sharp screech of microphone feedback announces, "It's time to switch things up!"

Then, before my eyes, my little group of four is scrambled. One of the coordinators grabs Allen and Mitch and replaces them with two new men, one of whom makes Judith blush like a schoolgirl. The other is actually within my age range, and better yet, I don't recognize him. He's wearing worn Wrangler jeans and a white button-down with pearl snaps. He's a little more cowboy-esque than I usually go for, but after my earlier prospects, he might as well be an oasis in the middle of the desert.

He introduces himself as Dan and doesn't seem to be much of a talker, but he does bring me a fresh beer from the concession stand, so that's a win.

"Have you lived in Hamilton long?" I ask, trying to strike up conversation while Judith takes her turn. Dan and I are sitting beside each other and when his thigh brushes mine, I don't move away.

He swallows his sip of beer and shakes his head. "Nah, just moved here last year. I work over at Longhorn Ranch."

My interest in piqued. "What do you do over there?"

He shrugs and glances down, like he's not used to being asked direct questions like that. "Ranch hand, nothing fancy. I tend to the horses and help out where they need me."

It makes sense. His chin is sporting a couple days' worth of stubble, and his skin has a healthy glow from being outdoors. I can see it now: him taming wild mustangs with patience and masculinity. I bet he knows how to use a lasso for other, more nefarious reasons too. I'm imagining just that when he reaches forward, grabs an empty cup, and spits black crud into it. Chewing tobacco. I try not to cringe as my dream of riding him off into the sunset is shattered. I have very few deal breakers, but mouth cancer is definitely one of them.

When he's done, he sets the empty cup back down and turns to me, and then I notice the lump in his mouth where he's left a bit more of the disgusting substance. It's not my thing, especially when he leans closer to ask what I do for a living and I catch the scent on his breath. Call me crazy, but I prefer minty fresh to stale tobacco.

"Oh, um, I'm a real estate agent," I mutter, right before I hop up to take my turn again.

I don't even bother lining up my feet before letting the ball loose and turning back for my seat. I know the ball is going to end up in the gutter anyway, but then I hear the telltale sound of bowling pins getting knocked down and I whip around. I hit them! Not all—I'm not suddenly an Olympic bowler—but I've knocked down four of the pins. FOUR.

Judith is jumping up and down with glee. "You did it! You did it, Madeleine!"

I chance a glance over at Adam to see if he's witnessed my athletic prowess. He hasn't, because Tori is regaling him with a story and he seems to have turned his attention solely to her. It takes the wind right out of my sails. Suddenly four pins seem just as bad as zero pins.

"You get one more turn to knock down the rest," Judith says as I walk past my seat and continue on.

I tell her to take my turn for me and then I head for the bathroom.

I just need a little break, five seconds to stare at my reflection in the hazy bathroom mirror and assess where my life took such a sharp turn for the worse. I only manage three seconds of my existential crisis before Daisy pushes the door open and joins me.

"I hope you and Lucas are happy," I say, crossing my arms and meeting her gaze in the mirror.

"About what?"

"Inviting Adam and Tori. Why is he here anyway?"

She steps up and props her hip on the sink beside mine. "Lucas wanted to include him. I think they're friends or something now."

"So as his friend, he decided to set him up with Tori?"

She frowns and narrows her eyes, doing her best to pry into my brain. I sigh and turn away, pretending to fix my makeup in the mirror.

"We didn't want him to feel like the third wheel, so it made sense to invite her."

"But not me?"

"I *tried* to invite you, but you shut me down before I could even finish telling you the plan."

That part I can't argue with.

"Would you have *wanted* to be invited?" she asks, poking me in the side.

I snort. "Obviously! Look at how dismal this singles night is. I'd rather be hanging out with you guys than trying to avoid getting caught in that cowboy's tobacco breath."

"Ohh, that sucks. He seemed like such a good prospect."

"He *was*, right up until he spit a bunch of dip into a cup right in front of me."

"All right, well, I forbid you from going back. C'mon, come have fun with us. I don't even really like Tori, and Lucas can barely tolerate her outside the office. I think we're both regretting asking her to tag along."

"What about Adam?"

"Huh?"

"Is he annoyed with Tori?"

"I can't tell. They seem to be talking a lot."

"*Awesome*."

"You're into him, aren't you?"

Her question pisses me off, so I don't bother replying. Instead, I push past her and head out of the bathroom, on a mission to do the one thing I've wanted to do all night. Adam is sitting at their lane, checking his phone while Tori takes her turn. I don't pass go. I don't collect 200 dollars. I march right up and don't stop until I'm only a few inches away from him. He's leaning forward with his elbows on his legs, and when he locks his phone and glances up at me, it suddenly feels like I'm too close. I'm almost standing between his knees, but if I back up, I'll look like a coward. He leans back in his chair, makes no move to shift his legs, and then glances up at me with a self-assured smile.

"Why haven't you returned my calls?" I ask, my arms crossed as aggressively as possible. "I left you a bunch of voicemails."

"I called you back."

I roll my eyes. "Sure you did."

"I called you this afternoon and left a message on your

work phone."

I can't verify if that's true or not; I was showing Mr. Boggs a few houses.

"Right, well, I have no clue if you *did* leave a message or what you might have said, but here's the deal, Adam: you're going to buy a house from me."

"That was the deal."

"And you're not going to feed me any lines about how I didn't hold up my end of the bargain, because I did. It's not my fault your mom moonlights as a polygraph examiner."

"I couldn't agree more."

"And I don't want to hear any arguments."

He leans forward and pushes to stand. For two seconds we're chest to chest, but I cave first and step back, giving us both a little bit of breathing room. Tori is buzzing behind us, trying to get Adam's attention, but his gaze is on me. His eyes are searing into mine, and my knees are suddenly weak. He takes my elbow and leads me away from the group so we can talk in private. I think it'll also give me the opportunity to regain some of my personal space, but he doesn't allow it. He's right in front of me again. His cologne, his chiseled jaw line—all of it seems to be the best thing I've encountered in months.

"Are you listening to me, Madeleine?" he says, his hand still on my elbow. "I'm going to buy a house from you."

"Oh, right." I nod, trying to keep my voice neutral. "Good."

"When do we get started?" he asks, fending off the smile trying to make a comeback on his lips.

"How about tomorrow?" I ask, glancing down at his grip on my arm.

He releases me just before he replies, "Perfect."

"I'm assuming you'll need to schedule it in the

evening? After you finish seeing patients?"

I'm all business, *very* professional.

"We can go on my lunch break. I can give you all the time you need."

Hope and happiness wrap themselves around me like a warm hug. This might actually happen. I might actually sell him a house and Helen will have to take me off probation. I could cry, but I manage to keep it together.

I hold my hand out, and he wraps it up in his tight grip. We shake and shake, holding each other's eye contact until I finally cave and crack a smile.

"That was pretty bold of you to march over like that," he says.

"It felt like an out-of-body experience," I admit.

He smiles wider, still shaking my hand.

"You know you didn't have to feed me that whole line the other day about you 'not being ready to date'—you clearly have no problem hanging out with Tori."

His grip tightens ever so slightly around my hand. "It wasn't a line. Daisy invited her to tag along, nothing more to it."

I already know this, but I'm having an insecure, weird moment and I wanted him to corroborate Daisy's story. It feels disturbingly good to hear he didn't invite Tori himself—so good that I can't help but push the conversation one step forward.

"Yeah, well, have you fed her the line about not wanting to date yet?"

We shake and shake and shake.

"There's no reason to tell her that. She's not someone I'm interested in."

"Oh, but you told *me*?" I quip.

Something flashes in his green eyes just as the

significance of my statement settles over us. He doesn't reply, and he doesn't let go of my hand. It's the strangest, most charged exchange I've had in years. It's just a handshake, but I wouldn't be surprised if in a few months I look down and have a big ol' baby bump.

"Adam?"

"Hmm?"

"I should get back to singles night," I say, my voice weak and useless.

"Right."

"You can let go of my hand now."

He doesn't. "Are you going to go home with that guy in your bowling group?"

"Why do you care? Worried some big cowboy is going to have his way with me in a barn full of hay?"

He finally releases my hand and steps back. "I'll see you tomorrow."

CHAPTER THIRTEEN

Adam

MY MORNING AT the clinic is spent with three dogs, two cats, and a wily parrot. My patients demand my attention, but I still manage to carve out a little bit of space in my head to delve into my weird feelings for Madeleine. I came to Hamilton with no intention of digging in and growing roots. For the last eight years, I've had nothing but roots. I need time to myself, to adjust to a life that isn't shared with Olivia. We only broke up a few months ago—isn't there some kind of rule for this? If we were together for eight years, shouldn't it take me at least eight months to move on? So then why does it already feel like Olivia is a distant memory?

Even the pain I endured through the breakup seems to have faded away.

It's Texas.

I swear the humidity sucks the feeling right out of you. Who can stand to hold a grudge when it's already hitting above 90 in the early afternoon? They say crime rates go down in the summer because no one can endure the endless heat. Maybe my anger with Olivia can't endure it either.

Or maybe it's just Madeleine.

The woman has an uncanny ability to pop up when I least expect her. Hamilton is small, but not that small, yet Madeleine is everywhere—and somehow, it's not enough. I accepted the invitation to go bowling with Lucas yesterday because I thought Madeleine would be there. She's his sister, and she's Daisy's best friend. It would make sense for them to invite her, but then they surprised me with Tori and I had to make the best of the situation.

I bowled for shit, too busy trying to steal glances of Madeleine and the cowboy one lane over. I knew about cowboy boots, but I thought pearl snaps were just another hacky Texas stereotype. I'm surprised he didn't light a campfire in the middle of the bowling alley and pull out a harmonica.

I'm checking out my last patient before lunch—an old, docile golden retriever. Maybe if he were a bit more rambunctious as I listen to his heart and lungs, I wouldn't be wondering why Madeleine was at a singles night in the first place. She's beautiful and funny, there's no getting around it, and I doubt there's a man in this town who would deny it—so why is she trying to find dates at a bowling alley?

I bring it up to Sasha, the receptionist, and try to act casual about it.

"Oh, Madeleine Thatcher? Yeah, I know her. She was one grade below me in school."

I'm reminded how small this town is.

"Did she date much?"

Her brows hit the ceiling. "Madeleine? No way. She

was too busy heading up every club in school. She was the classic overachiever, just like her brother, except he went off to become a doctor, and Madeleine sort of...fizzled out."

I frown. "What do you mean?"

"I mean in college she majored in something crazy like global finance, and yet here she is, back in Hamilton, switching dead end jobs every few years."

Interesting.

"But even if she wanted to date, guys at Hamilton High were a little intimidated by her. I mean, she's not exactly *Miss Congeniality*. Most guys want someone who's a little more upbeat, someone with a little personality."

I laugh before I can stop myself. "Oh, she's got personality all right."

Sasha shrugs. "Well then it's wasted on men here in Hamilton. If you ask me, I think she should move somewhere else. She could get some fancy job and meet a guy who actually appreciates her *quirks*."

Quirks. *Jesus.* Just because she doesn't titter at everything a man says doesn't mean she has quirks. She's confident, smart, and somewhat cynical, but then again, so am I.

I realize I'm defending her in my head and shove away from the front desk.

"Thanks for the info. I'm headed to lunch."

"Want some company?" she asks, hopeful.

"Already have some."

I drop my white coat in my office on the way out the door and then start to walk to Hamilton Brew. Madeleine emailed me this morning, confirming our lunch meeting and giving me the address for the coffee shop. I'm starving, and when I push through the door, I'm greeted by the smell of fresh baked bread.

My stomach grumbles on cue, and then I scan the room and find Madeleine set up with her laptop and notes at a table pushed up against the side wall. She looks more professional than I've ever seen her in a fitted dress and nude flats. Her long hair is pulled into a high ponytail and she's typing away at her laptop, and I almost agree with Sasha—in Chicago, men would be flocking to her. In Hamilton, her "*quirks*" are completely wasted.

I weave through tables to get to her and she glances up, a wide smile breaking out across her face. She's radiant despite the overcast day. I reach her and lean down, pressing a kiss to her cheek. She always smells like lavender, I realize, just before I feel her stiffen. I jerk back to standing.

Why the hell did I just kiss her cheek?

"Oh! Um, hello," she says.

A deep blush creeps up neck and I clear my throat.

"Hey, did you already order?"

She can't meet my eyes. She's focusing on a point just over my right shoulder as she shakes her head. "I was waiting for you."

I nod toward to the counter. "C'mon, I'm starving." She drops her papers onto her laptop and reaches for her purse. I hold out my hand to stop her. "It's on me."

She frowns and shakes her head. "I like to treat my clients when I invite them to meet me at a restaurant for business."

"And I like to pay when I take a friend to lunch," I say, closing the subject.

She doesn't argue, but she doesn't drop her purse either. That's fine. When we order, I tell her to go first, and when she orders the same turkey club I was eyeing, I tell the cashier to make it two and then slip him my card before she can unclasp her wallet. She laughs and reaches for one of the massive chocolate chip cookies on display beside the cash register.

"For that, you're buying me a cookie too."

The coffee shop fills up for lunch fast, and by the time we've taken our seats with our sandwiches, no less than five people have come up to say hello to Madeleine.

"You're pretty popular," I comment, unwrapping my sandwich.

She shakes her head. "It's just how life is here in Hamilton. Stay here for another few months and you'll see. You can't make it through a turkey club without ten people coming up—"

"Maddie Thatcher, is that you!?"

I turn just in time to see a small woman with short blonde hair bolting for Madeleine.

"Mrs. Bell!" Madeleine says, leaping out of her chair. "When did you get back in town?!"

They're hugging and talking too fast for me to catch up, including mention of an RV trip and newlywed bliss. I finish half my sandwich before they finally extricate themselves from their conversation and notice me sitting here, watching them with amusement.

"Oh, Adam! I'm sorry, this is Mrs. Bell, Daisy's mom."

I can see the resemblance as soon as she mentions it. She's a little shorter than Daisy, obviously older, but they have the same delicate bone structure, the same mischievous gaze.

"Adam!" Mrs. Bells says, turning back to Madeleine and lowering her voice. *"The vet, Adam?"*

Madeleine rolls her eyes. "Clearly Daisy has been filling you in. Yes, this is *the vet, Adam* but right now he's *my client, Adam."*

Mrs. Bell squeals. "Oh, how amazing, Madeleine! Daisy told me you were having a rough go of real estate for a little bit. I'm so happy to see you with a new client."

I see Madeleine's smile falter. Is she having a rough go of it? She was obviously desperate to get me as a client if she was willing to accept my proposal the other day, but I just thought she was being an overzealous agent—going the extra mile for her job, that sort of thing. Now, I'm not so sure.

"Well once Madeleine sells me a house, I'll recommend her to everyone I know," I add, trying to ease her frown.

The fact that I don't really know many people in Hamilton is completely lost on Mrs. Bell. Her eyes glow with approval.

"What a kind man." She turns to Madeleine. "And *handsome* too, don't you think?"

Madeleine laughs. "I don't think you're supposed to say that in front of him, Mrs. Bell. It'll go to his head."

I smile. "I don't mind, really."

Mrs. Bell laughs and tosses me a wink. "I wish I could stay and chat, but I don't want to keep you two from your date—"

"Lunch meeting," Madeleine corrects.

Mrs. Bell smiles. "In my day, we called them dates, but whatever floats your boat."

"He's a *client*!"

Once again, they seem to have completely forgotten I'm sitting here, listening, but I don't mind. It's the most entertainment I've had in weeks.

"Well I've never had a client eye me the way he's eyeing you."

I smile, but Madeleine groans and shoos her away,

threatening bodily harm if she keeps it up.

"Don't pay attention to her," Madeleine insists, sitting back down at our table. "She likes to stir up trouble. It's kind of her thing."

I shrug, finishing off the last bite of my sandwich before I reply, "I like her."

She reminds me of my mom, but somehow that kind of teasing is more charming when it comes from someone you aren't related to.

"She means well, but you should have seen the way she manipulated Daisy and Lucas before they finally got together. I thought Daisy was going to kill her."

I laugh, imagining it for myself. "I'd like to hear about that someday when we have more time."

Her eyes flash and she slaps her forehead. "Ugh, right, of course. We need to get down to business. You have to get back to work soon, I'm sure, and we haven't even started to talk about real estate."

I wish we didn't have to. I want to hear more about Mrs. Bell, about Madeleine's life in Hamilton, but she insists. Her untouched sandwich gets pushed to the side as she turns her laptop so we can both see the screen.

"So first we'll go over the details about what you're looking for—y'know, what your price range is, that sort of thing."

"I don't know the answer to that."

She balks. "Which part? The price? Or the type of house you're looking for?"

"All of it. Price shouldn't be an issue since I sold my house back in Chicago before I moved, but I haven't put much thought into the house I'll buy here."

"That's okay. What was your house like back in Chicago?"

I sit back in my chair, thinking it over. It was modern, and sparse. Olivia and I picked it out together and while I liked the open floor plan, the contemporary furniture and white rooms left the house feeling a little bare. I explain this to Madeleine and then I add, "I'd like to look for something a little more…homey, if that makes sense."

She smiles. "Of course it does. What about lot size? You probably didn't have much land in Chicago, but here, you have a lot of options. Downtown living will afford you standard lot sizes of about 10,000 to 15,000 square feet. Outside of downtown, people usually sit on at least a few acres."

I like the sound of having a bit more space. In Chicago, my neighbors were right on top of me.

"What about a middle ground? Somewhere not too far out, but maybe still on an acre or two?"

She jots down my request and nods. "That's definitely doable. I can already think of a few homes that come to mind."

"And I'd prefer an older home that's been remodeled. I'm not afraid of a little renovation work, but I don't have time to build from the ground up right now."

Her pen flies as I continue outlining what I'd want in a house. It feels good to decide everything for myself instead of having to compromise.

"A porch would be nice."

"Mmm."

"Maybe two stories? At least four bedrooms."

She smiles. "I thought you said you weren't sure what type of house you were looking for."

It's another thirty minutes before I feel like I've told her everything that comes to mind. The whole process doesn't seem so daunting anymore, and I want to start looking right away.

"How about we start this Saturday?" Madeleine asks, looking at her calendar on her laptop. "That'll give me enough time to compile a list of homes, and you can sit on some of the decisions you made today and see if they change."

"Sounds good."

It's Thursday, so Saturday is only two days away, but it seems like too long.

"Could I come by and run Mouse tonight?"

She stops taking notes and peers up at me from beneath her lashes. "Really? You don't have to run with him just because I offered."

I insist, though I know I'll be regretting my decision in the morning. I've worked out, but I haven't run any long distances since I left Chicago. My legs are already burning just thinking about it.

"Okay." She smiles shyly, focusing once again on the notes in front of her. "You can come by around six. And I might have you sign a waiver—I think Mouse has put on 10 or 15 more pounds just this week."

CHAPTER FOURTEEN

Madeleine

I HAVE NO earthly idea why Adam wants to come over and run with Mouse. Sure, he mentioned that he loves running, but he can run by himself any time he wants. Does he really like Mouse that much, or is there more to it? I ponder this question while zipping around my small apartment, tidying up at warp speed. The only person who ever comes over is Daisy, and I never bother picking up for her. She has seen this place in its full glory, but Adam hasn't, and he shall *never* see the full extent of my bachelorette barbarian lifestyle—not if I want him to think of me as a functioning adult. I start with the vacuum, but that takes twice as long as I thought it would thanks to all the puppy hair Mouse seems to shed at alarming rates lately. I zoom through the house, tripping over the vacuum cord three times before I'm finally finished. I am sporting nice bruises on my knees and a seriously jammed baby toe, but there isn't a speck of hair on my floor.

After that, I scrub the bathroom and the kitchen. I take out the garbage and load up another trash bag with things I should have been tossing on a regular basis: empty shampoo bottles, old magazines, an adult coloring book Daisy bought for me that I never got around to actually using. I *did* rip the pages out and use them as gum receptacles a time or two, which had a very soothing effect on my stress levels. *Thank you very much, adult coloring.*

The second trash bag is remarkably heavy—like drag it on the floor and groan heavy—and I decide right then and there that I'm going to clean my house more.

"Do you hear that Mouse?! We're cleaning this place up at least once a week—well, if we don't get kicked out first!"

He doesn't respond, and when I walk out of the bathroom, I find him chewing on the vacuum cord. *Good dog, save me from the prospect of weekly cleaning.*

I am losing my mind and suddenly it's 5:50. I'm still in my work clothes, and I can't decide how that makes me look. I consider changing, but Adam is due any minute and I still have to take out my second bag of trash, put up the vacuum, light a candle, and somehow teach Mouse how to behave like a good dog before Adam arrives.

It's no use. I'm running back to my apartment when I spot Adam pulling into the parking lot. If possible, his car is shinier than it was the last time I saw it. I really wish he wouldn't park next to my clunker. It's just cruel.

"Hey Madeleine," he says as he opens his door and steps out.

He's in running shorts and a t-shirt, sneakers and a ball cap. He is suddenly sexier than I've ever seen him, which makes no sense considering half his face is covered by the hat and his aviators.

"Oh hey Adam. C'mon, Mouse is inside waiting for you." *And probably terrorizing my apartment in some new and creative way.*

"Where did you just come from?" he asks, turning behind me to look at the apartment complex.

"Oh, the dumpster. Had to take some trash out."

"Ahh, that explains the ice cream wrapper stuck to your dress."

I look around, and sure enough, there's a Snickers ice cream bar wrapper stuck directly to my hip. When I pull it off, chocolate sludge clings to the fabric.

"Ugh…gross…that must've come from someone else's trash. I don't really do desserts, just lean protein and broccoli."

He chuckles and follows me inside. Mouse goes crazy when he spots Adam, jumping and whining until Adam eventually gets him under control. I don't even bother apologizing or trying to explain away the behavior. Adam knows what kind of beast Mouse is by now, and unless a miracle occurs, he's not going to come into manners overnight.

"I'm going to change really quick so I can wash this thing," I say over my shoulder. "Make yourself at home, give yourself the grand tour, whatever."

I shut the door to my bedroom, rip off my sheath dress, and rummage through my drawers until I find a pair of workout shorts and a tank top. I'm not actually planning on working out, but I like the illusion it creates.

"I like what you've done with the place," he calls from the living room.

"Thanks! There's water in the fridge if you need it!"

Two seconds later, I hear a crash and come running, yanking my tank top down as I go. Half of the contents of my refrigerator are on the floor. Adam is standing, frozen—no, *horrified*.

"Oh god, I forgot to warn you—"

"I just opened the door and everything came tumbling out."

I have a tiny refrigerator, like half the size of a normal one. I'd complain to Mr. Hall about it, but y'know, beggars can't be choosers. Anyway, I make do. I shove all my food inside of it and carefully stack it in a way that it doesn't come tumbling down if I open the door slowly enough.

Adam, of course, didn't think to do that, and now he's bent over picking up my yogurt and apples.

"It's a small fridge," I offer lamely as I try to help.

"Yeah, sorry, I was trying to get some water and didn't think to prepare myself for an avalanche."

I look up to find him smiling.

"Are you *mocking* me?"

"I feel like someone has to. The amount of accidents that happen to you on a daily basis must break some kind of Guinness World Record."

Yeah, yeah, yeah. I stand and start shoving food back into the fridge before I hand him the water pitcher.

"There you go, Mr. Hydration. Have as much as you want."

He accepts the glass I hand him and then leans back against the counter. I lean back against the opposite one, and my galley kitchen feels small with him inside of it. I mean, it always feels small, but now it feels *microscopic*. If I reached my foot out just a little, I'd bump his shoes. I wonder what he thinks. He's probably used to something a little more spacious, more up to date. My appliances are from the stone ages, and the dishwasher, though intact, doesn't even work. I store my winter clothes in it because

I'm resourceful like that.

"You can come running with us if you want."

I refocus my attention on his face, having just stared at his legs for the last thirty seconds. Have I ever cared about a man's legs before?

Adam is smiling, mocking me still.

"I'd rather get stuck on a deserted island with Lori."

He laughs.

"Not much of a runner?"

"My brother got the running genes. I got—"

"The clumsy genes."

I smirk. "Exactly."

He finishes off his water and turns to open the dishwasher. This time, I react fast enough to stop him.

"Oh! No worries," I say, retrieving the glass from his hand. "I hand wash everything."

Mouse goes crazy once I grab his leash. Adam hooks it to his collar and then salutes me on his way out the door, promising not to be gone too long. I close the door after them, press my back to the door, and then slowly, my gaze falls on the one thing I forgot to clean: my dirty clothes hamper in the middle of the living room. It was in plain view for Adam, and sitting right on top is a sheer pale pink bra I bought ages ago and only pull out when I have no other options. It only takes a second for me to calculate the odds of Adam having seen it—100%. *Perfect.* Now he probably thinks I put the hamper out there on purpose, like I'm trying to seduce him with my delicates. I groan and carry the hamper into my bedroom then force myself to pull up a workout video on YouTube. It's either that or continue to clean; I can't watch TV while Adam is out exercising my dog. It feels wrong.

By the time he knocks on my door 45 minutes later, I'm

lying in a heap on my floor, sweating and refusing to stand.

The yoga video I picked was called *Intermediate Yoga*, or so I thought. A quick check after I've finished proves that I read it wrong. *Insanity Yoga* is listed in the description box, which, to me, seems like an oxymoron.

Adam knocks again and I know I have to get up off the floor. I try to move my legs, but they don't budge. I groan and try again, forcing myself to get up. Every step to the door is painful, and my forearm burns as I turn the handle.

Adam, bless him, looks like a sweaty God on my doorstep with his t-shirt clinging to his chest and arms. Mouse stands beside him, panting and happy as a clam.

"Looks like you two had fun," I say, opening the door wide enough for them to step through.

"Did you just take a shower?" he asks, amused by my current state, no doubt.

"Insane yoga," I whisper on a pained breath.

He laughs. "Sounds like you should have just come running with us."

He unhooks the leash and Mouse takes off for his water bowl. I limp into the kitchen and pour Adam another glass of water then get one for myself as well. We're back to standing across from each other in the tiny space, just like earlier, except now we're both dripping with sweat and I think I need to tell Mr. Hall the air conditioning in my unit is on the fritz again because the air is hot, stagnant.

Neither one of us talks as we finish our water, and I'm not brave enough to meet his eyes. Instead, I focus on Mouse, who laps up water from his bowl and then plops down right between us.

"Was he a good running partner?" I ask Adam.

"Terrible at first, but after the first mile, he seemed to get the hang of it."

I smile down at my dog. "Hear that Mouse? You were only terrible *at first*. That's progress!"

Mouse wags his tail.

Adam laughs and I brave a glance up to him. He's watching me—studying me, more like. I want to smooth my hand over my hair. Fix my ponytail. Tug my tank top up a bit. I think it shifted while I was working out and I can't be sure, but I think I'm now rocking a little more cleavage than is appropriate. But, if I adjust my tank top, I'll be drawing *more* attention to my breasts, and that won't do. After the sheer bra fiasco, I'm trying to convince Adam I'm *not* desperately trying to seduce him.

"Why are you looking at me like that?" he asks, tilting his head.

That damn smile is there. So confident. So appealing.

I look away. "What? I don't know what you mean."

"Your eyes almost looked like you were…"

Turned on?!

"Bored," I quip, moving around him to drop my cup in the sink. We need to move out of my kitchen. I've never thought so before, but it's basically a muggy sex den. Such a confined space, with all those pots and pans and spatulas…I shiver.

Adam's phone rings and I tell him to take the call, but he shakes his head.

"It's not a call, it's a reminder I set a week ago to alert me about a chamber of commerce meeting I have to attend tonight."

"When is it?"

"In 20 minutes. *Shit*."

He probably doesn't have time to go home and change.

"I still have my work clothes in my car…" he says, thinking out loud. Then his gaze drags to my bathroom, and

I catch on after an awkward amount of time.

"Oh! Oh, yeah, do you want to shower here?"

He drags a hand through his hair. "I don't want to intrude. I just completely forgot about this thing—"

I wave away his concerns. "No, you aren't intruding. You just exercised my crazy dog! The least I can do is let you shower."

He thanks me and runs out to his car for his clothes. I use the thirty seconds to scramble around and confirm that nothing embarrassing is left in my shower. When he walks back in, I've just finished hiding my bikini trimmer. I whip around and smile.

"Sorry, I don't have any manly shower products. You're going to end up smelling like lavender."

He shrugs. "It's either that or B.O."

I catch a whiff of the sweat and manly musk wrapped up with a hint of his body wash. I'm half inclined to tell him he'd be fine going to the meeting as is, but I don't say that because he nearly accused me of being turned on and I don't know what would happen if he knew I *was* turned on. Would he still let me sell him a house? Would he feel awkward around me from then on?

I don't want to find out.

"All right, so I'll just be right out here," I say, pointing to the hallway.

He nods and turns the shower on. Even after he closes the door, I can hear him moving around. My apartment is too small.

Clothes hit the floor then the shower curtain gets tugged to one side. Feet step into the tub and water splashes down Adam's naked body. I pinch my eyes closed just as a bottle gets uncapped.

He's lathering himself up, maybe washing his hair, and

I can't take it. I turn on music and hand wash the glasses we used for water. It only takes me a second, so I wash them again.

Mouse is staring up at me.

He knows my secrets.

He knows my shame.

I shoo him away and wash the glasses again.

The shower turns off and the shower curtain gets pulled to the side again. I sigh with relief. In a few minutes he'll be dry and clothed and out of my apartment, and if I happen to crawl into bed and pull out Señorita Vibrator, well, that's a secret I'll take to the grave.

"Uhh, Madeleine?"

His voice shocks me enough that I drop the glass in the sink. Thankfully, it doesn't shatter.

"Yeah?" I call out, my voice shakier than I would have liked.

"Do you have any towels in here?"

Of course I forgot to put one out for him. Add *poor hostess* to my list of deficiencies.

"Check the middle cabinet," I shout. "There should be one in there."

"I already checked."

My eyes dart to the dirty hamper in my room. One, two, three dirty towels are stuffed inside. I cringe. I had to use them yesterday when Mouse came back muddy from our walk. *Right. I have no clean towels.* Adam is naked in my bathroom and I have nothing to hand him. I yank open the kitchen drawer at my hip and pull out all the tea towels I can find. There are five in total—maybe if he uses them conservatively, they'll dry off his whole body.

"Adam?" I ask, stepping toward the bathroom door. "I realize this is going to sound weird, but—"

"You have no clean towels."

"It's Mouse's fault! Listen, crack the door and I'll hand you some of my kitchen towels. They're small but clean, so they should work."

He laughs, and I know he's adding this to the list of things he wants to mock me about. *Who doesn't have a single clean towel in their whole apartment?* Madeleine Thatcher, that's who.

"All right, hand them over," he says, cracking the door and holding out his hand.

The exchange was supposed to be smooth. I slip the towels through the crack, he grabs them, shuts the door, dries off, and gets the hell out of my apartment.

But I don't consider Mouse. I don't consider the fact that he would desperately miss Adam in the few minutes he was in the shower. I don't consider that Mouse would come bounding forward with enough force to push the bathroom door wide open. It's the slowest slow-motion experience I've ever witnessed.

My hand is stretched out in an attempt to pass Adam the towels.

He's standing at the threshold of the bathroom, naked and dripping wet. He's tan from head to toe, and I know this because in the second I have to take in all of his naked glory, I see every inch. EVERY. SINGLE. INCH.

My jaw drops.

The man is miles of toned muscle, tight abs, strong thighs. My gaze roves everywhere—and I mean *everywhere*—before I come to my senses, dramatically slap my free hand over my eyes, and announce, "You have a scar on your hip!"

He yanks the towels out of my hand. "Bike accident when I was seven. Would you like to see the one on my back as well?"

I shiver at the thought of seeing his butt.

"No—please—I mean no, thank you," I chirp.

"I was kidding."

"*I'm so sorry.*"

"So are you going to turn around? Mouse is standing in the doorway and you're blocking him, so I can't shut to the door."

I jump into action, grab Mouse, and whip around, trying my hardest not to die of mortification. The bathroom door shuts just as I run into the wall. Even then, I'm too scared to take my hand away until I'm safely back in the galley kitchen. I press myself against the refrigerator and try to calm down, but my heart is beating a wild rhythm in my chest, thump, thump, thumping so hard that I feel like my arteries might burst.

My hand finds my mouth and I bite down on my fist to keep from making a sound.

A groan.

A moan.

A laugh.

Anything could spill out, and I don't want Adam to think I'm losing my mind. I squeeze my eyes closed and I see it all there again. It's like the residual effects of staring directly at the sun. I turn to face the refrigerator tug it open, swinging the door back and forth, fanning my flushed face.

To be fair, it has been a *long* time since I've seen a naked man, but I know that's not why I'm reacting the way I am. I've dated some cute guys, but I've never seen a man like Adam in the flesh. That one second of accidental flashing basically ruined me for any man that might come after him.

The bathroom door opens and I jerk forward toward the

sink. By the time Adam walks by, I'm pretending to wash my water glass *again*.

"That glass looks squeaky clean."

I drop it on the drying rack and turn, forcing myself to look his way. *I can do this. I can be normal.*

He's back to wearing his work clothes, but what does it matter? He's the sun, remember? Every time I blink, he's back in the doorway of that bathroom.

"I'm really, *really* sorry," I say again, hoping he won't hold this against me.

He smirks as he uses one of the kitchen towels to dry his hair. "It took you quite a while to look away."

"Did it?" I croak.

"I guess I know where Mouse gets his manners."

"Well you weren't exactly quick to cover up!"

"I mean, you basically catalogued all of my scars."

There's no point in trying to hide my blush. "Yeah, well, sue me. I was frozen in shock."

"Were you? Or was it something else?"

His green eyes find mine and I want so desperately to look away as I ask, "What do you mean?"

He sighs and shakes his head. "Never mind. I need to run or I'm going to be late."

Oh, right, the meeting—the whole reason he showered here in the first place.

I walk him to the door and try to find something to say to ease the awkward tension between us. Real estate is the only subject that seems acceptable. "So Saturday is still good for you?"

"What?" he asks, confused.

"For houses?"

"Oh, right. Yeah. Send me a text and let me know where to meet you."

I hold the door open and he steps past. I think he's going to leave without either of us saying another word, but something makes me want to be brave, to catch him off guard. I think he wanted me to be honest earlier, to say what I was really thinking.

"And Adam?"

He looks over his shoulder.

"If the tables were turned, I doubt you would have looked away either."

I think my line is killer, one of those moments in life when you say the exact right thing at the exact right time—right up until I get a text from Adam Saturday morning, canceling our meeting.

CHAPTER FIFTEEN

ADAM HAD A good excuse for canceling on me: one of his patients' owners called with an emergency and Adam agreed to go into the clinic to check it out. He didn't mention what the emergency was in his brief text, but it's not like I could question it. He dropped everything on a Saturday to aid a helpless animal. Like I said, it's a good excuse.

The problem is, he hasn't bothered to get back to me about a rain check. Over the last few days, I've called and left him voicemails, shot over a pair of professionally worded emails, and even slipped and texted him twice when my common sense had already gone to sleep for the night.

In return, I've received nada. *Zilch*.

We are right back to square one, and it makes no sense. When we're together, he's friendly, even borderline flirtatious. When we're apart, he doesn't just act different, he falls off the face of the earth altogether.

At first, I give him the benefit of the doubt. Maybe he's really bad at communication. Maybe he likes to live his life unencumbered by technology. Maybe he's so embarrassed about me seeing his *nether region* that he can't work up the courage to text me back.

Too bad none of those lame excuses stick. There's something up with Adam, and I think I know what it is.

He likes me.

The clues fit. He flirts with me when we're together, he got jealous over the cowboy at the singles event, and he came over to run with Mouse. Why would he do any of that if he didn't like me?

Daisy doesn't agree.

"It sounds like you're trying to fit a square peg into a round hole."

I wave away her pessimism. "Listen, you didn't see the way he acted around me the other day. He came over to run with Mouse and he was looking at me almost like he *wanted* me."

She hums in disbelief. What a good friend. "Are you sure he wasn't just horny? I mean, how well do you know this guy? If he liked you, he'd text you back."

I check my phone and the only text waiting for me is from the local pizza shop, offering me a coupon for being such a loyal customer. That's it, no more giving my number out to pizza places; the only text I want to receive is from Adam. Still, I save the coupon.

"Shouldn't we go in?" Daisy asks, leaning over to eye the front of the YMCA through my passenger-side window.

It's the day of the second puppy training class and we're sitting in the parking lot, waiting for class to start. We stopped for sandwiches on the way over. I think I told

Daisy it would be a picnic, but instead we sat in my car. I finish off the last bite and sneak a small piece of turkey back to Mouse.

"Not yet. Last time Mouse was overeager with all the other puppies and everyone acted so offended. I want to minimize the amount of time I have to be around them."

"Is that Lori?!" she asks, pressing her face closer to the glass.

"Oh, yeah." I roll my eyes. "She came last time to try to convince Adam to hire her as an agent. I'm not sure why she came back."

"Her dog looks really old."

"That's because it is."

I brought Daisy with me to puppy training class because I need someone else to evaluate the situation with Adam and tell me if I'm reading too much into things or not. She's the perfect person for the job because she isn't one of those friends who only tell you what you want to hear. When I tried to pull off bangs in eighth grade, she politely told me I looked like a buffoon and instructed me to immediately grow them out. I've trusted her implicitly ever since.

When we walk in, there are even more women than there were for the first class. The twelve measly chairs positioned in a half-circle have long been claimed, and the unlucky few who weren't able to grab a seat linger around the perimeter.

"Wow. Is Adam a world-renowned dog trainer or something?" Daisy asks, eyeing the group of women as we head toward the back.

I level her with a knowing glare. "No, he's an eligible bachelor in a small town."

As if to prove my point, when Adam walks through the

gymnasium doors a few minutes later wearing jeans and a Hamilton Animal Clinic t-shirt, a hush falls over the crowd. Everyone sits up a little straighter, pushes their boobs out a little more. Daisy laughs and the sound carries around the entire room. Adam follows it to the source and his green gaze locks with mine. My stomach flips and I hold my breath. It's been nearly a week since he was in my apartment, and I'm not quite sure how to act. I want to be annoyed with him for not replying to my texts, for completely disappearing yet again, but then he breaks out in a wide, devastating smile. He's happy to see me. My heart soars and Daisy has to elbow me in the side to get me to look away.

"See?!" I tell her.

"Yeah, okay. He looked really happy to see you, but remember how he hasn't bothered to call or text you back in the last few days?"

I remember, but now that he's here in the flesh, I can't seem to hold on to any of the anger that was brewing over the last few days. Adam is here, and that's all that matters. The training class starts and he spreads us out around the room. There's more clicker training, and he adds on a few new tricks to today's repertoire. We're supposed to be working on the stay command when he makes his way over to Daisy and me.

"How is Mouse coming along?" he asks, reaching down to pet him.

I beam. "Really good. He'll sit and stay for a few seconds now before going crazy."

He laughs. "That's to be expected in the beginning. He'll get better at it the more you work with him."

"Well then, we better get back to it."

He nods, but he doesn't drop eye contact, doesn't move

to check on the next student.

"I'm sorry about the last few days. I know you've been trying to get in touch about a rain check date and—"

"No worries." I smile. "Really, it's fine."

His brows furrow as if he's surprised to be let off the hook so easily. "Right, okay. Well maybe I'll catch you after class?"

I smile. "Of course."

Daisy has a bone to pick with me as soon as he's not within earshot.

"Way to cave within the first five seconds of seeing him!"

"He seemed remorseful," I say with a shrug.

"No," she whispers, "you just saw those eyes and that jawline and you turned into putty."

I consider her accusation. Adam *does* have a good jawline.

"Have you ever considered that maybe I'm a mature adult who knows how to handle herself in public?"

"No. I've never once considered that."

Silly Daisy. If she were in my position, she would have laid into Adam and demanded some sort of excuse, but I don't need an excuse.

"You can see that he's interested though, right?"

She narrows her eyes, mulling over her answer before replying, "He does seem overly friendly with you compared to the other students."

"*And* did you see the way he smiled at me when he first walked in?"

She nods reluctantly. "I saw."

I try not to squeal.

"But why do you want him to like you so bad? Are you going to do something about it?"

"Oh." I hadn't thought that far ahead; I just wanted to be right about him liking me. "No, I probably won't do anything."

"Really?"

"Do I have to do something about it?"

"Not necessarily, but aren't you on all those apps and attending singles events because you want to find someone to spend time with?"

"Right, sure, but Adam told me the other day that he's not ready to date."

She laughs. "Bullshit. He's been eyeing you all class like you're dipped in chocolate sauce and he's got a serious sweet tooth."

"Gross."

"I'm serious. Whatever he meant by that dating comment, I don't think it still applies. He wants you."

When she puts it that way, it makes a lot of sense. Adam is single. I'm single. He seems interested, and I'm *definitely* interested. The only problem I foresee is that I will be working with him at the agency. Daisy doesn't seem to think that's a problem though.

"So you show him a few houses, earn a commission, and then date him. He agreed to be your client prior to you being interested in him. It's not really a conflict of interest, in my opinion. Has Helen mentioned anything about a non-fraternization policy?"

I snort. "Are you kidding me? She actively wants us to get close with our clients. I think Lori has dated like five of the men she's sold homes to in the past."

"See?! It's perfect."

I nod, absorbing her suggestions. "So you think I should stay after class?"

"You have to. I already asked Lucas to come pick me

up."

Thirty minutes later, Daisy is gone and all the other attendants are filtering out of the gymnasium doors toward the parking lot. I linger behind with Mouse as Adam chats with a woman who has a question about clicker training. It feels a bit awkward, especially when she drags on and on, acting as if she's never even heard of the concept before. It's just the three of us and she doesn't seem to be in any hurry to leave.

"I tell you what, why don't you come early next class, and we'll go over it a little bit more," Adam suggests.

"Oh really?" she asks. "That would be great. Thank you so much."

She's overly eager and I want to shoo her away. Instead, I focus on Mouse and give him a little bit of overtime training—Lord knows he needs it.

A few minutes later, the gymnasium door closes and I look up to see Adam walking toward me. For a moment, I think maybe I shouldn't have stayed behind.

"Need help cleaning up?" I ask, tilting my head toward the dozen chairs. There are also a few cones set out for walking exercises. In all, it would take someone five minutes to clean it up. Together, we do it in three.

"Thanks," Adam says, accepting the last chair from me so he can stack it against the wall.

"No problem."

"So…"

He laughs and stuffs his hands in his pockets. "So."

It's my chance to make a move. It's either now or never.

I take a step toward him and bite the bullet.

"Listen, Adam, I was wondering if you'd want to get dinner or something this week?"

My invitation appears to catch him off guard. He tugs a hand through his hair, looks away, and then glances back with narrowed eyes. "To go over house stuff?"

I smile. "We can talk about that if you want, but I was thinking something a little more personal."

"Like a date?"

"Sure, like a date," I reply, my voice a little more flirtatious than I'm used to. "I know you told me the other day you weren't really ready, but you and I don't have to make a big deal—"

He sighs and glances away just for a second before shaking his head. "No, I don't think it's a good idea."

My smile doesn't even falter because I don't think I've heard him correctly. It's ten long seconds before I register his response and my smile slowly fades.

"Wait, did you say *no*?"

"I'm not dating right now."

I take a tiny step back and regroup.

"So just to be clear, you're saying no."

My voice is still deceptively calm, though every nerve ending is firing off inside of me, telling me to run. It makes no sense. He likes me…doesn't he? Isn't that why he's been acting so weird lately?

"Madeleine, listen." He comes closer. "It's not you. Believe me, it has *nothing* to do with you."

I hold out my hands to block him from getting nearer. "Oh God, please stop while you're ahead."

"What? It's the truth. You think I'm spouting off bullshit? I'm not dating right now. I just got out of an engagement. I need some time to figure out my life."

I hear nothing but stale, useless words. "You need some time to *figure out your life*? Go hike the freakin' Appalachian Trail! If you're not ready for anything, why have you been flirting with me? *Running with my dog?*"

He reaches out, but I take another step back.

"I admit, I might have led you on a little bit, but that wasn't my intention."

I point my finger at him accusingly. "You were jealous about that cowboy. You didn't want me to go home with him."

His expression looks pained, like he doesn't want to hurt me. "You're right, I didn't want you to go home with him."

I laugh, and it sounds aggressive and cruel. "So just to get it straight—you don't want to date me, but you don't want other people to date me either?"

He doesn't reply.

"Do you like me or was I deluding myself?"

He steps forward and grips my arms so I can't pull back. Finally, I'm as close as he wants me to be, and I have no choice but to stand right there in front of him, inhaling his body wash. It's nauseating and perfect. I can't stand it, and yet I want to let my head fall against his chest and sigh.

"I like you. If I were dating right now, I'd want to be with you, okay?" He bends down so his gaze meets mine. Even still, I do my best to focus on the gym floor. "The reason I've been ignoring your calls and emails is because I like you *too much*. Of course I want to date you. Of course I want to go to dinner. I want to go back to that night in your apartment and skip the stupid chamber of commerce meeting. Do you get it? I want you, but it's not the right time. I've been trying to give us both some space."

"I get it. If we were to date, I'd just be your rebound girl." He bristles at the assessment, but it's the truth. "Have you dated anyone since Olivia? Have you even had a one-night stand?"

He barely shakes his head.

I yank my arms free from his hold. This is too much. I'm at my limit. My apartment, my car, my job, my love life—there isn't a single thing that isn't in shambles.

"This makes so much sense," I say, more to myself than to him. "Why wouldn't I go for a man who is completely uninterested in dating? This is perfect."

I toss my hands in the air and whip around to grab Mouse. I want to leave *now*.

"Madeleine—"

He's following behind me, trying to get me to listen.

"*It's not you, it's me*," I mumble under my breath. "Daisy is going to have a field day. I can't believe she talked me into this."

"Madeleine, you're taking this personally."

"Of course I'm taking this personally!" I shout just as I reach Mouse and grab hold of his leash.

It's a couple dozen steps to the exit and Adam beats me there, barricading the door so I can't leave.

"Oh, *very mature*," I chide, crossing my arms and waiting for him to move.

"I'm not letting you leave until you understand where I'm coming from."

I squeeze my eyes closed as warning bells start to ring in my head. I'm going to cry. The tears are forming, and if I cry right now, in front of him, there will be no going back. *I'll* have to go hike the Appalachian Trail.

"Madeleine, listen to me," he implores, his voice so soft and comforting.

He thinks he will be able to explain away my anger, but what he doesn't understand is that I get it: he isn't in a place to date, he doesn't want to lead me on, and he respects me too much to use me to get over Olivia.

I repeat all of that out loud to him, just to verify.

"Do I have it right?"

He shakes his head. "I *am* over Olivia, but that doesn't mean I want to jump right into another serious relationship."

"I get it."

I really, *really* do.

He groans, and there he goes again, tugging his damn hand through his hair. Each time he does it, it gets a little more messy, a little more irresistible.

"Let me leave, Adam."

"No."

I try to scroll through the few self-defense moves I know from the action movies I've seen over the years. I could go for the jugular, maybe stomp on his foot, but that seems too cruel, even in this situation.

Adam tugs Mouse's leash out of my hand and tosses it to the ground. Mouse, for all of his dog instincts, walks a few feet away and goes back to lying down and ignoring us. I sear him with my gaze. *What if I was in real danger, Mouse? Some dog you are.*

I step to the left, right, left again and I think I've outsmarted Adam, but then he grips my shoulders and spins me until my back is to the door. I'm stuck between a rock and a hard place, literally. Adam's thigh is pressed between my legs and his hands hold both of my arms captive against the cold metal door, like two goal posts. This exact pose has happened in a dream before, but it was Michael Fassbender standing where Adam is, and Michael didn't have quite as much emotion in his eyes.

"I *told* you I didn't want to date," Adam says, his hands tightening on my arms enough that I don't even think of trying to break his grip.

"Yes you did," I bite out. "And then you proceeded to flirt with me incessantly. Sorry your signals got crossed! Usually guys who aren't interested in dating don't eye me like I've been dipped in chocolate sauce!"

His eyebrows furrow in confusion. "What?"

"Nothing. *Ugh.*" I try to jerk free, but it's no use. I should have been doing *Insanity Yoga* for months leading up this standoff; maybe then I'd have enough strength to break free. "Just let me go so I can salvage what's left of my dignity."

Who am I kidding? There is none left. This gymnasium now contains my last remaining ounces. I might as well march down to the local salon and tell them to give me 'the Lori' because there is no hope for me.

"I feel bad," he says, bending closer.

You should, I want to say. *You made me like you. Why did you have to make me like you?*

Instead, I look away and say in a monotone voice, "You're hurting me."

I think that will be the end of it. No guy wants to hurt a woman; it's engrained in their twenty-first century brains to respect women. That said, Adam doesn't budge. Worse, he argues. He must have been raised by wolves—it's why he wanted to become a vet.

"No, I'm not hurting you. I'm barely holding you."

"I have weak wrists."

He laughs.

LAUGHS.

I jerk my head back and glare at him. "You're holding me against my will. I think this is called assault."

His gaze drops to my lips. "*Assault?*"

It's like I've just given him a brilliant idea. He inches closer, and his body wash tortures me a little bit more.

"Why are you looking at me like that? You aren't ready to date, remember?"

He nods. "I know."

He's still studying my lips, and there's fire lighting up his green gaze, fire and...*lust*.

"Adam?" I say on a shaky breath.

"I'm going to kiss you," he announces.

"Don't!" I snap. "*Adam Foxe*, do NOT under any circumstance—"

He kills the rest of my sentence with his lips.

He kisses me, and for a second or two, I refuse to cooperate. He can move those lips all he wants. He can grip my wrists tighter and hold me hostage, but I will not play along, not even when he takes my bottom lip between his teeth and bites down ever so gently. Well, maybe then...but I only moan and kiss him back because it's a knee-jerk reaction. Anyone would do the same, really.

The second I give him an inch, he takes a mile. He runs his tongue across the seam of my mouth, demanding entry, and I open up for him because I'm helpless. I've never been kissed like this before.

One of his hands releases my wrist so he can move down and grip my waist between his fingers. He draws me right up against him and I sink my hand through his hair, finally weaving my fingers into the silky strands I've been eyeing for the last few weeks. They're short and soft, easy to tug. He tilts his head, taking the kiss deeper. There are groans and thrusts, and what's worse is that they aren't just coming from him.

Soon there's not a single millimeter between our bodies. His leg is still between my thighs and we're rolling our hips, trying to grind our bones down to dust. I feel feverish, hot. I think my knees would give out if he weren't holding me up. This has got to stop, but I trail my fingers down his neck and hang on for dear life.

"*Madeleine*," he groans against my lips.

I think I have a mini orgasm just from the way he says my name, like he's coming apart at the seams.

Take me. Take me here and be done with it.

His hand snakes up from my waist and he drags his palm up my body, over my stomach and then over my breast, slowly…painfully. I shiver and he does it again, this time a little slower than before. Goose bumps bloom along the trail he makes and I'm thankful my clothes keep his hand from my skin. I feel raw and sensitive just from this. If he were touching me skin to skin, I think I'd do something embarrassing like break out in a sob.

His lips leave my mouth and descend down to my jawline, to my neck. My head falls back against the door—the same one I was attempting to flee through just moments ago—and I squeeze my eyes closed, savoring every sensation rippling through me.

"*Yes*." I sigh when his mouth descends even farther and he kisses my breast through my clothes.

We are *this* close to going past the point of no return against the hard metal door when a shrill whistle blasts through the gymnasium. We leap apart. I pry my eyes open and spot a middle-aged coach standing in the doorway on the opposite side of the gym. He has a volleyball in one hand and his whistle in the other—the whistle he is still blasting at full volume.

"*Jesus*," Adam mutters under his breath.

I reach down to straighten my shirt and then brush the back of my hand across my mouth. I'm shaking—maybe from being caught, maybe from what we were just doing.

The coach finally lets his whistle fall back against his

chest.

"We've got competitive volleyball practice in here in 20 minutes," he shouts. "Clear out."

Mouse barks at him, and I leap for his leash before he can take off running.

We heed his orders and 'clear out', awkwardly and silently. Adam follows me out into the parking lot, but I have nothing to say. He just finished telling me he wasn't ready to date, and then we made out hardcore. Makes sense.

"Listen, back there—"

I groan. I'm mentally and physically exhausted. If he starts up again about how much space he needs or how *unprepared* he is for dating, I won't be able to control my temper.

I whip around and cut him off. "Adam, save it. We aren't dating. I get it. Whatever that was—" I shake my head. "It was nothing, okay? I've already forgotten about it."

He doesn't speak up to correct me, and I'm thankful for that. Out here, in the empty parking lot, he's partially cast in shadow. He doesn't look like Polite Adam, the man who loves animals; he looks like Seductive Adam, the man who just pushed me up against a door and had his wicked way with me. In other words, we're in dangerous territory.

"I'll see you around," I mutter, turning straight for my car.

I don't release my breath until Mouse and I turn back out onto the main road. That was…the most confusing half hour of my life. A therapist would have a field day with that exchange. Me? I don't want to touch it with a ten-foot pole.

The traffic light in front of me turns yellow and then

red. I slam on my breaks and glance down at my right arm propped on the steering wheel. It bears the mark of Adam's hand, from where he held me against the door. Already, it's fading. By the time I get back home, it'll be gone, but I can't wait until then. I scrub at the skin with my other hand, making my entire forearm red until it all blends together.

There. He's gone.

The light turns green and the car behind me lays on its horn.

"I'm GOING," I shout to no one.

When I turn down the street toward my apartment complex, I don't turn in. I pass the parking lot twice, looping around the block and contemplating my options. I could leave right now. It's not as if I have a life going here. I could drive until I hit Houston, Austin, Dallas. I could keep going until I hit another state, another country. I could start over somewhere and wipe the last few years from my memory.

And maybe I would have if Mouse hadn't whined from the back seat, reminding me of my responsibilities here, of all the reasons I'm stuck in this tiny town and this tiny life.

CHAPTER SIXTEEN

"**ADAM, WE WOULD** have invited a mannequin to lunch had we known you'd be this quiet."

I glance up from my untouched turkey sandwich and find my mom and Kathy eyeing me suspiciously, waiting for my reply.

"Oh, yeah. Sorry," I say, shrugging off their concern.

It's been a few days since my incident with Madeleine at the YMCA, and she hasn't replied to my phone calls or text messages. The tables are reversed, and I don't like it.

This morning, I was summoned to lunch by my mom and Kathy, and I couldn't turn them down. I don't have room in my schedule for another impromptu appointment courtesy of my mom and a stuffed bird.

We're eating at a deli down on Main Street, just across from Madeleine's real estate agency. I didn't pick the restaurant, but I did pick my seat at the table, facing out, toward the agency. We've been here for thirty minutes and

I haven't seen Madeleine once. She must be eating at her desk or out with a client.

"If it's nothing, then why aren't you eating?" my mom asks. "I'm almost finished."

To prove her wrong, I pick up my sandwich and take a massive bite.

"Alrighty then." Kathy laughs. "Diane, did I tell you I saw Madeleine at the grocery store the other day?"

I pretend to be enthralled by my sandwich.

"Oh? No, you didn't."

Kathy nods. "Yeah, just for a second. We were both about to check out, but she stopped and struck up a conversation with me. I half expected her not to remember me since she and Adam weren't at the barbecue that long."

My mom hums. "She's such a nice girl."

"*So* nice."

It doesn't feel like they're trying to get under my skin, and yet they are.

"Can we talk about something else?"

My mom laughs. "Sure. Why don't you come up with something to talk about?"

"How are the girls?" I ask Kathy, knowing exactly what I'm doing.

Kathy is obsessed with her daughters, and she'll talk about them nonstop if you get her started; it's a tool I've used quite a few times at awkward family dinners when my mom is intent on aiming the focus on me and my life.

"Oh they're good! Did I tell you Allie lost another tooth?"

For the next thirty minutes, I tune them out and slink back into my thoughts about Madeleine. I know I screwed up last week. From the beginning, I knew Madeleine was someone I could be interested in, so I did my best to respect that. I tried to be polite and distant. Obviously I had moments of weakness, but nothing as terrible as what I did to her in that gymnasium.

I was trying to do the right thing. I was so sure that turning her down and explaining that I wasn't ready to date was the gentlemanly course of action, but then why did it feel like the exact opposite? Seeing her expression when I turned her down for a date broke something inside of me. She looked so defeated, so utterly embarrassed. No woman wants to be made to feel undesirable.

But that's not Madeleine's problem.

She's *too* desirable.

I want to be with her. God, I would have taken her against that metal door if that coach hadn't interrupted us.

And that's the problem. I tell her one thing and do another. I can't blame her for being angry with me—*I'm* angry with me.

From here on out, I should leave her the hell alone. I should stop calling her and get someone else to cover the puppy training classes. I should bury my head in work and focus on myself.

Instead, as I walk back to the clinic after lunch, I try calling her work phone, half expecting her to screen my call.

On the third ring, she picks up.

"Good afternoon, Madeleine Thatcher at Hamilton Realty."

"Madeleine."

There's a long pause, and I wonder if she is about to hang up.

"Can we talk for a second?" I ask before she can.

She sighs. "I'm at work, Adam. What do you need?"

She clearly wants nothing to do with me, but that's to be

expected.

"I think we should talk."

"Okay, and I *don't* think we should talk. Is there anything else?"

I've never heard her voice so devoid of emotion.

"So you're not upset with me about the other night?"

"Not at all."

She's bluffing.

"All right, then I'd like to come by and run Mouse tonight."

"I have plans."

Another bluff.

"I'll come by *before* your plans."

Someone on her end of the line warns her about a meeting starting in five minutes in the conference room. She tells them she's headed there now.

"If you say no," I continue, "I'll assume you're still upset about the other night."

I'm not proud of myself, but my underhanded tactic works.

"Fine," she says. "Be there at six."

Okay, maybe I'm a little proud.

• • •

I'm standing on her doorstep at 5:55 PM and I can hear her shuffling around inside. After I knock, she scurries to the door and unlatches the lock. I'm a little taken aback to find her standing on the other side in a skimpy red cocktail dress. It's fitted around her waist and the short hem falls to mid-thigh—barely.

She's putting in her second earring and waves me in

with a small nod.

"Come in. I'm almost done getting ready."

"For what?"

Maybe she doesn't hear me, or maybe she feels she doesn't owe me an answer. She disappears into her room and I hear her shuffling through her closet. Mouse tries his best to monopolize my attention, winding through my legs while holding a ball in his mouth, desperate to be pet. I rub behind his ear, sinking my fingers into his soft puppy fur, and crane my neck to get a look inside Madeleine's room. She's sitting on her bed, strapping on high heels. Her dress has ridden up, barely covering her upper thighs.

"Do you have a date?"

She jerks up and sees me watching her.

"*No*, I just like getting dressed up like this for fun."

Her words drip with sarcasm. She pushes off her bed and closes her door, cutting off my view. She might as well be telling me to fuck off.

It's just Mouse and me for a few minutes. I could leave and get started on our run. Instead, I help myself to a glass of water and take a seat back on the couch. Her apartment seems smaller than the last time I was in it, or maybe I didn't pay attention before. Now, with her hidden away in her room, I have nothing to do but snoop.

Her antique coffee table is cluttered with books. There are stacks of paperbacks piled underneath and layered on top. There's no bookshelf that I can see—it's not like one would fit—and it seems she uses the table instead. Spines face me and I scroll down the list, recognizing one out of the ten titles: *All the Light We Cannot See* by Anthony Doerr. On a whim, I reach for it, appreciating the worn spine. There's a yellow sticky note tucked between the pages and I flip to it, wondering what passage she found important enough to refer back to. Maybe I liked that passage too.

"Rooting through my things?"

I drop the book like it's on fire.

She chuckles and comes over to pick it up, and her silky dress brushes my leg as she bends down, straightens. My fingers catch the hem and I brush it between my thumb and pointer finger; it's softer than I could have imagined. I drop it before she can notice.

"Aren't you going to apologize for snooping?" she quips, finally meeting my eyes. I realize I've been waiting for her to acknowledge me ever since I first arrived. Now that she has, I have nothing to say. I lean back on the couch, taking in every detail she's prepared for another man. Her long brown hair falls in loose, silky waves. Her makeup is heavier than I've ever seen it, though it's still not much. Her lips have a soft pink color on them and as I stare, I remember what she tastes like.

"Guess that's a no," she says with a shrug.

She's turning to back away, and I reach out for her hand. I don't have the right, and her expression confirms that.

"Who are you going out with?"

Her brow arches in annoyance. "Why do you care?"

I tug her hand and she stumbles forward. It's a warning: *Tell me or I'll pull you down onto this couch and you won't make that date and I won't run with Mouse. We'll repeat the same mistake we made a few days ago.*

"It's just a guy," she answers lamely.

"Where'd you meet him?"

She looks away. "The singles event."

I drop her hand.

"Which one was he?"

"Tall, blond."

I scrunch my brows, trying to recall someone with that description. *Was the cowboy blond?*

"I don't remember him," I finally admit.

She smiles, but it looks more like a sneer. "Probably because you weren't at the event. You were on a double date."

I have a hundred more questions, but she heads back into her room and comes out a second later with a small clutch. Mouse rushes over; he knows she's about to leave and doesn't want to be left behind. She leans down and reassures him she'll be back.

"It's kind of chilly out," I say, pointedly staring at her spaghetti straps.

She laughs and stands. "I think I'll manage." She's heading to the door when she adds, "Listen, don't wait around for me after your run. I probably won't be back until late, if at all."

With that sendoff, she's gone, and I'm left sitting on her couch while Mouse whines at the door, sad to still be here when she's gone.

"Yeah," I mutter. "Tell me about it, buddy."

CHAPTER SEVENTEEN

"THIS IS THE *best* date I've ever been on," I announce with a sated sigh.

I've got a hot pepperoni pizza propped up in a box in front of me, enough chocolate ice cream to last me for days, and best of all, old reruns of *The Office* playing on the TV. I couldn't ask for anything more.

"Don't ever say I don't know how to wine and dine a girl."

I smile and glance over to Daisy, who is currently wearing a hideous pajama dress, fuzzy socks, and some of those weird under-eye moisturizer strips. My slinky red dress is tossed across the back of her couch, replaced by an oversized t-shirt and Daisy's pajama shorts. I'm rocking my own pair of fuzzy socks, but I drew the line at moisture masks. After all, my makeup looks killer and I'd like to preserve it, even if no one but Daisy and Lucas will see it.

That reminds me.

"Hey Lucas! Could you bring us another bottle of wine?"

He groans in the kitchen, none too thrilled about his role as butler for the evening. I'm quick to remind him of all I've done for him in *his* time of need.

"Remember when you and Daisy had that massive fight and I housed you for like *a week*?"

Silence.

Then a few minutes later, a bottle of chilled rosé drops in my lap.

"Open it yourself," he says before heading upstairs to his man cave.

"What does he even do in there?" I whisper to Daisy. "Have you checked his computer history?"

She grabs the corkscrew from the coffee table and gets to work on the bottle. "I kid you not, he's into basketball now. He's watched every single Spurs game this season."

I shiver at the thought of suffering through a sporting event. "Make with the wine. I think we can get through another couple episodes before I need to head back."

"I still don't get why you had to pretend to go on a date tonight."

"I'm not pretending, Daisy, this *is* a date. I've been in love with you for the last 20 years."

She tops off my wine glass. "Funny."

I shrug. "I had no other choice. Adam was coming over and I couldn't just greet him in my pajamas. He's already seen how pitiful my life is, so I wanted him to think I had some semblance of a love life outside of him."

"But you don't."

I wave my hand in front of me so it encompasses our wine glasses, pizza, and fuzzy-socked feet. "What do you call this?"

"A friendship with unhealthy, codependent tendencies."

I smile. "Well to me it seems like the start of something really, *really* special."

"You have issues, and sorry, I can only watch one more episode. I'm ovulating and Lucas and I need to—"

"STOP. Jesus. That's my brother you're talking about."

"Our fertility specialist said we need to go at it like rabbits."

My fingers are stuffed in my ears. "La la la la la."

"And if we don't conceive this month, then we have to start to talk about other options."

I drop my fingers and peer over at her. She's staring down at her hands and nibbling on her bottom lip, clearly distraught. She and Lucas have been trying to have a baby for over a year. I've sat with Daisy and watched her read pregnancy test after pregnancy test—always negative, always a disappointment.

I nudge her with my elbow. "I'm sorry."

She shrugs. "It's okay. I mean, we haven't even scratched the surface. We still have a lot of options."

"Yeah…I just know how hard the last year has been for you. Remember, I can connect you to Adam's sister-in-law, Kathy, if you want me to. She took Clomid and that's how she conceived her twins."

She doesn't meet my gaze; I think she'll cry if she does. Instead, she reaches over and squeezes my hand. We sit like that for a while, watching *The Office* and pretending like everything's okay.

• • •

By the time I head home, I'm sleepy from wine and ready

to crawl into bed. It was hard enough to put my dress back on; I didn't even attempt the heels. They're sitting in the passenger seat when I pull into my apartment complex.

Sitting in the parking spot beside mine is a familiar black Audi.

What the hell.

I throw my car into park.

Why is he still here?

An optimistic part of me assumes his car crapped out and he left it here and headed home. I know that's not the case though. Nice cars like that don't crap out—just mine—which means Adam is still inside my apartment and I'm pissed as hell. Can't a girl pretend to go on a date and come home in peace? Why is he so insistent on making my life a living hell? The fact that I've been ignoring his calls and emails should make it pretty clear that I want to be left alone.

I groan and flip down my visor, checking my reflection. The situation isn't as dire as I would have assumed. Thanks to the amount of pizza I devoured at Daisy's house, I look thoroughly ravished. *Good. Let him think my date couldn't take his hands off me.*

Then I look over and see my heels mocking me from the passenger seat. I have to take off my cloudlike fuzzy socks and put my heels back on, all because Adam doesn't know how to give me space. I groan and reach over for the offensive footwear. I take my time strapping them on, hoping Adam will stroll out and leave at this precise moment. I'll wave from my perch in my car and we'll be nothing more than two ships passing in the night.

No such luck. A few minutes later, I finally have to face the music. I march up the path to my apartment and stick my key in the door, but Adam unlocks it before I can. *How thoughtful.*

He stands on the other side, holding the door open for me. His hair is damp from a shower and he's changed into clean clothes: jeans and a soft t-shirt. *Oh, by all means, make yourself at home.*

"What are you still doing here?"

He flashes me a small smile. "Mouse didn't want me to leave."

Mouse is snuggled up in a ball on the couch, too comfortable to get up and greet me—*his mother*.

"Okay, well, I'm tired…" *Hint. Hint.*

"You're back pretty early," Adam assesses, completely ignoring my implied suggestion for him to leave my apartment. Has he never had to take social cues before? Do social cues even apply to hot people? The probability is low.

I roll my eyes as I step past him. "Gotta leave them wanting more, Foxe. You of all people should know that."

"Yeah? Tell me about your date. Was he nice?"

Something in his tone sounds off.

I yank off my heels and derive just a little too much pleasure from flinging them into my closet.

"He was a perfect gentleman, thank you for asking," I reply as I make my way back out into the living room.

Adam is sitting on my couch looking like he owns the place. I bet if I sit there after he leaves, it'll smell like him. How disturbing. He can't just come into my life and change the scent of my furniture.

He's watching me with a half-smile.

He tilts his head and asks, "Where did you go?"

I prop my hands on my hips. "A little Italian restaurant."

"What'd you order?"

"Pizza."

"And what did you two talk about?"

"Books. Politics. Culture." I wave my hand in the air to encompass all of the made-up subjects. "The conversation *really* flowed."

His brow arches in disbelief. "And what about a second date? I'm sure he asked about that before he dropped you off."

I resist a sneer.

"Already scheduled for next week."

"Yeah?"

"Mhm." I brush my finger down my silky skirt. "I'm thinking about wearing an even sexier dress since we'll probably, y'know…"

"You can stop lying now," he snaps, his eyes full of the same fire I saw at the YMCA.

I toss my hands in the air. "*WOW*. What is it like to wake up every day with your level of arrogance? I've asked you to leave like ten times and yet there you sit on *my* couch, petting *my* dog, accusing *me* of lying!?"

"Lucas told me you were over at his house," he says with an even, cool tone.

My brother is now dead to me.

I offer him a condescending slow clap. "Way to go, Sherlock. You figured it out. I didn't have a date. Nope, I just couldn't stand to be in your presence for longer than five minutes, so I lied. Do you feel good about yourself now?"

His brows furrow and the fire in his gaze blazes just a little hotter. "He only told me because he knew I've been trying to reach you the last few days."

"Oh, so you and my brother are confidantes now? Well why don't you do me a favor and tell him to fuck off, and then you can pass the message along to yourself as well."

He has the audacity to smile then. If I were still holding my heels, I'd fling one at his stupid, magnificent head.

"That's it. Mouse, *attack*!"

Mouse licks his butt.

It was worth a try.

Adam pushes to stand and stalks toward me. I back up. For every step he takes, I take two, but still, his strides somehow eat up the distance between us. I hold my hands out to keep him at arm's length and his muscled chest hits my palms. It feels like I'm trying to hold back a tidal wave.

"I misspoke the other night," he says, wrapping his hands around mine and keeping them pinned against his chest. I was fending him off, but now it seems like the exact opposite.

"Oh?"

"Obviously, I'm interested."

I reply with a very unladylike snort. "*Obviously*? You could have fooled me."

"C'mon Madeleine, I'm very interested," he repeats, his steady gaze holding mine. "But I was trying to do the right thing. I just got out of an engagement. I moved across the country. I'm a mess." I nearly laugh—his life is infinitely less messy than mine. "You aren't someone I want to fuck around with."

"So you're saying I'm not fuckable?" I tease.

"*Madeleine*."

His hands tighten over mine as he tugs me closer. This proximity is starting to be a problem. The tension between us is growing, and I'm scared we're about to have a repeat of the YMCA make-out session—except now we're alone in my apartment and my couch is just a few steps behind him. Worse, my bed is even closer.

I need to extinguish the fire between us *stat*.

"I'm kidding! Adam, listen, you don't have to explain anything to me. I heard you loud and clear the other night, and I've moved on. That kiss was nothing—pfft, less than nothing."

I think I'm doing a good job of diminishing my feelings, right up until his eyes flare. *Oh no.* I think I've just swung a red flag in front of an angry bull.

"*Nothing?*" he asks, sidling even closer. "*Less than nothing?* Huh."

My eyes have to be as round as saucers. I'm scared of what he's capable of…or maybe I'm curious.

"Adam, c'mon. You said you wanted to do the right thing, remember? Go home—that's the *right* thing."

He smirks and steps closer. We're hip to hip when he bends down and brushes his lips against my ear. "You haven't been listening."

I shiver and then insist, "I have."

"I don't want to do the right thing anymore."

I squeeze my eyes closed, willing myself to wake up from this bizarre dream. Adam's hand releases my wrist and he skims the back of his finger up my forearm and bicep until he hits the thin red strap of my dress. It's loose and easy to tug down my shoulder. The front of my dress falls with it and the swell of my breast is hit with cold air-conditioning.

"I really, really don't want to do the right thing anymore," he says just before his lips hit my collarbone.

My head falls back until it hits the wall, and my fingers sink into his hair just like they did last week. We already have old habits. His lips on my skin feel familiar, right. He peels down another inch of my dress, and I'm too nervous to open my eyes. I know how much he can see. I can feel his mouth on my breast. I should have worn a bra. *Two bras.*

"Hold on to me, Madeleine."

My eyes jerk open. "Hold on to you?!"

Before I get a reply, Adam picks me up off the ground and forces me to wrap my legs around his hips. He pushes me up against my apartment wall and crashes his mouth to mine. *Holy shit.* We've gone from zero to 60 in seconds. We're making out like savages. The popcorn texture on the wall is scraping my back, maybe leaving marks, who knows—I don't feel a thing. Adam is a painkiller.

His hand is in my hair, and then it's sliding down and tugging on the other strap of my dress until the fabric is pooled at my waist. With my skirt shoved high on my thighs and my top peeled away, I'm nearly naked and blushing scarlet from my navel to my chin.

"We should slow down," I sputter just before his mouth falls to my chest.

He swirls his tongue around my nipple and my eyes pinch closed.

Or, y'know, speed up even more.

I've never been taken like this before. This apartment and these walls have seen purely PG action over the years. All sexual activities were relegated to the bedroom—lights off, music on, blankets covering body parts.

At this moment, Adam has me pinned against the wall. My legs are coiled around him like a snake and he's in charge. I'm helpless. I don't even think my fingers have feeling anymore. I can only focus on his mouth. On my breast. The cool air he blows before covering the sensitive skin with his lips. Sucking and tasting and doing his best to draw out every ounce of resistance.

But it's not enough.

I can't do this.

Nothing good will come from having sex with Adam.

Well, I can think of *one* good thing—but no, I can't.

"Adam…we have to stop."

He pulls back and his damp hair is tousled, courtesy of my fingers. It's adorable, and I nearly cave.

"What's wrong?" he asks.

With his brows tugged together and a concerned frown playing on his lips, I want nothing more than to lean forward and continue right where we left off. Instead, I hold my ground.

"We aren't dating. This is a bad idea."

It becomes clear then how funny it is to be having this conversation while we're poised in this position. I can feel how hard Adam is between my legs. My chest is still completely exposed to him. His hand is, *yup*, still on my boob.

I reach down for the straps of my dress and tug it back up as best as I can.

He lets me down gently, no groan or protest. My knees nearly buckle, but he keeps hold of me until I have my footing. It's a sweet gesture, and it makes the next few minutes all the more painful.

We're silent as he gathers his stuff and heads for the door, but it's not an angry, tense silence. There's a resolved, solemn feeling in the air, like maybe we both agree that this is for the best.

I trail after him, holding the door open as he steps through. He turns back and catches my eye. I smile. He smiles, and then he steps closer, dropping his forehead to mine. My eyes flutter closed and for a few seconds, there's nothing to hear but the sound of our breaths coming in unison.

The unspoken words fill the gap between our bodies.

"Good night Madeleine."

He brushes my cheek with the back of his hand, and then he's gone. I close the door and sink down to the floor. His car revs up in the parking lot, and I stare at the wall where he just had me pinned. There might as well be a white chalk outline etched there. After all, it's a crime scene. Theft in the first degree.

CHAPTER EIGHTEEN

I SHOULD HAVE let Adam seduce me. We could have stayed right there, pinned to that living room wall, and I would have let him give me an orgasm, maybe even two. It would have done me good to let loose and have fun. It's been so long since I've fooled around with anyone, I've probably forgotten how to do it properly.

"Madeleine?"

Adam didn't seem to mind though. I mean, he minded when I forced him to leave, but up until that point it seemed like he was enjoying himself just fine. Maybe I'm not so rusty after all.

"Madeleine? Yoo-hoo? Have we lost you?"

I look up to find every set of eyes in the conference room focused on me. I'm at work, stuck in an endless loop of meetings, and apparently, sometime within the last ten minutes I drifted off into Adam-land. Helen is standing at the head of the long table, uncapped dry-erase marker in hand. Behind her, she's scrawled three words on the white board: *Real Estate Mixer*.

I sit up straight and try to offer an apologetic smile. "Oh, sorry about that Helen. I must need a little more caffeine this morning."

She doesn't laugh, so I uncap my pen and glance down at my notebook. I haven't jotted down a single word from the meeting. Lori probably has a binder full of notes taken within the last five minutes.

Helen sighs and turns back to the white board. "Right, well, as I was saying, we are going to shake things up around here. As you know, I like to host a company event once a quarter to engage the community and expand the Hamilton Realty brand. Next weekend, instead of hosting a brunch over at Hamilton Brew, we'll be hosting a mixer at the local microbrewery!"

Lori claps so fast and so loud that I think her wrists are going to snap. "Such a brilliant idea, Helen!"

Then, of course, we all take turns kissing Helen's ass before she can continue explaining the logistics.

"I'd like each one of you to commit to bringing three clients or potential clients to the mixer. They don't have to currently be in the market to buy or sell a home, they just need to have *potential*!"

I'm already running through a mental Rolodex of people I could possibly invite, and I'm coming up embarrassingly short.

"Can I count on you all to send out invitations today?" she asks, pointing her marker out at us. "We want to give people plenty of time to RSVP before next week."

"Absolutely!" Sandra says, pumping her fist in the air.

I'm left nodding mutely, agreeing to bring people though I have absolutely no clue who I'll be able to coerce into attending. I could ask Adam, but I don't think that's a good idea. Hell, I don't even think I should be showing him houses today, which is why I've taken it upon myself to invite his mom and sister-in-law to tag along for our lunchtime appointment. It's a brilliant plan: they can offer their input on the homes we tour, *and* they'll provide a buffer so Adam doesn't get any ideas about continuing where we left off.

I saw him at the training class last night. He was polite, and handsome, and so good with Mouse. He was the one to suggest house hunting today, and I was relieved to know he wanted to continue on as my client given how tumultuous the last few weeks have been for us.

Still, given the circumstances, it's best if we aren't left alone together. The other week, when I ran into Kathy at the grocery store, she gave me her number and made me promise to call her if I ever wanted to hang out. I used that number this morning for more self-serving reasons, but she didn't seem to mind. In fact, she sounded incredibly excited to tour houses with us.

I meet Diane and Kathy at Hamilton Brew as planned, then the three of us caravan over to the first home. Adam's black Audi is already parked out front. He's leaning against the driver's side door, checking his phone, and I appreciate—and abuse—the few seconds of uninterrupted gawking. He looks ridiculously good in a set of navy blue scrubs. His jaw is clean-shaven, his skin is tan, and every hair on his head is perfectly in place. *How does he do it*, I wonder as I park my car behind his. He looks up and smiles, and then that smile slowly fades as his gaze shifts to his mother in the passenger seat.

"Uh oh, he doesn't look too happy to see us," Diane comments with an amused grin. She takes no offense at the fact that her son is so annoyed by her presence.

"Ah, yeah..." I turn to face Diane, prepared to face the music. "I might not have informed him that you two would be joining us, but it's for his own good. You two bring a female touch to the process, and you might be able to provide valuable insight that Adam wouldn't have thought of himself."

When I explain this to Adam, he heartily disagrees. "No. No way. Too many cooks in the kitchen."

"Pfft." I wave away his concern. "That's nonsense."

Diane and Kathy stand behind me, smiling and waiting for us to stop arguing.

"Why didn't you tell me you invited them?" he asks, stepping closer and lowering his voice. "Is this about the other night?"

Jesus! He might have lowered his voice a smidgen. Everyone this side of the Atlantic Ocean just heard his question.

"Ah—" I turn to face the lot, ignoring his question and refocusing the group on the subject at hand: real estate. "As you can see, this house is a redone ranch-style home with plenty of modern amenities." I jerk open my folder full of housing specs and quickly hand out an info sheet to everyone present. "The lot is oversized for this neighborhood, and the previous owners have taken great care in preserving the oak trees around the property."

Diane and Kathy ooh and ahh. Adam crosses his arms and puts on his best scowl, annoyed with me for bypassing his question. I walk them around the entire exterior of the home and then we proceed inside. Adam is barely glancing around the place. His attention is on me, not the shimmering granite countertops the owners installed just last year.

"And did I mention the farm sink?" I ask, sweeping my

hand across the appliance like Vanna White. "They're very in demand right now."

"Oh!" Diane squeals. "I've been wanting to put a farm sink in my kitchen for years. Look at all that space!"

Kathy agrees. Adam says nothing.

I smile over at him, trying to ease the tension. "Do you like farm sinks, Adam?"

He grunts and walks away.

"Now I see why it was important to invite us," Diane says, metaphorically patting herself on the back. "He probably doesn't even care about the kitchen sink, but any future wife of his will want this farm sink."

"I'M SINGLE AND I DON'T CARE ABOUT FARM SINKS!" Adam shouts from the next room.

As if we've agreed on it beforehand, the three of us act as if we can't hear him at all. I usher them through the door and we proceed without Adam.

In all, the showings aren't half bad. While Adam is the absolute worst, moodiest client I've ever had to work with, Diane and Kathy are a pleasure. They listen to my short spiel about every property and ask questions I know the exact right answers to. I am definitely convincing them of the advantages of each property we tour, but unfortunately, they aren't the ones ultimately purchasing a house through me. That would be Adam, the man who is taking a phone call out on the back patio as we walk through our fourth home of the afternoon. I'm disappointed; I saved the best for last.

"Wow. I'm *SOLD*," Diane declares, waving her hand around the spacious kitchen. "This one is my absolute favorite."

I smile—and since Adam isn't the room—admit that it's my favorite too. The property is located a few minutes north of downtown Hamilton and sits on two acres of land with a shallow creek that runs through the back yard. It's a redone white farmhouse with a metal roof and a wraparound porch, and it has four bedrooms, three full bathrooms, and top-notch finishes throughout the house. The builders were meticulous about design details, and if I had even one penny to my name, I'd be putting in an offer on the house in a heartbeat. As it is, I probably won't ever get the chance.

The house went up on the market two days ago and word on the street is that there are already a few buyers buzzing around, prepared to send in offers. I would hurry Adam along in the purchasing process if he seemed even halfway interested, but I don't even think he's bothered to look inside.

"Who is he talking to out there?" Kathy asks.

Diane and I shrug.

"Maybe I should have let him know you two were coming along."

Diane levels me with a hard stare. "Don't you let his little tantrum sway you. He doesn't get to just stomp his foot and have his way. I've been easy on that man his whole life, and maybe it's time to start pushing back a little."

While I can agree with her tough-love stance, I'm not related to Adam. I'm his real estate agent—at least for right now—and it's my job to ensure he's getting the most out of the showing.

I let myself out onto the back patio just as he's wrapping up his phone call.

"Work," he explains with a curt nod, stuffing his phone back into the pocket of his scrubs before he tries to move past me.

"I invited them as a buffer," I admit, hoping to end the tension between us. My words stop him in his tracks. "After last week, I was nervous to be around you...and I thought if they came along, you and I wouldn't be in danger of picking up where we left off."

His green gaze catches mine, and I see that amusement has taken up where anger has left off.

"We're in other people's homes, Madeleine," he mocks. "Even I have *some* self-control."

Like that's stopped anyone before.

I mash my lips together and nod.

He steps closer and presses his hand to the small of my back. "C'mon, show me the house. I like what I've seen of the exterior."

"You do?!"

"It's my favorite so far."

Yes. Yes. Yes.

I lead him back through the house while Diane and Kathy wait for us in the kitchen. We weave through the three bedrooms and the living room, and then I sweep my arm around the massive master bedroom.

"It's great, isn't it? The French doors open up right out onto the porch and there's a ton of natural light."

He nods. "It's a little big for one person."

"The room?"

He smiles. "The house."

Does he think I'm pressuring him into a big house? Maybe he doesn't want children. Maybe I'm assuming too much.

"I know four bedrooms seems like a lot, but you'll fill them up quick. You could have a home office and a gym if you wanted to."

"Until kids."

I avoid making eye contact at all costs. "Yes, err...until that."

"Madeleine?"

"Hmm?"

"Why can't you look at me?"

I focus intently on an old oak tree I can see through the French doors. "I'm just really enjoying the view."

"I'm not asking you to have children with me." He laughs.

"Ha! I know!" My voice sounds strained, and I want to hide my face from his view. "This is just all *so* awkward. I don't usually have hardcore make-out sessions with clients before I show them houses."

He steps closer. "Weird. I *always* make out with my real estate agent before I let them show me homes."

I try to laugh at his joke, but it sounds hollow.

"You're overthinking this."

"*Am I?*" I finally turn to face him. He's standing a few feet away, his hands propped on his hips. There's a playful gleam in his eye and a smile waiting to break free across his lips. "Maybe you're not thinking enough. Have things changed? Are you suddenly ready to date? Or are you just done trying to keep your distance?"

He smiles ruefully. "Both? Neither? Madeleine, it doesn't have to be so black and white."

Maybe not for Adam, but for me, it does. I'm done playing in the gray area. I don't have the luxury of romping around with Adam until he comes to his senses. I spent most of my 20s dating the wrong kind of guys: the bad boy, the egoist, the womanizer. No more. Now, it's time to go down a different path. I need someone who doesn't balk at the idea of marriage, who isn't going to cringe every time I bring up children.

"Can't we just take it one day at a time?" he asks.

If I were 22 and fresh out of college, his proposition would sound like a dream. Now, I need to know what to expect in the next month, the next year. I have to start planning for the future or I'm going to wake up 40 and alone with Mouse as my only companion.

I sigh and shake my head. "Let's just focus on real estate for right now. You only have a few more minutes before you have to get back to work."

"But when am I going to see you again? Can I take you out?"

Out? On a date?

It sounds too good to be a true. *Because it is.* I drag my hand down my face. "Adam, c'mon. This isn't the right time."

"Madeleine."

He steps closer and I shake my head. He's doing it again—crowding my space until I give in. Twice this has led to an inappropriate make-out session; I won't let it happen a third time.

I turn back to the porch and he comes to stand beside me.

"There's a mixer thing that my agency is hosting," I relent, focusing on the oak tree. "I have to invite three people. You can come."

"When is it?"

"Next week."

He shakes his head. "That's too far away. Let me come and run Mouse."

Run Mouse is nothing more than a euphemism at this point.

"Adam, I'm giving you the mixer." I cross my arms to emphasize my point. I'm not budging. "Take it or leave it."

I can see him smirk out of the corner of my eye. "I've never had to beg a woman to spend time with me before."

I smirk. "You haven't been on the market in a while."

He reaches out and smooths his hand beneath my hair, resting it on the base of my neck. Goose bumps bloom down my spine, but he plays coy. "Maybe I've lost my touch."

I shrug. "Maybe."

He laughs and then bends to press a kiss to my hair. "I'll play this game, Madeleine. You want me to wait until the mixer? I'll wait."

But he doesn't take his hand off my neck. He turns me until I'm facing him. My breath is coming in short, weak spurts, and my knees are starting to feel shaky. I'm rooted to the spot, staring up at him with my fists clenched by my sides.

"It's next Saturday at the brewery downtown," I volunteer.

His hand skims higher and his fingers weave through my hair. He barely tugs and yet I stumble toward him, catching myself against his chest.

"At the brewery?" he asks, leaning down and pressing another kiss to my cheek, this one just at the corner of my mouth.

I nod mutely.

"What time?" he asks, wrapping his other hand around my waist.

"7:00 PM," I croak.

He hums as he bends down and presses a chaste kiss to my lips. It's over so fast that my eyes are still closed when he pulls away. I wilt toward him like a flower, desperate for a little more sunlight.

"Madeleine? I'm not going to kiss you again."

I blink my eyes open. "You're not?"

I sound upset about it.

"No," he says, tucking a few strands of hair behind my ear.

Oh, what perfect torture. I could write off our past indiscretions as unsolicited attacks, but if I ask him to kiss me now, there's no shirking my half of the responsibility.

"Maybe just a short one?" I offer. "Your mom is waiting for us in the kitchen."

He laughs at my justification, like a short kiss is hardly a kiss at all. Then he steps back and releases me.

"Show me the master closet."

What about our kiss? I want to ask. Did he not like my compromise?

"Madeleine, show me," he says again, and this time I catch the insistent tone, the subtle desire he's barely keeping under wraps.

I play along as he ushers me toward the walk-in closet to our left.

"It's one of the largest ones I've seen. There are..."

My sentence drifts off as the closet door closes and locks behind me. We're draped in darkness, and I think Adam is going to reach up and turn on the light, but his hands find my hips instead.

"Go on."

"What?"

"Tell me about the closet."

I laugh. "I can't see my papers anymore."

He squeezes my hip, and with his other hand, he takes my papers and drops them to the floor. "You've seen it before. Tell me what you remember."

"Oh...um..."

He steps closer and my brain starts to scramble. Is he

going to kiss me?

"There are built-ins for shoes and folded clothes…"

His mouth finds my cheek and I inhale sharply.

"What about the folded clothes?" he asks, and though I can't see his face, there's no mistaking the amusement in his tone.

"They're plenty of drawers for them…"

My voice is fading. I can't concentrate with his mouth so close to mine. His hand hooks around the nape of my neck and he tilts my head back. I shiver when his fingers weave into my hair.

My eyes flutter closed and he steps closer, sliding right up against me until our bodies meld together like matching puzzle pieces. When I press up onto my toes, our hips meet, and his hands find my waist, keeping me there. My chest brushes his and he takes my earlobe between his teeth. I claw at his shirt, suddenly impatient for more.

"Do you want me to kiss you, Madeleine?" he whispers against my ear.

I nod, but he does nothing.

"Tell me," he says.

My hands grip his biceps. "*Kiss me.*"

In that instant, his lips find mine and he kisses me like he intends to leave a mark. He bites, drags, and sucks the life right out of me. It's passionate and heated—kissing that feels more like fucking. His name is in the air, moaned by someone who sounds a lot like me. His hand is in my hair, my shirt, my bra. There's no slow lead-in, no polite invitations or barriers crossed over weeks of polite foreplay. I feel crazy, and then his palm is on my breast and I don't feel crazy anymore. I feel alive in the dark closet as we sink down onto the carpet.

Adam is over me, holding his weight up just enough for

my lungs to expand a little, but not nearly enough to fill them. I can't draw a full breath, and his hips are rolling over mine and my fingers are digging into his shoulders, ensuring that he doesn't back off even one inch. I don't want air; I want the kiss Adam is delivering to my stomach. I want the feeling of my silk blouse sliding up and over my head. We barely fumble in the darkness, our movements intuitive.

We were moving fast last week, but in this closet, it's as if all bets are off. We're frenzied and wild. Shirts are flying and pants are getting unzipped. His mouth is on my breast. My nipple. He bites down and I arch off the ground.

"*Adam.*"

He moves his mouth to the other side, bestowing the same soft kiss, hard bite combination on my other breast. My nipples are so sensitive and he takes advantage, rolling his tongue over them until I'm near tears.

I'm aware of how wrong this is, of how unethical it is to have sex in a client's closet.

"We can't, Adam, not here—"

"Yes, *here*," he bites back, enraged by the idea of stopping. His hand shoves my skirt up to my hips. Our clothes are crumpled around us. The carpet is scratchy against my back, my shoulders, my bare thighs. His hand digs into my flesh, feeling every inch that he's claiming. Minutes tick away like seconds, and then Adam finds the soft center of my underwear and brushes it aside without an invitation.

I don't recognize myself. I don't know this woman lying in a dark closet letting a man brush his thumb across her most intimate area. Reality slips away. I'm nothing but a bundle of nerves and firing synapses as Adam drags his finger up and down between my spread thighs. He doesn't have to hold me down or spread me wider; I do everything for him—*with pleasure.*

"Hold here," he says, taking my hand and guiding it down to where my underwear is pressed to my thigh. He'd been holding it to the side, exposing me, and when my hand replaces his, suddenly it feels like I'm offering myself to him.

Here.

Take it.

Have it all, my body says as he bends low and blows cool air against my wetness. My hips jerk off the carpet, trying to ease the mounting tension. His hand finds my thigh and he uses gentle pressure to keep me still as he does it again. Cool air. A kiss pressed against my upper thigh. A finger skimming my folds. He sinks his finger inside me slowly, like he wants to savor the sensation. I'm tight around him and I try to relax. He adds a second finger and stretches me. I'm arching for him, letting him fuck me with his fingers in this dark closet because I'm not Madeleine Thatcher anymore. This is someone new, someone who left her inhibitions at the closet door.

"Could you come for me like this?" he asks, and I laugh.

Can't you feel me starting to shake? I want to ask. *Can't you feel the way I'm starting to crumble beneath you?*

He bends down and I have his hair in my hands. I'm tugging on the strands as his lips draw closer and closer to where I desperately need them. A lick. A taste. It's hardly more than a few seconds of sensation, but the pleasure tears through me. He adds his thumb to the mix, swirling it across my bundle of nerves, and I'm crying out for him.

His free hand clamps over my mouth, trying to muffle

my cries. His tongue drags across me. I try to stay quiet, but his fingers are working inside me, sliding in and out even faster. It's like he's telling me to stay quiet and moan louder all at once. I'm shaking. I'm close. The first few ripples of pleasure warn me that I'm going to crash and burn in a few seconds, that soon his hand will need to suffocate me completely to keep me quiet.

"Madeleine," he whispers. "*Madeleine.*"

My name has taken on another meaning. It's a plea and a command, and when I come for him, he says it a third time, pressing each syllable to the inside of my thigh.

I come back to earth slowly, putting together the pieces of our closet rendezvous as Adam crawls off me and tugs my skirt back into place. My shirt is still missing. My bra is unhooked, sitting askew on my chest. I'm pretty sure I have second-degree carpet burn on my back.

Adam is already standing.

"What about you?"

I think I see him smile in the dark. "There's not enough time."

Of course there's not enough time!

"Oh God. I can't believe we did that while your mom and sister-in-law were in the house." I groan as he pulls me up to stand beside him.

He chuckles and helps me straighten my clothes.

The closet door is unlocked and pushed open. I have no clue how long we were in there, but it was long enough that I have to blink my eyes as they adjust to the light in the master bedroom.

"You look great," he says, fixing his now-wrinkled scrubs.

He looks sexy, but his hair is tousled and his lips are red. A quick glance in the master bathroom mirror proves that I look a million times worse. My makeup is smeared. My clothes are creased. My hair is frizzy, and no amount of finger combing will flatten it back down to normal.

"Relax," Adam says, eyeing me from the doorway. "They probably haven't even realized we've been gone that long."

Oh they realized all right. Diane has a knowing smile on her face when we stroll into the kitchen a few minutes later.

"And so that's the house," I announce to Adam as though I'm trying to conclude a fake tour.

"Wow. That was some tour," Kathy says with a laugh. "We've been sitting here for almost thirty minutes."

Adam nods. "Yeah, I really liked the house. I wanted Madeleine to show me every nook and cranny."

"And did you, Madeleine?" Kathy asks with feigned innocence. "Did you show Adam *every nook and cranny*?"

Adam tries and fails to cover a laugh.

I pretend like I don't understand subtle innuendos.

In all, it's the most embarrassing experience of my entire life, and I decide that I won't be able to look Diane or Kathy in the eye for at least a month.

Maybe a year.

CHAPTER NINETEEN

Adam

I KEEP MY promise and don't see Madeleine until the real estate mixer the following weekend. I'm not happy about it, and my office staff isn't either. They don't know the source of my moodiness, why I'm suddenly quick to snap and annoyed by minor mistakes, but I can tell they're all scared to be around me. One morning midweek, I am about to wish one of the assistants a good morning and she scurries out of the reception area so fast that she spills half her coffee on the floor.

I get it. I'm not that fun to be around, and Madeleine is to blame.

Each day, I count down to the mixer. I wake up and I think about the closet back at the farmhouse. Even after a morning run, an extra intense boxing session in the gym, and an exhausting pick-up basketball game, the memories of what she tasted like are right there, clearer than ever.

The night of the mixer, I head straight home from work

and shower quickly. I feel like I'm right back in high school, about to take my dream girl out on a date. I rush getting ready, and when I show up at the mixer on time, I assume I'll be one of the first guests there.

Unfortunately, the brewery parking lot is nearly full—a side effect of free beer.

It's a cool venue, rustic and old, nothing like I'd find back in Chicago. Instead of building from the ground up, the brewery took over an old granary, complete with rusted silos out back, old red bricks, and industrial beams. Right now, since the weather is still nice by Texas standards, they've pushed aside all of the glass-paneled doors so the patio stretches right into the main room, where the Hamilton Real Estate team has decked the place out for the evening. I spot one of the agents, Lori, right by the entrance, and she latches onto me before I even manage to step inside.

"Adam!? I didn't expect you tonight," she says, hooking her elbow through mine.

"Madeleine invited me."

"Did she now? Funny, I didn't think she'd be able to scrounge together any guests other than Daisy. Me, *well*, I had a hard time limiting my list—though Helen didn't mind when I said I was bringing *ten* potential clients."

I extricate myself from her grip and nod, feigning interest. "Right, well, that's great. Listen, have you seen Madeleine?"

She rolls her eyes. "Yeah, she's over by the bar, trying to chat up Carter just like the old days. They used to date, I think. Honestly though, when is she going to learn that you can't throw yourself at every man you see? I mean, she's pretty, but she just reeks of desperation if you ask me."

I didn't ask her. In fact, I started wandering away

halfway through her rambling reply. Madeleine is by the counter, wearing a royal blue dress and nude high heels. Lori was wearing the same color, and a quick glance around the room shows that all of the agents must have been instructed to dress in the color for the evening. They're easier to spot that way, though Madeleine needs no extra help in that department.

There's a line of men winding around the bar trying to get their turn to talk to her. Oh sure, a few of them nurse beers and pretend to check their phones, but I know they're just biding their time until she kicks the current guy to the curb so they can sidle up and talk to her under the guise of discussing real estate.

The current guy, some macho man in a black t-shirt and jeans, is staring at her with hearts in his eyes. Lori mentioned his name but I already forgot it. Fortunately, Madeleine reminds me just as I walk up.

"Carter, I can't believe you let Lori talk you into coming tonight."

He leans closer. "I knew you'd be here and I wanted to check up and see how you were doing."

I clear my throat and the two of them turn to look at me in tandem.

Madeleine lets loose a heartbreaking smile. Carter's smile is a bit more forced.

"What's up, man?" he asks. "Do you need something?"

For that, I lean forward and kiss Madeleine on the cheek.

"You look great," I say, letting my gaze rove down her body. She really does. Her dress is tight enough to show off her killer figure, and her heels only make it that much harder to pry my attention away from her legs.

She's flushed from my compliment by the time I glance

back up at her face. "Oh, thanks. Um, Carter, this is Adam. Adam, Carter."

I extend my hand to Carter and he does the classic asshole move of gripping my fingers instead of my whole hand so I'm left looking like a dainty girl. I counter with a hard clap to his shoulders. "Good to meet you, man."

It's not good to meet him. Didn't Lori say he and Madeleine used to date? Clearly the guy isn't over her. I was wondering when this would happen; Madeleine's too amazing to go unnoticed for long.

"Madeleine and I were just catching up on old times," he volunteers, shooting her a wink. "I was telling her the only reason I let Lori talk me into attending tonight was because I knew Madeleine would be here."

Madeleine smiles and shakes her head. "Oh c'mon, it's fun to catch up, but I'm sure you know everyone here."

He shrugs and takes a step closer. "I'd be lying if I said I didn't miss you. What have you been up to lately?"

Before Olivia, I might have walked away, been the cool guy. Now, I stake my ground.

"She's actually been seeing me," I volunteer, reminding him I'm present. "Madeleine, can I talk to you for a second?"

Her gaze flickers back and forth between us. "Oh, of course."

"I thought you were about to show me a few houses?" Carter asks, and like that, he plays the trump card.

Tonight is about business, and Madeleine is desperate to pick up new clients.

"No problem. Come find me after." I shrug. "I'd like to put in an offer on that farmhouse."

We all have a trump card, Carter.

Her mouth drops. "WHAT?! Adam, are you serious?"

I take her wine glass before she spills it. "Of course. It's a great house and I'd be a fool to pass it up."

She looks back at Carter, her hands pressed to her mouth in shock. "I can't believe this."

Neither can he. I don't have to look at him to feel the disdain rolling off him. I shouldn't be proud of my behavior—it's juvenile and petty—but then, all is fair in love and war, and this feels like a little of both.

"I guess I'll come find you later, Madeleine," Carter says with a nod before backing away. The other guys flocking around her get the hint and disappear too. I take Carter's spot at the bar and lean in to kiss her, but she turns her head at the last second. Rejection feels like a hard slap in the face.

"*Adam*. Not here," she says, scanning the room from beneath her lashes. "You're only the second client I've sold a home to since Daisy and Lucas. I don't want Helen to get the wrong impression."

"Oh? And what would that be?" I ask, helpless at fending off the repressed anger building up inside of me. "That we're together?"

"That I had to spread my legs to get you to buy a house!" she hisses, stealing back her wine glass and downing the rest of it in one go.

"Is that what you really think?"

"Of course not!" She doesn't meet my eyes. "But that's what *they* would think."

"Oh c'mon, Madeleine. You rejected me when I asked you to go out on a date and now this? I came to this mixer to spend time with you, and now I'm not allowed to act like we're..."

My voice trails off as I realize I don't have a label for us. *Friends, lovers, significant others?*

She uses my falter as ammunition. "*Exactly.* Considering *we* don't even know what we are, it's probably best not to make out in front of all of my coworkers."

"Fine." I straighten up, wave over the bartender, and ask for one of the beers on tap.

We stand silent for the next few minutes. I can tell she has a million words left to say, but it's not the right time. I sip on my beer and peer over at her. She's staring down at the bar, contemplating something serious from the looks of it.

"I wasn't kidding about the house," I add, knowing she needs confirmation. "Regardless of what's going on with us, I still want to put in that offer."

She presses her lips together to keep from smiling, but I know it won't work for long.

"Do you think it's still on the market?"

She nods gleefully. "I checked this morning. They've had offers, but the owners are waiting for the full ask."

"Then let's give it to them."

Her eyes widen. "Are you serious?"

"Compared to the Chicago real estate market, that house is too good to be true. It costs a fifth of what my place sold for back in the city."

She squeezes my arm and her gaze drops to my lips. I think for a second she's going to break her own rule and kiss me right here, but then she shakes her head and turns to survey the crowd. "I have to go tell Helen. She's not going to believe it."

She's right; Helen doesn't believe it. In fact, she acts as if Madeleine is mistaken.

"And *you* showed him the house?"

"Just the other day!"

"Wow." She glances between us. "And you're the only

agent he's been working with?"

She beams. "Yes."

Why is it so hard for Helen to believe?

"She's been excellent," I add, offering Helen a smile.

She nods. "Of course. I've always thought Madeleine had great potential with our company."

When she strolls away a few minutes later, I turn and arch a brow. "That seemed weird, no?"

She frowns. "What? Helen? No. I mean, truthfully, she's been on the verge of firing me for the last few months. I don't think she thought I had it in me to sell a house."

"But you sold one to Lucas and Daisy."

"Yeah, months ago, and really, that doesn't count."

"You haven't had clients since then? How is that possible? Carter was about to buy a house from you just a second ago."

She stares down at her empty wine glass. "There have been a few—like Mr. Boggs. He's here tonight and I've probably shown him a thousand houses, but he's never going to buy anything."

"Why do you continue entertaining him then? He's probably just bored."

Or worse, he wants to spend time with Madeleine any way he can. I wouldn't put it past some men.

"Yeah, well, I feel bad." Her finger traces the rim of her wine glass. "Maybe he does want to buy a house and he just hasn't found the right one yet."

Ah, I see her problem. When it comes to real estate, Lori is a snake and Madeleine might as well be a rabbit. A few things make sense now.

"That's why you were so eager to talk to me about real estate at that first training class."

She nods. "Helen put me on probation and I knew if I didn't make something happen soon, she'd give me the axe."

A waiter passes, and I take her empty glass and trade it for two fresh ones. "Well, here's to proving them wrong."

She beams and clinks her glass with mine. "And to buying the farmhouse of your dreams."

"Madeleine, there you are!"

"Mr. Boggs," she says with a smile. "I was just going to come over and show you a few listings."

He groans and shakes his head, acting every bit the old miser his name suggests. "Don't bother. Already looked. There was nothin' good. I'm going home. Tell that boss of yours she needs to serve more food at these things. Wine and beer galore, but not a damn bread roll in sight."

Madeleine laughs. "I couldn't agree more. I actually stuffed some granola bars in my purse if you want one."

He perks up a bit at the mention of food. "They're not those healthy ones are they?"

She laughs. "C'mon, you can pick which one you want."

Without Madeleine, I weave my way through the party, recognizing a few faces in the crowd from the puppy class and the clinic. A few of them even stop to chat with me, but I try to keep an eye out for Madeleine the whole time. After she finishes up with Mr. Boggs, Carter grabs her attention again, cornering her over by a table with all of Hamilton Realty's current listings. I swear she shows him every damn house twice before the man is satisfied, and though I'm tempted to step in like I did before, I know it won't do any good. She needs to make sales if she wants to get Helen off her back.

By the time I've finished my second beer and

strategically covered two yawns, she's moved on to another potential client. I'm ready to head out, and I don't want to interrupt. She scans the room and finds me so I gesture toward the parking lot and mouth, "I'm leaving."

She juts out her bottom lip and mouths back, "Stay."

I'm tempted, but I don't want to take up any more of her time. She needs to mingle with clients and I need sleep. I wave and her bottom lip juts out a little more. I sigh and turn for my car, knowing if I don't leave now, I probably won't.

When I get home, I unlock the door to my rental house and flip on the light. Everything is quiet inside, not a single item out of place. The housekeeper must have come by today because the rooms seem even more sterile than usual. I toss my keys in the bowl by the door then flip on the TV and the living room light, not because I want them on but because they help disguise the fact that I'm home alone. The soothing sounds of ESPN barely do the trick.

I take a seat on the couch the previous owners left behind. The whole place came furnished, which is part of the reason why it feels temporary and, well, sad. Take the couch, for instance. It's made out of fake red leather, a color that burns my eyes every time I look at it. The potpourri on the coffee table has likely been sitting in the same glass bowl for the last thirty years. A tapestry of *Dogs Playing Poker* hangs on one wall. In short, it's not my style. I feel like I'm a guest in someone else's home, which was the intention in the beginning. I didn't want to dig in too deep too fast, but how long can I keep skimming the surface of my life?

Olivia and I had a house and a dog, two great careers, and a large circle of friends. I doubt anyone would have guessed we'd break up a few months before the wedding, that she would sleep with my best friend instead of telling me she wanted to end it.

And Molly. The fact that I let her have Molly has been eating away at me for the last few weeks. Maybe this house and its tacky furniture would feel a little more like a home if Molly were here to greet me at the end of the day.

Then again, maybe not. My life in Texas won't start to feel right until I push myself out of this weird holding pattern I've fallen into. I set up parameters for my life—no dating, no getting too attached—because it seemed like the right thing to do after getting out of a long-term relationship, but maybe there's a little more to it. Maybe Olivia didn't just take scissors and shred our relationship, but did a hack job on my confidence as well. Hell, after eight years, I should have known what she was capable of, but I was blindsided and I don't want it to happen again.

However, I also don't want to sit on this stupid red couch for another day, pretending I don't have feelings for Madeleine. She doesn't want to be led on, and I don't want her to slip through my fingers. So, it's simple: it's time to man the fuck up.

I text her.

Adam: Tomorrow. 8:00 PM. Be ready because I'm taking you out on a date.

I expect some sort of protest; instead, I get a joke.

Madeleine: UGH. A little heads up would be nice. All my sexy panties are in the dirty clothes hamper.
Adam: Do laundry. Or don't...no one said you had to wear underwear.

Madeleine: ADAM FOXE, I think my phone just blushed.
Adam: Is that a yes?
Madeleine: ....Fine. Okay. ONE DATE.

CHAPTER TWENTY

"**WHERE HAVE YOU** been? I've been calling your office phone all morning!"

"Oh, sorry," I reply. "I was just showing my *new client* a few condos downtown."

Daisy squeals. "Are you serious? A new client other than Adam?"

I lean back in my chair and run my fingers across my desk calendar. It's not as full as I'd like it to be, but it's getting there, and tonight, after *Company meeting*, I have *Date????* penciled in with a little heart. The four question marks seemed necessary this morning; a period at the end was too presumptuous. Sure, Adam called it a date last night, but I'm not naive enough to take his words at face value. Maybe he wants a date, maybe he wants to find another dark closet—either way, I'm game. I'm just going to keep my heart and my expectations in check. Simple.

"Madeleine?"

I cover the calendar with my keyboard as if Daisy is looking over my shoulder instead of lingering on the other end of the phone line.

"Yes! It was another new client. I met him at the mixer, the one you showed up to for five minutes before leaving. Still, I owe you."

"Oh yeah, that sucked, but you don't owe me. I stole some wine on my way out."

"Classy."

"It was the sauvignon we both liked."

Genius.

"Good. Save it until we can drink it together."

"I can't promise it's going to last beyond tonight. Just come over after work. I see my last patient at 4:30 PM."

Date???? taunts me from beneath my keyboard.

"I can't. I have plans."

"Plans? With who? I'm your only friend. That's how this works."

"Lori."

I hear her do a very ladylike spit-take. "Jesus, I just got coffee all over my computer screen. Tell me you're kidding."

I smile. "Yeah. I'm actually seeing Adam."

"*Seeing Adam?*"

"Yes, for a get-together."

"Just call it what it is."

"He called it a date, but I'm calling it a casual dining experience between two consenting adults."

"God, you're annoying," she groans. "Can't you just let good things happen to you? Why do you have to sabotage this before it even starts?"

"Sabotage it!?" I lean into my cubicle and lower my voice. "Have you already forgotten the scene at the YMCA when I asked Adam out for dinner and he turned me down? That was barely two weeks ago! And now suddenly he's all 'let's date' and 'let's get it on in dark closets'."

She hums. "I see your point, that is a quick turnaround time. Maybe he's suffering from a psychotic condition? Bipolar disorder? Depression?"

My eyes widen in alarm. Daisy is a doctor; she would know this sort of thing. "Are you serious?"

She laughs. "No! C'mon, I was kidding. He's well within his rights to change his mind. It's not like he proposed to you. He asked you on a date. Relax. Actually, if anyone is suffering from a psychotic condition, it's you."

"Thank you for the diagnosis, Dr. Thatcher. You might need to work on the bedside manner."

"Speaking of bedside manners, have you guys boned yet?"

I jerk forward in my cubicle as if her voice can somehow carry through the office.

"Daisy!"

"Oh c'mon, don't hold out on me now."

"No, as a matter of fact, we haven't yet."

She hums and takes her time before replying, "That's smart. Better to not have sex until you're both ready to commit."

"Why?"

She sighs. "Don't they teach kids the whole milk-and-cow adage anymore?"

"Daisy, it's not the 1950s. I'm an independent woman who can spray her milk all over town if she so chooses."

She snorts. "And far be it from me to interfere with that. But if that's the case, there's another adage you should remember: don't cry over spilled milk."

"What the hell? Are you trying to be some freaky spirit

guide?"

"Maybe."

"You're not even spiritual."

"I took a meditation class a couple months ago, Madeleine. Name one person in your life more spiritual than me."

"My mom. My dog. My mailman. The lady that passes out bibles outside the grocery store."

She hangs up on me, and it's just as well because Sandra walks by my cubicle a second later and clicks her tongue. *Oh, save it, Sandra. I've had to listen to you take personal phone calls for the last year and guess what, my hilariously witty conversations with Daisy trump your weekly phone calls with your podiatrist. Newsflash: no one wants to hear you talking about bunion cream.*

"Nearly finished for the day, Madeleine?" she asks, attempting to surreptitiously spy on the papers sitting on my desk. What does she think I keep in here, the nuclear codes?

"I just have a few things to finish up."

It's true. While I'd love nothing more than to leave work and start primping for my "casual dining experience" with Adam, I still have to fire off an email to Kyle Foster—my new client who's in the market for a condo—and recap the options we toured earlier this morning. I have another round of showings scheduled with him later in the week, but I want to make sure we're both on the same page.

Mr. Boggs has demanded another list of houses, and though everyone will say it's a waste of time, I compile all the new listings on the market and send them over.

Then, after a few phone calls and a short chat with Helen where she informs me that I'm "on the right track" and "won't be on probation for much longer!", I'm heading out the door, giddy to see Adam.

My attention is on my phone, though I tell myself I'm not checking for a text from him. *Surely he wouldn't cancel this last minute, right?* As soon as I think the question, a dog bark snaps me back to reality. I glance up and freeze, completely taken aback by the sight in front of me. Adam's car is parked in front of the curb and he's leaning back against the passenger side door *à la* Jake Ryan from *Sixteen Candles*.

"Well this is a surprise," I say, stepping closer and taking in the whole tantalizing image first presented to me a few yards back: his sexy jeans, the white button-down, the bouquet of sunflowers wrapped in brown paper he has clutched in his right hand.

I try to keep my smile within normal, sane limits as I raise my gaze to meet his. He's been watching me study him.

"Do you like sunflowers?"

"Oh those are for *me*?"

He tilts his head and his adorable smile nearly kills me. "Well, I could try giving them to Mouse, but he'll probably try to eat them."

I nod, playing along. "He's more of a roses guy."

He bends down to kiss my cheek. "I'll remember that for next time."

Next time. NEXT TIME. My heart explodes.

"I love them. Thank you." He hands me the sunflowers and I cradle them to my chest as he opens the car door for me. "You know you're a few hours early."

His fancy car purrs to life and we pull out onto the main road.

"I figured there was no point in waiting."

"Oh yeah? Maybe I wanted to change or reapply my

makeup or something," I joke.

"No need. You look great."

"Hmm...in my work dress? I look like I'm about to go to a board meeting."

"Then I want to sit by you in a board meeting."

I follow his gaze to where my dress has ridden up. When I'm standing, it's a modest length, but the leather seats in his Audi have hiked up the skirt and a few inches of my thighs are now on perfect display. I lay the sunflowers down across my lap and smile when everything is covered.

"Thanks for the flowers," I say with a smirk.

"Maybe I should give them to Mouse after all."

"No, they're too pretty. Where are we headed?"

"To the grocery store. I thought we'd grab a few things and then head back to your place to cook."

"Oh? No fancy restaurant for the first date? Whatever happened to wining and dining a woman?"

His green gaze locks with mine as he slows the car to stop at a red light. "I'm a *really* good cook."

"Oh yeah?"

"Any man can take you to a restaurant and pay for a meal, but not everyone can make my famous lasagna."

"*Fancy*—a veterinarian *and* a chef."

"Do you need me to turn the A/C on? You look flushed."

"Ha ha, how about you just drive, funnyman."

A few minutes later, we head into the grocery store and I suggest a strategy. "Let's divide and conquer because I'm already hungry and lasagna takes forever."

As it is, I'm already planning on peeling open a bag of chips to eat while I peruse the aisles.

"Okay, here." He rips his grocery list in half and hands

me one of the slivers. "I'll grab the vegetables and then meet back up with you."

I glance down and admire his chicken-scratch handwriting.

"What a romantic date."

"Pretend like I'm there with you, being charming."

"Maybe our hands would have brushed as we reached for the same box of lasagna noodles and we would have blushed and looked away—now we'll never know."

He starts to back away, smiling and shaking his head. "I thought you were hungry."

I reach for a bag of sour cream and onion chips stashed on the end cap of an aisle. I tear them open and pop one into my mouth. *Delicious.* And if I imagine it's a healthy green juice, it's a win-win.

"You have to pay for those, you know."

"I will," I say with a shrug. "Now *go*. I bet I can finish with my list way before you can."

His brow arches. "Is that a challenge?"

I stuff another chip into mouth, nod, and then take off running in the opposite direction before he even realizes what I'm doing. Technically it's cheating, but I ignore his shouts behind me as I narrowly avoid a cart being pushed along by an elderly woman. She bats her fist at me like I'm some no-good youth, and hell, maybe I am. I'm running in a grocery store while eating stolen merchandise, but it's for the greater good—or at least for good, healthy competition.

I realize my mistake a minute later when I glance down at Adam's list. His messy handwriting might have seemed adorable before, but it's going to be my downfall in this race. What the hell does he mean by "crosted tumatues". I squint and gather that the second word is actually tomatoes. *Still, what the hell are crosted tomatoes?!*

I ask everyone in the tomato and pasta aisle who will humor me.

"Lady, I have no clue. I'm just trying to get to the spaghetti sauce."

I try someone else. "Excuse me, sir, have you heard of crosted tomatoes?"

He shakes his head and keeps careful watch of me as he scoots his cart past, like he assumes I'm going to reach out and grab it.

"I'm not crazy!" I tell him, like any sane person would. "I just don't know what crosted tomatoes are!"

Then I fling my arms up in hopeless abandon and knock down one of the display towers so carefully arranged in the aisle. I scramble to keep the cans from rolling too far away and succeed in recreating the display at least half as well as the person who did it before me. *Mission accomplished.* I look down and read what the cans say: crushed tomatoes. CRUSHED, not crosted! I mistook Adam's *u* and *h* for an *o* and a *t*. I shout that to the man who thinks I'm crazy and he tells me I better leave him alone.

I know I'm running behind. Adam is probably done with his list and heading toward the checkout by now. I make a mad dash for tomato sauce and lasagna noodles, and then I spend a solid five minutes in the cheese section trying to decipher his handwriting. Parmesan and mozzarella are easy enough to make out, but there's a third type of cheese that's plaguing me. I'm scanning through all the possible options on the shelf when someone says my name behind me.

"Madeleine? Is that you?"

I turn to find Carter grocery shopping in his police uniform. *Well damn.* I now realize that if he'd worn this getup on our first date, there would have likely been a second.

"Carter! Hey!"

I'm excited to see him for two reasons: he was in the market for a house the last time I checked, *and* I think he can help me decipher Adam's handwriting. I start with the latter.

"Oh, yeah, that says ricotta."

I slap my forehead. "Of course! Duh. Thank you."

He finds it on the shelf before me and then adds it to the growing pile of ingredients stacked in my arms. I should have grabbed a basket, but in my rush to get going, I forgot one.

"You got it?" he asks with a laugh.

"Yeah. It's all very strategically balanced and should stay in place as long as I don't make any sudden movements."

He laughs again, and I ask how he's been since the mixer.

"Good. Just picking up extra shifts whenever I can, keeping busy."

"Sounds fun. Did any properties catch your attention?"

I'm nothing if not direct. I still have a grocery-shopping contest to win, after all.

"Y'know, to be honest, now probably isn't the best time to invest in real estate. I'm going up for a promotion soon and if that happens, I'll have a bit more income to play around with."

I'd hold up my hands to stop him if they weren't full. "Of course! Believe me, I understand. I have dreams of moving out of my crappy apartment one day too."

He smiles and catches the attention of another shopper, who passes *extremely* slowly with her cart. Like I said, it's the uniform.

"I am in the market for a date though."

My attention jerks back to him. "What?"

"C'mon, Madeleine. I know the timing didn't work so well last time, but we had a good time, didn't we?"

"You never called me about a second date," I admit sheepishly.

His brows arch as if in shock. "I must have been busy with work or something, because believe me, I was interested then, and I'm interested now."

"Oh…ha. I don't think…I mean, I'm flattered."

I am, seriously. Up until the last few weeks, I would have crawled on my hands and knees for some male attention, and now suddenly I'm at the grocery being asked out *while* on a date. Is Mercury in retrograde or something? *Wait, what does that even mean?*

"C'mon, you aren't seeing anyone, are you? I asked Daisy at the mixer and she said you were dating, but it was nothing serious."

At that precise moment, I spot Adam push a cart around the corner, and for some reason, I panic. It feels like I'm cheating on him, like I've snuck off in the middle of our date to have a rendezvous in the dairy section with Carter. Adam's expression as Carter and I come into view only solidifies my guilt. It sits like heavy sludge in my stomach.

"Madeleine?" Carter asks, trying to figure out why I've suddenly gone mute.

Adam stops his cart beside ours and glances back and forth between us.

"Cameron, hey."

"Oh, it's Carter."

"Right. Madeleine, did you get all the stuff on the list?"

I look down at the pitiful stack in my arms. I still have a ways to go, and now it looks like I've been here dilly-dallying with Carter instead of shopping.

"I had trouble finding the right cheese," I offer lamely.

Carter laughs. "I helped. No worries."

Adam doesn't laugh, and I can't be sure, but I think most of the cheese melts off the shelf when Adam's laser-beam gaze slices through Carter.

To cut the tension, I drop my stack of ingredients in Adam's cart. Carter notices and holds up his hands in innocence. "Sorry, are you guys…together? I would have never—"

"Oh, yeah. I mean—"

"You didn't say you were here with someone."

Now Adam's laser beams are aimed at *me*. I fire mine right back at him.

"I didn't really have the chance."

My excuse sounds pitiful even to my own ears.

"Umm." A short middle-aged woman with a baby strapped to her front tries to shove past us. "Would it be possible for me to get to the cheese for a second?"

"Oh yeah, of course."

I step away and give her room to browse.

Carter backs up and nods. "I'll see you two around. I need to get these groceries home before my stomach growls at me again."

I laugh and wave him off, hoping the tension will drift away with him.

Shocker—it doesn't.

Adam is moody as we push our cart through the store, finishing up with the second half of the list. I try to distract him with my most winning smile, and when that doesn't work, I throw some Oreos in the cart. Everyone loves Oreos, right? His scowl doesn't budge, not even with the promise of double-stuffed cream filling.

"It took me a while back there because I got caught up in the tomato section." I laugh. "You realize you have the *worst* handwriting ever, right?"

He takes the list out of my hand without returning my smile. "My staff at the clinic can read it just fine."

He might as well be Mr. Freeze with the way he gives me the cold shoulder through the rest of the store.

I don't even bother trying to create idle chitchat after that; I just finish off my bag of chips and mind my own business. If he wants to play Mr. Jealous, he can play by himself.

At checkout, he refuses to let me pay for half, and seems somehow insulted that I would even offer. I think I could do just about anything at this point and he would find fault with it. *Plastic?! Who gets plastic bags?*

"Oh, and these," I say to the cashier, holding up the barcoded side of my chip bag. She scans it without a second glance, and I stroll out of the store and head for Adam's car wearing a gratified smile.

When we both slide into his car, the tension and silence are nearly unbearable. I'm tempted to lean forward and turn on music, but there are a million buttons on this stupid dashboard and for all I know, I could press one that expels me from my seat like I'm in a cartoon. I sigh and lean back, crossing my arms so I'm not tempted to touch anything.

My sigh doesn't get to him like I hoped it would, so I have no choice but to lose the silent game we've both been secretly playing.

"This is ridiculous." I turn and work up just enough courage to glance at his fists clutching the car's steering wheel. "If you're angry with me about something, just tell me so we can move on."

"I'm not angry with you."

I snort. "You could have fooled me."

His fists tighten on the steering wheel and I look away.

"I'm annoyed that Carter made his way into our date, that's all."

"Well, he's gone now and the only person ruining this date is *you*."

He lets out a heavy sigh and then pulls the car onto the first dusty dirt road we pass. We're only a few minutes away from my apartment, but now we're headed into the middle of nowhere. I want to ask him what he's doing, but I'm scared to hear his answer.

We make another few turns and end up parked beside the old water tower. It was originally painted sky blue to match the colors of Hamilton High, but most of the paint near the bottom has worn off. There's a perimeter fence blocking trespassers from reaching the ladder, but that never stopped me in the past. In high school, we all went to the top at least once as a rite of passage.

"I'm not doing a good job at this," Adam admits quietly, and his soft tone catches me off guard.

I was prepared for a fight, not a surrender.

I turn and take in his profile. His eyes aren't on the water tower—they're focused straight ahead. Tonight, here, they seem more like two raw emeralds than anything else, hard and unyielding. His jaw is locked, his mouth is pulled into a harsh line. His hands are still clutching the steering wheel even though the engine is off.

"I guess I'm not either," I admit.

He nods and looks out the window then, finally, at me.

"I was never jealous with Olivia." Apparently my expression betrays how shocked that statement makes me because he shakes his head and turns away. "I've never been that type of guy, the kind that needs to stake his claim and beat his chest. With Olivia, we had a really easy relationship and I was confident in what we had together. I never thought to be jealous of another man. We were together for eight years, and then she fucked my best friend. I don't know, maybe if I'd been a bit *more* suspicious, more aware of other men, I wouldn't have been so shocked to find them in bed together."

Suddenly, I get it. His whole macho-man routine makes sense. He feels like he didn't do enough to protect his last relationship, so he's trying to overcompensate this time around.

I lean my head back against the headrest and smile. "I don't mind the jealousy, it's the accusations and the lack of trust that infuriate me." He opens his mouth to respond, but I continue. "I know it's going to take time for us to build trust with one another, but right now, at the very least, you have to give me the benefit of the doubt. I'm not Olivia. I would never sleep with your best friend, not even if he happened to be Chris Pratt." His fists loosen on the steering wheel. "He's not Chris Pratt, right?"

He smiles and shakes his head, finally turning to face me.

"You were screwed over royally, Foxe. I'd expect there to be some collateral damage."

He nods. "When I left Chicago, I thought I was leaving all of that behind as well, but I guess I brought some baggage with me."

"How much?"

"What?"

"How much baggage did you bring with you? I'd rather know now. The jealousy and the machismo act I can handle, but I'm wondering if there are other things too."

He looks out the window, past my shoulder, as if trying

to bring to mind any other faults.

"I guess I have a short fuse lately as well."

I smile. "Yeah, I've seen that a little bit, but it's nothing I can't handle."

"What about you?" he asks, reaching out for my hand. He laces his fingers through mine, and I like the way it feels. He has big, masculine hands; mine look puny by comparison.

"No baggage." I shrug. "Perfectly well-adjusted adult over here."

He grins. "Yeah?"

"Adam...I stack food precariously in my refrigerator and I store my winter sweaters in my dishwasher. Believe me, there's a whoooole lot of baggage that comes with dating me. Fortunately, though, I haven't had any horrific relationships in the past. There aren't any old wounds that have yet to heal or angry ex-boyfriends lurking in the shadows. In fact, I haven't really dated anyone serious in a long time."

"Not even Carter?"

"We only went out on one date," I admit.

He seems surprised by that.

"Now I kind of feel stupid for getting worked up about him."

I shrug. "It's the uniform, it makes him seem more threatening than he is."

He laughs and nods, turning out to look at the old water tower. "Maybe I should get one of those."

My mind does the work for me and the image of Adam in a police uniform is nearly enough to short-circuit my brain. Suddenly, the car feels clammy. I want to roll down the window, but I can't because I have no clue which button to press.

I turn to Adam and find that he's been studying my profile. His eyes aren't gemstones anymore, but they're just as threatening.

"Should we go home?" he asks, bringing our clasped hands to his mouth and kissing the back of mine.

I shiver and shake my head. "Not yet."

We should head back—we have perishables in the trunk—but I like sitting in his car with him. I unlatch my seatbelt and turn to face him. There's a small console separating us, but nothing else.

"Do *you* want to head back?" I ask, and it sounds like an invitation.

His gaze drags down, pausing on my lips for a moment before he trails down my neck and chest. He's studying my dress—no, he's studying my body beneath the fabric. His smile is slow to spread, a little haunting...sexual. "No."

"Can I kiss you?" I ask, my voice barely above a whisper.

He wraps his hand around my neck and tugs me closer. Our lips meet over the center console, and at first, it's harmless, just a little peck. His smile presses against mine. We laugh and his hand gets tangled in my hair even more. He's holding me there as I kiss him again, and this time, I add heat. My teeth bite down on his bottom lip and his hand tightens. His kiss devours me.

I pull back and our eyes meet. A silent challenge passes between us.

Here? he asks with a tilt of his head.

Now, I say with small smirk.

There are inconveniences about having sex with Adam in a car. When he tugs me over the center console, I lose my heels and my elbow bangs against the steering wheel. My knees barely fit on either side of his hips, and when his hands trail up my inner thighs, I arch my back so hard that I hit the horn. It blares so loud I jump out of my seat, and Adam is laughing and tugging me down again, kissing me. The space is awkward, but Adam isn't. His hands know exactly how to hike up my dress so my light blue panties are revealed. They're such a soft, delicate material against his jeans. I grind my hips back and forth as he kisses me, and the sensation is torturous for us both.

One hand falls to my hip, and he's tilting and timing our movements as if he's inside me, as if he's showing me how good it will be in a few minutes. Maybe next time we'll be fully naked in a bed, with soft candlelight and a sexy playlist in the background, but right now we're in the cramped space of his front seat and Adam is sliding my panties to the side so his middle finger can sink inside me. My head falls to his shoulder and I pant, actually *pant*, like I can't get enough air. The windows are foggy and Texas is too humid for this kind of activity. I'm sweating, and my heart is hammering hard. He slides a second finger inside and I bite down on his earlobe, whispering his name.

"Say it again," he commands, and I do.

I whisper his name every time he drags his fingers out and sinks them back in slowly. Right when they're so deep inside of me that I feel like I'm breaking in two, *that's* when I say his name.

"Spread your legs," he says, but he doesn't wait for me to listen. His hands are on my thighs, spreading me like I'm an elastic band, and maybe my knees are digging into the door and the center console, and maybe he's ripping my delicate blue panties—the pair I covet every time I find them tucked away in my drawer—but then his fingers are back on me, *in* me, and I don't care about bruises or panties. I want what he's offering.

"I'm so close," I promise him, and his thumb swirls across my clit.

I've had first times with men before. They're awkward and clunky, like a new pair of shoes you haven't worn in yet, but this, Adam making me come with his fingers as I arch back and cry out into his silent car—there's no room for anything but heat and passion. His mouth is on my neck, and the zipper of my dress is tugged down. My bra is blue too, and it belongs to a matching set that was pristine up until a few minutes ago. Adam notices and swears he'll replace it for me, saying it against my breast as his lips close around my nipple. He could be promising me the Taj Mahal and I wouldn't notice.

"Who cares. Who cares."

My fingers are in his hair and when I tug, he swirls his tongue across my nipple. I like the give and take. Maybe he does too.

"I'll make you come again," he promises with a heavy breath. "But I need to be inside you."

I nod because of course he needs to be inside me; this night was never going to end any other way. When he showed up outside my office with sunflowers, he could have just taken me right then against the brick building.

His jeans are unzipped and barely pulled down, just enough for him to position himself beneath me. I push up onto my knees and he brushes across my wetness. A shiver runs down my spine from the sensation and he does it again, and again, coating himself until he's slick.

My nails are digging into his shoulders. "Adam, *stop*. You're killing me."

He doesn't stop. He hits my clit and my stomach quivers. I'm going to come again, and he's not inside me. *No!* I want to feel myself come around him, so I reach down and position him right beneath me. Before he moves, I sink down. He's only barely inside, stretching me slowly, but my thighs are burning and my eyes are pinched closed. I can't focus—I've lost track of every sense except for touch. I think I'm begging him for something, but I barely hear my words and I don't hear his reply. He holds me up, teasing me inch by inch. I don't think I can wait any longer. Pleasure is already ripping through me and behind my closed lids, I see stars.

"Madeleine?" he asks.

I let out the breath I've been holding and the stars lose their shimmer.

"Yeah?"

"Look at me."

His hands prop up my chin, waiting for me to blink my eyes open. I can't. Once those light green irises meet mine, he'll see it all. This is the first date and I'm pretty sure I'm not supposed to be straddling his lap, digging my fingers into his shoulders, slowly losing my mind.

He leans forward and presses a kiss to my cheek. It's so romantic and soft. I want to capture it in a mason jar and preserve it for later, for a month from now when Adam and I have dissolved into nothing. I could pry it open every now and then for old times' sake and feel just like I do in this exact moment. He's buried all the way inside me and I'm shaking and finally, our gazes meet and there's no going back. He moves in me, grinding and rolling his hips in such a deliciously erotic rhythm. I think there are tears brimming in my eyes, but I refuse to acknowledge them. Maybe he sees them too because he pulls my face forward and presses his mouth to mine.

In this position, he saves me the trouble of trying to stay composed. My moans disappear on his lips. My body shatters and he holds me together, whispering against my cheek.

Later, when I've safely settled back into the passenger side seat and am trying in vain to straighten my clothes, fix my hair, wipe my mouth, he reaches over and grips my thigh. It's subtle and reassuring.

"Still hungry?" he asks with a lazy little smirk.

It's the smirk of a man who's just successfully seduced a woman, the smirk that will keep me up later tonight as I lie in bed, wide awake and buzzing from the best night of my life.

CHAPTER TWENTY-ONE

"YOU HAD SEX."

I drop my muffin. It hits the floor and rolls beneath the table beside ours.

I toss up my hands and glare at Daisy. "You made me lose my muffin."

"I think you lost something else too."

"What's that supposed to mean?"

"You had sex and you aren't telling me about it."

A few seconds pass as I run through the pros and cons of retrieving my muffin. Pros: I wouldn't lose the $2.70 it cost me, I'd get to eat it, and I could avoid looking at Daisy for another few seconds. Cons: the table is occupied, the muffin is definitely covered in dust and dirt by now, and I would *only* get to avoid Daisy for a few seconds—not nearly long enough.

"Can we talk about something else?" I ask, leaning back in my chair and crossing my arms.

Daisy breaks off half her muffin and slides it over to me on a napkin. It's a peace offering, and I take it.

"All right, fine. Your brother and I have been having a lot of sex."

I want to let my forehead fall and hit the table, preferably hard enough to cause some short-term memory loss. "How about we skip over the topic of sex altogether?"

"What? It's all I think about. Fertility this, fertility that."

I feel bad for snapping at her. "How's it going?"

She shrugs. "I'm supposed to take a pregnancy test in a few days. Last night I had some cramping on my right side which could be implantation cramping—an early sign of pregnancy."

I frown. "C'mon Daisy, you know better. You can't read into things like that. You'll just drive yourself insane. Remember a few months ago when you swore you were slightly more bloated than usual?"

She picks at her muffin. "Yeah, well, this feels different."

I don't have the heart to burst her bubble, not when she's struggled for so long.

"Well in a few days, we'll know for sure."

"Yeah." She nods, not meeting my eyes. "If only I had something to distract myself until then. It feels like torture having to wait that long…"

I groan. "Fine! Fine. We had sex last night," I whisper. "In his car."

She claps her hands together. "YES! I knew it. Your poker face is shit. I mean, you were smiling down at your muffin, and no one likes lemon poppy seed *that much*."

I try hard to keep the smile off my face, but it's impossible.

"Did he stay the night after?"

"No. We went back to my place and cooked dinner, drank wine, played with Mouse. It was remarkably normal considering what we'd just done a few minutes before, but I didn't invite him to stay over. I thought it was better if we had some space."

"Huh. Makes sense I guess. Was he good?"

My cheeks now resemble the red brick wall beside us.

"Damn! I knew he had it in him. No one looks that good and doesn't know what he's doing in bed. It would be such a waste of—oh! Speak of the devil!"

I turn over my shoulder and spot Adam strolling into the coffee shop in workout shorts and a t-shirt. I mentioned to him last night that I had a standing coffee date with Daisy on Saturday mornings at Hamilton Brew. I'm sure he's here on purpose, and when he scans the room and finds me, his smile confirms it.

"Did you invite him?" Daisy asks, curious.

"No."

Yes.

"Huh. Then you must have been pretty good too. He can't stay away."

But he does stay away. After he orders at the counter, he picks up a newspaper and takes his coffee to a table across the room, near the window. I find it incredibly annoying. Surely he came for me...right?

Daisy thinks he's doing it on purpose. "It'd be weird if he came and interrupted our coffee date. Maybe he wants to see you, but doesn't mind waiting until I leave."

"Then leave!"

She stands and steals back the last of the muffin. "For that, I'm eating this. Have fun with Mr. Audi."

Everyone at the surrounding tables hears her—hell, *Adam* probably hears her—and it takes all my willpower not to trip her on her way past my chair. The only reason I resist the urge is because she *could* be pregnant.

"I'll call you later," I promise.

She waves at Adam as she walks out and then he glances over to my table. I tilt my head and nudge Daisy's empty chair. He stands, collecting his coffee and newspaper.

"Just passing by?" I quip as he takes her seat.

He smiles. "I was in the neighborhood."

"Mhm."

"I hope I didn't cut your coffee date short."

"Nah, we've been here for a while."

It's true. That was our *second* round of muffins for the morning.

"Then I don't feel so bad."

I don't think he feels bad at all.

"Daisy thinks you can't stay away because last night was so fun."

"Which part exactly? You straddling me in my car?"

I swear the woman sitting behind us gasps under her breath.

I roll my eyes. "*Yes*, that part."

"Maybe I just wanted coffee."

"Or maybe you couldn't stay away."

He tilts his head, studying me. "Maybe."

I smile. "Figures."

"What are you doing after this?"

"Taking Mouse to the park. It's pretty out and I've been promising to throw the ball with him for the last few days. Want to come?"

"Can I finish my coffee first?"

I nod and stand. "Yeah, I need another muffin anyway."

• • •

Three days later, I have to take Mouse back to the clinic for a round of shots. I have exactly thirty minutes to get in and out, drop Mouse back home, and make it to work on time. Adam doesn't care about my time crunch. We're in the exam room where he's supposed to be inoculating my dog, and instead, he's pinning me against the door, sliding his hand up my dress…like any proper vet should.

"Do you do this with all your patients?" I tease, only halfheartedly batting his hand away.

There's not enough time for this, not to mention I have no brush, no makeup, nothing to touch myself up with if he decides to ravish me before work.

He strings kisses down my neck and my eyes flutter closed.

"*Adam.*"

Someone knocks on the door of the exam room and we fly apart. It's just his assistant, coming in with the shots for Mouse.

I brush my hand across my neck, which is definitely pink from his lips, and take a seat in one of the chairs.

"How are you today, Ms. Thatcher?"

I smile at the assistant. "I'm good." I tug down my skirt that's riding a few inches higher than it should be. "Good, yeah. How are you?"

She tries in vain to quell her smile. "Great. Dr. Foxe has been in a really good mood lately."

Adam is busy administering the shots and then showering Mouse with treats. Still, I can see the smile he's trying to hide.

When the assistant makes a move to exit the room, I stand. "Is that all? I'll follow you out to handle the bill."

The assistant glances between Adam and me. "Oh, he didn't tell you? You get the family and friends discount."

I arch a brow at Adam. "Lucky me."

When I leave a few minutes later, every pair of eyes in the reception area is trained on me. The gossip is going to get around town quickly enough, and though I should mind, I don't—not one bit.

Tonight, Adam is going to make roasted chicken with rosemary potatoes, and then after, I'm going to seduce him on my couch. I'm not sure which part I'm more excited about.

No, the chicken.

Definitely the chicken.

• • •

Adam closes on the farmhouse a week later. We spend all morning at the title company as he signs the documents and finalizes the last few loose ends. I can hardly sit still in my chair knowing I'm seconds away from carrying a commission check to the bank. I have it all planned out: I'm going to pay my rent (*and* take care of all my overdue payments), sock away some money into savings, and maybe, *finally* take my car to get fixed. I don't know who's more excited about the last thing, Adam or me.

I offer to help him move in; he doesn't have much since the house he was renting came fully furnished. There are a few boxes filled with his clothes and personal items, and even still, transporting everything only takes us two trips. We drop the boxes in the living room, stacked out of the way, and I take a second to inspect the empty space.

It's a dream house—*my* dream house—but I haven't said that to Adam. It seems like a strange thing to announce to a man you've just started dating. *Oh, by the way, the house you just purchased is exactly the type of home where I want to raise my future family. Cool, huh?* I might as well slip him a piece of paper with my ring size on it. It's too much pressure. We aren't even officially dating. Daisy asked about it last night.

"He's not my boyfriend, per se," I explain.

"What do you mean? You guys have been inseparable lately."

"Yeah, well, it's still new and there's no rush to stick a label on it."

She hums like she doesn't quite believe me. "Do you want to avoid labels or does Adam *want to avoid labels?"*

"Me. Adam. We both do, I think."

"Don't you get confused?"

"What's confusing?"

"Are you guys exclusive?"

"I am."

"And Adam?"

I sigh, trying to convey how freaking annoying she's being. "I don't know, Daisy."

"YOU DON'T KNOW?!"

"I haven't seen him with anyone else! And to be honest, I don't know how he'd have the time. We're together every day." I'm 99% sure he isn't seeing anyone else, but I haven't asked. It seems like such a heavy and awkward conversation to have this early on.

"Sounds like you're setting yourself up for a lot of miscommunication."

"Weird, I think I'm missing some communication right

now. The signal is breaking up. Gotta go."

"Tell your boyfriend—oh, I mean your friend with no labels and no strings attached—that I said hi."

I hang up on her.

Now, 24 hours later, I'm annoyed to find that Daisy's seed has taken root in my thoughts. *Are we exclusive? Do I even want to be exclusive?* Ha. The girl who has been eternally single for the last few years isn't sure if she's ready to settle down; that's rich. A month ago, I'd have gone on a date with Mr. Boggs had he asked politely.

I'm pulled out of my thoughts when Adam opens the French doors that lead out to the wraparound porch and tells me to wait for him out there. Mouse runs out before me, taking full advantage of the fenced in acres that sit around Adam's house. The closest neighbor might as well be on another planet. Out here, it feels like we have the entire world to ourselves.

I take a seat on the porch steps and watch as Mouse tracks a squirrel and takes off. Then he spots a rabbit and doubles back. He is in doggy heaven.

Adam brings out a chilled bottle of champagne and two plastic cups.

"Time to celebrate?" I ask, taking the cups so he can pop the cork.

"Seems appropriate. It's not every day that you sell a house."

I smile. "It's not every day that you *buy* a house either."

He laughs and pours me so much champagne that it spills over the brim of the small cup. I squeal and lean back, but there's already champagne on my t-shirt. Adam makes clean work of it, stripping it off over my head "so it can dry" on the porch.

I laugh as he pulls me in close. "I don't think that's how

it works."

"It'll be dry in no time," he promises, nuzzling against the side of my neck.

"Oh yeah? And what about my bra?"

He's already trying to peel it off me.

"I think it got a little champagne on it, too."

"We should go inside."

Those words come out of my mouth, but they're nothing more than a halfhearted whisper.

"No one can see us," he promises, backing me up against the side of the porch. He moves his left foot and then his right, and mine have to follow. Soon enough, I'm caged in.

"Mouse can see," I joke.

His mouth drags down my chest, kissing across my collarbone and then lower still. "He's too busy with squirrels."

No, Mouse wasn't too busy with squirrels, he was rolling in a puddle of mud. I know because a few seconds later he runs up onto the porch and shakes out all over Adam and me. In seconds, we're both completely covered. We leap apart and Adam chides Mouse with feigned anger. Mouse responds by running right back off the porch, straight to the puddle, and rolling around some more.

"Are we sure he's not part piglet?" I ask, stepping up behind Adam and hooking my arms around his waist. My bare chest presses against his t-shirt and I turn my head, letting my cheek rest between his shoulder blades. We've never done this—casual intimacy, *cuddling.* We were on our way to fooling around on the porch and we will probably continue in a few minutes, but for now, I don't mind just standing here, feeling his heart beat beneath my palm.

He laughs. "Right now, I honestly can't tell."

I make a move to step back, and he reaches down to hold my hands against him so I can't pull away. I'm glad he can't see how big I'm smiling against his back.

• • •

The next morning, I wake up alone in Adam's new bedroom. His newly purchased air mattress is set up on the ground, and our blankets are sprawled out everywhere. We went to work christening the space right away. The wall, the door, the hardwood floor—they all played a role in our night. Hell, I'd have probably dangled from the ceiling fan if I was tall enough. *I guess there's always next time...*

But first I need food. All the pizza and champagne we had last night is long gone. I sit up in bed, wrapping the white sheet around my chest. That's when I hear the voices carry from downstairs, and I can't be sure...but I think I also catch a whiff of fresh bread. Pastries, maybe kolaches. *Oh yes.*

I scramble off the mattress as quickly as possible and throw on the only clothes I have: yesterday's mud-stained blouse and pencil skirt. I'm tempted to borrow something from Adam, but he's not here to offer it to me, and I'm not going to assume it'd be okay. Maybe he'd think I was crazy, trying to steal his t-shirts and leaving a toothbrush by his sink—although, a toothbrush would be *really* nice at the moment. As it is, I squeeze toothpaste on my finger in his bathroom and do a half-ass job of masking my morning breath. I tell myself it's better than nothing.

When I walk out of Adam's room, I verify that there are definitely voices coming from downstairs, and it's not from the television—I know because we didn't have time to set it up last night. See: sexual activities.

I make it halfway down the stairs before I identify who's talking.

Adam's mother.

Son of a—

"I was just as shocked as you are. I mean, she just showed up on my front porch! What was I supposed to do?"

"Put her on the first plane back to Chicago," Adam responds in frustration.

I want to scurry back up the stairs, but now I'm close enough to know for sure that there *are* fresh baked goods in that kitchen. My love of warm carbs outweighs my ability to heed social cues. Maybe they can keep on having their private conversation as I slink in, load up a plate, and slither right back upstairs.

"Madeleine! I had no idea you were here."

I freeze on the bottom stair as Diane takes in my dirty attire, my ruffled hair, and the hickey I just now remembered. I slap my hand up to cover it and she winks.

"Oh, yeah…" I fumble for a reasonable excuse. "I was just checking up on Adam to make sure he, uhh, knows where all the light switches are."

Adam shakes his head and laughs.

His mom arches a brow, humoring me. "What a fancy outfit for a Sunday morning."

I shrug. "Oh, you know, just because it's the day of rest doesn't mean you can't dress for success!"

I can drop the act. I'm not fooling anyone, not even Mouse. He's sitting beside Diane, staring at me with what I swear is a knowing grin.

"I think you have a sock stuck to your shoulder," she

points out.

It's actually a *pair* of socks, and they're Adam's. I peel them off slowly and lay them down on the counter. I think momentarily of making a *Dobbie is a free elf* joke, but I think the timing is all wrong. Instead, I smile awkwardly and shrug.

"Mom, Madeleine isn't here on real estate business. She's my girlfriend. For real this time."

GIRLFRIEND.

Take that, Daisy.

I offer Diane a smile, but I know it more closely resembles the straight-mouthed, teeth-clenched emoji I employ in moments of panic.

Diane slaps a hand to her chest and feigns shock. "What?! *No.* I could never have possibly guessed that."

I drop my hand from my neck. There's no point in trying to keep up appearances at this point.

"If I'd known you were here, I would have tried to make myself a little more presentable," I admit sheepishly.

"I think you look great. My son, on the other hand, could use a shower."

I glance over and smile. Adam is leaning back against the kitchen counter in a t-shirt and pajama pants. His light brown hair is sticking up in every direction, and he looks sleepy and adorable. I would maul him if his mother wasn't standing ten feet away.

"Long night?" she asks, and I turn into a strawberry.

"Mom, why do you ask questions you don't want to know the answer to?"

"Because I like to watch you squirm," she says with a confident smile.

"Could I maybe steal one of those pastries?" I ask, pointing to the light pink box on the counter. If I'm going to be subjected to interacting with my *boyfriend's* mother this early on a Sunday, I need to do it while I lick icing off a cinnamon roll.

She pushes the box toward me and then passes me a paper plate. "Take as many as you'd like. I brought them for you."

"I thought you said you didn't know she was here," Adam points out.

Diane grins. "I'm not half as naive as you seem to think I am, son."

He nods. "Noted."

I take a bite of pastry and silence falls across the kitchen. I'm reminded of the conversation I interrupted with my arrival. After I finish my first bite, I tell them I'll be on the porch with Mouse. Neither one of them tries to follow me. Clearly, they have something to finish discussing. Unfortunately, even outside, I can hear every word. The French doors do nothing to muffle the discussion about Olivia.

I gather up the details I missed while I was sleeping. Olivia apparently showed up unexpectedly at Diane's house last night. Diane let her in and gave her the guest room to sleep in for the night, a fact that makes me want to crush my cinnamon roll in the palm of my hand. I resist, though, because…cinnamon roll.

"What does she want?" Adam asks.

"To talk to you, of course."

He laughs and it sounds scary, menacing. "There's a little thing called a telephone. If she wanted to talk, she had the last five months to call me."

"She assumed you wouldn't answer."

"Well she was right about that," he says. "I probably wouldn't have."

"She brought Molly."

His beloved dog.

"Why the hell would she do that? Some kind of guilt trap?"

His mom tries to calm him down. "I don't know what she wants to talk to you about, but if you want me to tell her you aren't open to it, I will. However, I'm going to give you some advice that I think you should take to heart. You and Olivia left things in shambles. There was no closure, no little bow to tie up loose ends. Those are the things that haunt you when you get to be my age. If you want to move on, to leave Olivia in the past, I think you should have a conversation with her, in person. If you react in anger now, I think you'll regret it down the line."

NO. No you won't!

I hate Diane. I fling her cinnamon roll out into the pasture—I will not eat the bread of my enemies, and that's exactly what she is if she wants Adam to sit down with Olivia. He loved her for so many years. God, he probably still *loves* her. If they see each other, all those feelings are going to come flooding back, and the fact that she brought Molly—that underhanded bitch knew exactly what she was doing. I stomp out into the pasture and kick the cinnamon roll another ten feet. It feels good to demolish something, though I am now admittedly starving.

A few minutes later, when Adam shouts for me to come back inside, his mom is gone. Her stupid pastries still sit on the counter, but I'm not even a little tempted to take a new one.

"So apparently Olivia showed up at my mom's house last night," he volunteers.

He's getting ready to relay all the information I already know from snooping, so I hold up my hand to stop him. "I could hear you guys talking, even from out there."

"She thinks I should talk to her."

I can't meet his eyes. I stare down at Mouse, who is blissfully unaware of what it feels like to have your heart sliced down the middle.

"And are you going to?"

He drags a hand through his hair and turns away. "I don't know. I mean, I guess. She came all the way from Chicago."

My stomach churns.

"You should," I say, and the words taste like acid on my tongue.

"You think?"

I shrug. "Closure is always a good thing, right?"

"I don't love her anymore, Madeleine."

I finally meet his gaze and find that he's been studying me, his head tilted to the side. There might even be pity in his eyes. I suddenly want to get the hell out of Dodge.

"I know—I mean, I *don't* know, but it's..." I shake my head, trying to clear my scrambled thoughts. "You should do whatever you think is right."

Silence hangs over us, and I can't stand in his kitchen for another second.

"It's actually good timing, I need to head back to my place," I say, surprised by how confident I sound.

"Now? Already?"

"Yeah. I have a showing with Mr. Boggs soon and I need to shower and change."

He seems disappointed, or maybe it's my imagination throwing me a bone. "Right. Okay. I can drive you and Mouse home."

The car ride is laced with tension and unspoken words. We leave the radio up loud to drown out the silence, but it's not enough to quiet my fears, and when we arrive at my apartment, I try not to read into the fact that he only offers me a chaste kiss on the cheek.

Yeah, Daisy, I've got a label for you: *it's complicated*.

CHAPTER TWENTY-TWO

AFTER A FITFUL night of sleep and hours upon hours of fixating on what will or won't happen with Adam, I decide to play a game. In the morning, I wake up and pretend like Adam was never a part of my life. I walk Mouse around the neighborhood and then come home and prepare myself a healthy breakfast. I shower and get ready for work, grabbing my most flattering dress out of the closet. My hair curls like it's never curled before, and I apply my makeup with the gentle hand of someone who knows what they're doing. I feel good. Thoughts about Adam and Olivia hover in the periphery of my thoughts, but I refuse to let them get any closer than that.

When I stroll into Hamilton Brew to treat myself to a well-deserved latte, I appreciate the smile from the man behind me in line. It feels good to know that in a world where Adam never existed, I can still garner attention from the opposite sex. He even asks me what I would like to order. *Vanilla latte*, I say, and he nods to the barista. *Two of those then.* And even though I insist on paying, he insists otherwise.

I walk to the office with a little pep in my step, and it doesn't even bother me when Lori corners me around lunchtime with news of Adam.

"You and Adam Foxe are dating, right?"

That's the first thing she asks me, and I'm hesitant to answer. I can't leave though—my Lean Cuisine pizza is nuking in the microwave and there are only 45 seconds left on the clock, which means I'm 45 seconds from pizza heaven.

"It's nothing serious." I shrug.

She hums. "Oh, okay. It's just that I saw him last night at dinner with a stunning blonde."

Ice fills my veins.

"Why would I care?" I laugh, staring at the ticking timer on the microwave, hurrying it along with all my might. *Cook, pepperonis, COOK.*

"Well I would care if my boyfriend was seated with another woman at the lovers' table at Bellissimo. I was there with a few girlfriends for book club. We read *A Dog's Purpose* this month—very touching. As a dog lover myself, I could not put it down."

I hum, bored.

"And we were halfway through our discussion questions when in walked Adam and his date. I swear the whole restaurant was abuzz with gossip right away. *Who is she? Where did she get that dress?* It was beautiful, definitely high-end designer, not like what you wear around here."

I stab my thumb at the button for the microwave door and it swings open so fast that Lori has to jump back.

"Thanks for the information, but I need to get back to

work."

She puts her hand on my arm to stop me on my way out of the kitchen. "They seemed really cozy. She had her hand on his arm through most of dinner. I just thought that if *I* were you, I'd want to know."

I laugh sarcastically. "*No*, Lori, you wanted to rub my nose in the fact that Adam was on a date with a pretty blonde."

She feigns indignation. "Why, I—that's absolutely not the case!"

I shrug and walk out of the kitchen, proud of myself for finally standing up to her. She can pretend I'm wrong, just like I can pretend Adam taking Olivia out to dinner doesn't enrage me, but we both know the truth.

• • •

Later that night, Adam calls me while I'm making dinner. I'm hovering near the stove, heating up spaghetti sauce when his name lights up my iPhone's screen. I stare down at it on the counter. Technically, I can't answer because I have spaghetti sauce on my fingers, but I'm not a coward. I wash my hands and reach for the phone before it goes to voicemail. I sound out of breath when I say hello.

"Madeleine, hey."

"Hi."

"How are you? Did you have a good day?"

We've never done this. In the last few weeks, we weren't phone-call-at-the-end-of-the-day type people; we didn't have to be because more often than not, we were together. Now, I guess things have changed.

"I'm good," I reply, trying to sound chipper. "Work was

good." Good, good—apparently I don't know any other adjective to describe my life. "And yours?"

"Oh, yeah. Same. Good."

We both laugh because this is painful. This is blind-date levels of pain.

I want to ask him about his dinner last night, but I don't want him to think I'm snooping on him. Worse, I decide it's his responsibility to bring up the subject, not mine...but he never does. Over our short phone conversation, we don't discuss Olivia. We don't discuss us.

I want to go back to playing the game I invented earlier.

"Oh, my pasta is finished. I better go."

In truth, it's been done for five minutes, sitting in a colander in the sink, sad and droopy.

"Okay, yeah. You'll be at the training class tomorrow though, right?"

The training class, of course. I'd forgotten about it, and now that he brings it up, I'd love nothing more than to skip it, but Mouse doesn't deserve that. I don't want to be the reason that Mouse becomes a dog school dropout, turns to a life of doggy crime, and ultimately ends up in the pound for smuggling milk bones across the border.

"Yeah, of course. Wouldn't miss it."

I end the call and then I eat my sad dinner in my sad apartment. Turns out, I have thought of another adjective to describe my life: S-A-D.

• • •

I'm showing Mr. Boggs a house the next day when Daisy finally returns my phone call. I excuse myself and walk outside to answer.

"Daisy! *Finally*."

"Sorry, I was with a patient. What's going on? Why did you tell my receptionist 9-1-1?"

"Because I need you to come with me to Mouse's training class later."

"That's your emergency? You understand what those numbers symbolize, right?"

"Yes. This is an emergency," I insist. "Can you come?"

"Sorry Madeleine, I have a doctor's appointment."

I panic. "Are you serious? Reschedule—or better yet, just diagnose yourself."

She laughs. "Yeah, that's not really how it works. I appreciate the creativity though."

I walk another few steps away from the house and hold my hand over the receiver so my voice doesn't carry. "Daisy, I can't do this alone. I can't face him."

"Yes, you can. You're making this Olivia thing into a bigger deal than it is. Don't let Lori get into your head."

"I'm not making it a bigger deal, it IS a big deal! They were engaged for five years, Madeleine. They're probably soul mates, and tonight after class, he's going to pull me aside and let me down gently. I can't do it. I don't want Mouse to see me like that. My emotions will betray me."

"Yeah, God forbid you let him know how you feel."

"Yes, *God forbid*, Daisy! How pathetic will it look when he tries to break up with me and I start crying. I mean, I'm not even sure he owes me a breakup! Like you said, we weren't official or anything."

She sighs. "Yes, you were."

There's another voice on her end of the line—a medical assistant prompting Daisy about an appointment—and she lets me know she has to go.

I want to hate her for abandoning me in my time of

need, but I can't. She's right. I'm a grown woman and I can face Adam with my head held high, and I do just that, right up until I'm on my way to the YMCA with Mouse and get caught in a torrential downpour. All day, it was a cloudless, blue sky, yet somehow as I pull my car into a parking space, it has suddenly morphed into monsoon season. I stay inside, trying to wait out the worst of it, but minutes tick by and I'll be late if I don't make a run for it soon. Other attendees pull into the parking lot with umbrellas and galoshes, rain jackets that reach from their head to their feet. I rummage around my car and find the remnants of a plastic bag that just barely covers my head.

Unfortunately, it'll have to do.

Mouse and I dash for the front door. He diverts his path to splash in every puddle he can find, but I beeline right for the entrance. Even still, it's no use. When I pull the door open and walk inside, I'm soaked from head to toe. My once-perfect curls hang sad and limp. My jeans stick to my thighs, and my shoes squeak with every step.

Adam is already inside the gym with most of the other attendees. Everyone's unpeeling rain jackets and drying off as best they can. Mouse shakes and throws water clear across the room.

"Here, this'll help a little," Adam says, handing me a small gym towel he must have found in one of the supply closets. I use it to pat myself down and I go from sopping to just mostly sopping. Then Adam takes the towel back from me and uses it for Mouse.

"Thanks. I didn't think to pack my rain gear."

He smiles and glances up. We lock gazes, and those pale green eyes make my stomach flip. I haven't seen him in two days. It's nothing—hardly a blip—and yet the moment feels charged. I blink and look away first.

"I wasn't sure you'd come," he admits, standing.

If he can be honest, I can too.

"I almost didn't."

He sighs. "Yeah, I guess the last two days have been strange to say the least."

"Oh?" I sound casual, aloof.

"Adam," one of the other attendees calls. "Will we be starting on time or are we going to wait for the last few stragglers?"

Of course, puppy training class—the reason we're both here, the reason a dozen people are staring at us, wondering why Adam hasn't started teaching yet.

He looks back at me with furrowed brows, torn. "You'll stay after class, won't you?"

I nod. Of course I'll stay.

Unfortunately, I won't be able to keep that promise.

The first half of class proceeds as normal. Adam increases the difficulty of the commands and we work with our dogs—training, clicking, and treating each time they perform well. Mouse is getting the hang of sit, down, stay, and I'm mastering avoid, smile, nod whenever Adam comes around to check on me. I can tell he wants to pull me aside and chat, but there's no reason to do it in the middle of class. If he's going to tell me he and Olivia are back together, or that she's staying in Texas, or that he's going to propose to her again with an even *bigger* and *better* diamond, I want it to be in private, preferably in a room shrouded in shadows so he can't see me crumble before his very eyes.

"He's doing really well," Adam says, commending Mouse after a particularly long stretch of staying.

I bend down and pat Mouse's head when the gymnasium doors fling open and draw the attention of everyone in the room. A beautiful blonde steps in wearing a chic white blouse and black slacks. Both are impeccably fitted, probably tailored just for her bony little body. Whatever rain swept in while I was driving must have ended before she stepped outside because every single strand of short blonde hair is styled and in place. Her lips are covered in a bright shade of red and her heels look to be more expensive than my sofa. Around her wrist is a delicate brown leather leash attached to a medium-sized golden retriever. In short, she is the most put-together person I've ever seen in real life.

Olivia.

Of course she's Olivia, and the adorable well-behaved dog at her feet is Molly.

Adam's old family—Adam's *beautiful*, old family.

She beelines straight for us and my brain shouts at me to do something. *Run. Flee while you can!* I scan both exits, wondering if I can reach them before she reaches us, but it's too late. I catch a whiff of a light rose-scented perfume before I've even taken one step.

"Sorry I'm late. That rain wouldn't let up."

"What are you doing here?" he asks. "Did my mom tell you I'd be here?"

I have my eyes trained on the ground, too petrified to glance up and take in her glory from this close up. I bet she looks like a runway model, slicing her way down the catwalk.

"She mentioned it this morning, so I thought I'd bring Molly by for a refresher."

She sounds so confident with him, and I suppose she would. How many dinners have they shared? Vacations? Lazy Sunday mornings?

"Oh! Who is this?" someone asks behind me.

The other attendees are starting to gather around, curious about the goddess who just interrupted our class.

Olivia laughs and it sounds like a hundred baby angels. "Oh, I'm Olivia, Adam's fiancée."

"*Ex!*"

All eyes whip to me and I finally, finally glance up to Olivia. She's glaring at me with narrowed eyes, and I realize I've spoken out of turn. They were having a private conversation, and I was supposed to be nonexistent, a speck of dust.

"...*ex-cuuuuse me*," I correct. "Mouse just informed me that he needs to use the bathroom."

That's how I cover up my ridiculous faux pas—by using my poor, innocent dog as a scapegoat—but Mouse isn't meant to be a scapegoat, isn't trained enough for that sort of responsibility. I try to get him to follow after me so we can exit the gymnasium and continue on until we hit the Mexican border, but his paws are locked in place. His attention is singularly focused on Molly.

"He's really good at *stay*," I laugh, trying to tug him again. "Quit showing off, Mouse, *c'mon*."

He doesn't budge.

"I think he likes her," Olivia says, charming the pants off of everyone in the room.

Mouse whines excitedly and then offers a play bow, trying to gain Molly's attention, but she's playing hard to get, sitting politely at Olivia's feet.

"Madeleine, can I talk to you for a second?"

Adam is trying to draw me to the side of the room by the crook of my elbow, but like Mouse, I don't budge. My fight-or-flight instincts are kicking in, and I want to go—now.

I tug Mouse and finally, he listens.

"I'm just going to take him outside," I say, not looking at Adam or Olivia.

I want no part of this awkward exchange.

"Is that the friend you told me about?" I hear Olivia ask as I walk away.

I don't hear Adam's reply, and maybe that's for the best. As it is, I can fill in his reply with whatever I want.

Yes that's the friend I told you about, the one I'm madly in love with!

Ha.

When I walk out of the YMCA, I see that the rain has started again. Of course it has. It stops for women like Olivia, but for me, there's a little raincloud perched right overhead. I don't even bother rushing to my car. What's the point? My clothes are still damp from earlier.

Mouse tries to claw his way back inside the entire way to the car, and then his whining kicks up another notch when I open the passenger door for him. He doesn't want to leave, not while the new love of his life is back in that gymnasium.

"Believe me, it's just puppy love," I insist. "You'll get over it."

We both will.

I feel like a coward for leaving before class is over. Adam asked me to stay so we could talk, but how exactly would we do that with Olivia lingering nearby? I didn't expect her to still be in Texas. If all she wanted was some closure and an official goodbye, she wouldn't have brought Molly to the training class; she'd be halfway back to Chicago by now. And if she was still confident enough to show up uninvited with their dog, that means she still sees daylight, and whatever is going on between them is more complicated than I thought.

Complicated.

There's my favorite word again.

My car starts after the second attempt (thank God) and Mouse whines. I feel like I have to hold it together for the two of us. If I start crying, there's no going back. Rain beats down on my windshield as I drive the few minutes back to my apartment. I want to give in to the feelings of self-pity and sadness creeping in around the edges, but I won't do it. My life might seem just as complicated today as it was a few weeks ago, but things have changed.

I sold a house.

I paid my overdue rent.

Mr. Hall isn't following me around, hounding me for money.

I have an appointment on Monday at the mechanic.

Though it feels like all is lost on this short, sad drive back home, that's not the case.

The storm kicks up another notch by the time I pull into my apartment complex, and Mouse and I make a run for it just as a gust of wind nearly bulldozes me back. I fiddle with my keys quickly, push open the flimsy door, and usher Mouse inside as fast as possible. He shakes, sending water everywhere. Normally, I would care. Right now, I just want a shower. A hot, uncomplicated shower.

I take my time, letting the water turn from warm to scalding before I step under the stream. It doesn't solve all of my problems, but it helps. My lavender-scented body wash has a baptismal effect on me. In the ten minutes I lather myself up and rinse off, I decide things are going to be okay no matter what. If Adam and Olivia are back together and about to enter marital bliss, I can take it.

It's not as if he and I made a commitment to one another. We spent a few weeks having fun. Admittedly, I let myself fantasize about more, especially lately. I didn't want to indulge myself at the time, but it almost felt like a sign that he bought the white farmhouse. It's my dream house, and he bought it. Sure, I'm not crazy enough to move in with a guy after only a few weeks of knowing him, but eventually…I imagined us living there together, Adam, Mouse, and me.

The rain seems to grow even louder as I finish washing off. Thunder rumbles as if it's inside my apartment, a sign that the storm isn't going to let up any time soon, which is just as well. Rain suits my current mood just fine.

I step out and dry off, waiting for Mouse to rush in and lick the water droplets from my shins. He doesn't come, which probably means he's still pouting about having to leave training class without his beloved.

"Mouse, believe me, she would've just broken your heart! I'll let you have some chicken with your dinner. How's that?"

There's no jingle of dog tags, no sign that he's listening to me at all.

Stubborn dog.

I wrap a towel around myself and step out of the bathroom.

My front door is wide open, forced against the wall by the heavy wind and rain. I rush forward and close it, nearly wiping out on the puddle of water in the entryway. I must not have locked it before my shower, and it doesn't take much to push open the old door. *Yet another thing I need to bring to Mr. Hall's attention now that I'm a paying tenant again.*

I hurry back to the bathroom to retrieve a towel to wipe up the mess, and that's when it hits me.

Oh god, where's Mouse?

I turn and check the apartment. He's not in kitchen. He's not in my bedroom, or the bathroom. The apartment is tiny, and it takes me all of five seconds to conclude that Mouse is gone. He ran through the open door. He bolted while I was in the shower and now he's out there in the middle of a thunderstorm.

I yank open my front door and shout his name.

"MOUSE! *MOUSE*! Come here boy!"

I run to the end of the walkway and shout his name again, but he's nowhere in sight. There's no telling how long the door was open. He could have a ten or fifteen-minute head start on me. I rush back into my apartment and yank on the first clothes my hands touch. My keys are in my hand and I'm running barefoot to my car.

This isn't happening.

I refuse to acknowledge that Mouse has run away.

He's never done anything like this before. My front door has accidently flung open in the past and he's never cared. He's just a puppy. He was probably terrified when the door slammed open, and he bolted.

I force my key into the ignition and crank my car to life. It resists, but starts nonetheless.

First, I circle through the apartment complex's parking lot. I roll down my window and shout his name, ignoring the pellets of water hitting my face and soaking the inside of my car.

"MOUSE!"

Nothing, just more rain.

"MOUSE! C'MERE BOY!"

He's not here.

CHAPTER TWENTY-THREE

Madeleine

I TRY NOT to panic, but I can feel the worry rising up in my throat like bile.

He cannot run away.

He's my Mouse.

He's the one constant in my life.

He depends on me, and I depend on him.

I go back to my apartment to confirm that I'm not crazy, that he isn't just asleep on the couch. I harbor a false sense of hope that he's been there the whole time, that he would never leave me. Too bad it's not the case. I run back outside.

"MOUSE!" I shout once more before running back to my car and broadening my search. I turn right out onto the street. I want to be a math wizard, want to calculate how far he could have gone if he left my apartment five minutes ago, ten minutes, fifteen.

I stick to the right lane and creep along, shouting his name into the fading light of the day.

Cars honk and swerve by me, annoyed at my snail's pace.

I hardly notice them over my shouting and shouting and shouting.

I check the YMCA parking lot. It's far, but he has a motive for being there.

Class is over and the parking lot is empty. I loop around and check for Mouse's black and brown fur, trying to spot the little white patch near his eye. Another bolt of lightning lights up the sky followed by an ominous BOOM. The thunder is loud, too loud. Mouse has to be scared out here all by himself.

I give in to a wrecked sob, but just one—it won't help if I lose it.

I have to keep it together. I have to find my dog.

I loop around the surrounding neighborhoods then check outside Daisy and Lucas' house. I glance across the street, at Lucas' old rental house, but the lights are off and there's no dog sitting on the front porch. I put my car in drive and continue. There's no rhyme or reason to my search other than to check the spots I've frequented with Mouse in the past. There's Hamilton Brew; they have a dog-friendly patio out front, but he isn't there. I stare at their dog bowl getting pelted by rain and I remember not long ago when Mouse and I walked to the coffee shop early one Saturday morning. He waited while I went in to order a coffee, then we sat there together for hours. I read and he people-watched at my feet, accepting any free head pats or ear scratches that came his way. But now, the water bowl is overflowing from the rain and I need to keep going.

Next, I drive out to the dog park I've taken him to a few times. The rain is coming down in sheets, so hard that I have to squint to detect any movement outside. He's not in the fenced-in area. He's not roaming around outside. I pinch my eyes closed and try to think. He's out here in the storm, scared and alone. He could be anywhere. Terrible images of him cowering beneath a bridge or hiding in a ditch bring out another sob. *Don't think like that*, I remind myself. He's Mouse, he's probably having the time of his life getting wet and muddy. I just need to find him before the fun is over.

I take a deep breath, and because it feels so good, I force another.

I will find him, and I'll bring him home.

I put the car in reverse with plans to head back and check to see if he's returned to my apartment, but the car doesn't move. My tires spin in the mud, digging themselves deeper and deeper.

SHIT.

I bang my hands on my steering wheel.

SHIT SHIT SHIT.

My whole body is shaking. Panic is starting to creep up within me, overtaking logic and reason. I quell the sensation and assess the situation: I'm at the town's dog park, which is a couple miles away from my apartment. There is a raging monsoon taking place outside and now, my car is stuck in the mud.

I glance down and my heart lurches in my chest.

When I ran out of my apartment earlier, I was panicked. I assumed I would find Mouse within a few minutes. I didn't think to slip on shoes. No purse. No phone. I'm wearing sleep shorts and a tank top.

"Okay, okay, okay," I say to myself, trying to calm down.

My shaking hands clench the steering wheel and I let myself have three seconds to despair in my complete ineptitude. I have no phone. *I have no phone*, which means I can't call someone for help. I have no phone, which means I'm stuck out here until I can get my car out of the mud. My lungs won't inflate. I can't breathe. I think I'm having a panic attack, but there's no one around to confirm or deny that for me. I'm by myself, lost without Mouse.

CHAPTER TWENTY-FOUR

MADELEINE WON'T ANSWER her phone, and it's starting to piss me off. I understand that Olivia being in town has thrown our new relationship off balance, but it's not reason to go radio silent.

I dial again, and get nothing but voicemail.

It's an hour after the training class ended. Olivia is back at my mom's house, packing for her flight in the morning. She's leaving, and I'm not sad about it. In fact, I'm relieved to have her out of Texas. She came here under the guise of closure, but in reality, she came crawling on her hands and knees, trying to pick up right where we left off. After a few glasses of wine at dinner two days ago, she revealed that her life has taken a nosedive in the last few months. Ryan, my old best friend, left her a few weeks ago. Turns out starting a relationship with an affair isn't a great predictor of long-term stability. Evidently he was cheating on her—and she tried to spin it as God letting her know how I felt when it happened to me. As if her getting fucked over was going to be some bonding experience for us. It took everything in me not to laugh. I apologized and wished her well.

She didn't take me seriously at first. For so many years, Olivia had me wrapped around her finger. She said jump and I asked how high. I think she assumed she could fly down here and I would leap right back into her arms.

Her showing up to the training class was a last-ditch effort to convince me she was serious about wanting to get back together. Unfortunately, she went too far. Telling the class she was my fiancée was an underhanded way to stick it to Madeleine, the "friend" I told her about over dinner.

I'm serious about her, I said.

Olivia didn't believe me. In fact, she laughed at the possibility.

You think you're going to settle down with some Texas girl you met a few weeks ago? Can't you see it's just a phase, Adam? You're meant for so much more than this shitty town.

I smiled, asked for the check, and told her to book a flight back to Chicago.

We're done.

I stare down at my phone now, wondering how many calls I can make to Madeleine before I verge on stalker territory. Then I do one better—I grab my keys and head for my car. It's still raining as I head to her apartment. I could wait until the morning to see her, but there's no reason to continue on like this. She's assumed the worst, I know it. She thinks that because we've only been together a few weeks, I'm going to go right back to Olivia. That's on me, and I have to fix it. She might not want to take my phone calls, but she'll have to answer her door.

I park in my usual spot and head up the path. A bark snaps me out of my reverie and I glance up to spot Mouse sitting outside Madeleine's apartment. His fur is soaked and covered in mud; it looks like he's been rolling in puddles for the last hour.

"What are you doing out here, boy?"

He hops up as I approach and wags his tail. Most dogs hate thunderstorms, but he doesn't even seem to notice the rain pouring down beyond the covered walkway.

I turn and pound on Madeleine's door.

No one answers. I notice muddy paw streaks on the door.

"Madeleine, come on. Mouse is out here. What were you thinking letting him out in a storm like this?"

I knock again and wait a few minutes. There's nothing but silence on the other side of the door, and a sense of dread starts to fill my gut. Why would Mouse be outside alone? And where's Madeleine?

"Madeleine?" I call, pounding on the door harder than before. The flimsy thing rattles on its hinges, and I know if I hit it just little harder, the whole damn door would come loose.

"Young man, she's not home."

I spin around and spot an old man across the pathway, peering out at me from the sliver of space between his door and its frame.

"What do you mean she's not home?"

"She left a little while ago to find her dog."

I frown, confused. "Her dog's right here."

"Yeah, well, that's why it's strange that she's looking for him."

"Did you see where she went?"

He shrugs and steps back, closing his door just a bit.

"The dog's here so she'll be back soon."

"There's a flash flood warning in effect until the morning."

He shrugs. "Well you found the dog. I guess now you need to go find the girl."

With that, he shuts his door and leaves me out on the walkway to fend for myself. Mouse lies down at my feet, wholly unaffected by the fact that his owner is searching for him in the middle of a thunderstorm. I try to think fast. Madeleine isn't in danger. She's out in her car, looking for Mouse. She'll likely be back any minute, so I lean back against her door and wait. Mouse falls asleep. I check my watch. Another fifteen minutes roll by. I try calling her again, and her cell phone chimes in her apartment. *Well that explains why she hasn't answered any of my calls.*

Minutes slip past. Something doesn't feel right.

I run to my car and find a stray receipt in my cup holder.

Mouse is safe. I have him. Call me. - Adam

I pound on the neighbor's door until he answers and then I ask for some tape so I can put the note on her door.

"She's going to be back any time now," he says, shaking his head at me as he wanders off into his apartment. A second later, he comes back with a couple of pieces of tape that he ripped off the roll. *Stingy.*

I use every piece of tape to secure the paper to her door right at eye level so there's no chance she'll miss it, and then I load Mouse up in my car. With a pang, I remember the day of the barbecue when Madeleine insisted we take her car to avoid the scene before me now: a big dog making a mess of my interior. Right now, I could not care less.

A bolt of lightning shatters the sky a few yards ahead, followed by a booming clap of thunder. I pat Mouse—less to calm him, and more to soothe myself.

"We're going to find her," I assure him as we pull out onto the road.

CHAPTER TWENTY-FIVE

MY THREE SECONDS of despair turn into minutes. I don't know how long I sit there, frozen in panic. Thunder rumbles a few miles away, and I'm reminded that I have to act. I can't sit here while Mouse is out there alone, and I'm not naive enough to try to walk home alone, at night, with no phone, no shoes, and no purse.

My only option is to get my car out of the mud. I've seen my dad do it a couple times over the years. I need to find some wood and wedge it beneath my tire so there's enough traction for them to move. To do that, I have to get out of my car. I look out and wonder how long it's going to rain like this. Surely it can't keep up forever, but I don't have time to wait it out. I fling my door open and rush out, heading for the dense woods a few yards away. My hair is still wet from my shower, and the rain soaks everything else within a few seconds. I wipe the water from my eyes and search the ground. There are some sticks lying around in the mud, but nothing that will really give me traction.

I don't look for long. Truthfully, I doubt I'll find anything worth using. I need a massive piece of plywood, and I won't find that on the edge of the woods near a dog park. I gather together as many sticks as I can find and run back to my car, wincing when sharp rocks jab into my bare feet with each step.

Both of my back tires are stuck in the mud. The right one is worse than the left, so I start there, my feet sinking into the wet mud as I step closer. I drop my sticks on the ground and try to remember what my dad used to do. *I need to get the sticks beneath the tire, right? But how can I do that if the tire is stuck in mud?* I bend down and use my hands to haul away some of the mud, but it's like quicksand, filling right back into the hole as quickly as I can move it.

I'm so close to giving up. The rain is relentless, and now my hands are too muddy to wipe my eyes. I blink and try to clear them, but my vision is still cloudy. Maybe that isn't rain; maybe I'm crying now.

As I bend down, digging and digging, trying to haul away enough mud to make a difference, more fills in, making it impossible to get ahead of the problem. I'm struggling and working hard, and yet nothing I do seems like it's enough. There is no getting out of this hole, and I see that now. This hole, this stinking goopy mud pile is my life.

I understand that while other people slip into jobs they love and marriages that seem more like fairytales, I, Madeleine Thatcher, am destined for a tougher life. Nothing has come easy for me, and with every pile of mud that I move, I feel better. Most people would have given up already, but not me. I'm tough. I can do this. I dig and I dig, wedging the sticks beneath my car's wheels until I think there's enough to make a difference.

Before I step back into my car, I shake out my hands and feet, flinging off as much mud as I can manage. There are a few napkins stuffed in the driver's side door and I use them to wipe my hands. It's not enough, but it's something.

I start my car, shift it into reverse, and the tires spin and spin, spewing mud and sticks.

The clock on the dashboard reads 10:45 PM; I've been stuck here for an hour, and I'm no closer to getting myself free.

The rain continues on, relentless and unyielding.

I let my head fall against the steering wheel and I close my eyes against the tears.

I'm sorry, Mouse.
I'm so sorry.

• • •

Tap. Tap. Tap.

Raindrops drip down lazily on my window, barely pulling me out of a deep sleep.

TAP. TAP. TAP.

The sound is growing louder.

I groan and try to steal another minute or two of sleep. I don't know what time it is, but it's too early to be awake. Mouse hasn't nudged me with his nose, which means it must still be the middle of the night. He's more dependable than an alarm clock.

Mouse…

MOUSE!

I jerk awake and wipe sleep from my eyes, surprised to find myself in the front seat of my car, not back home in bed. I must have fallen asleep by accident. I was sitting here after attempting to get my car unstuck for the second time. I cried for a little, ate a smashed granola bar I found wedged between my back seats, played a sad CD and imagined it was the soundtrack of my life, cried more, and then at some point I must have put my head down on the center console and dozed off.

TAP. TAP. TAP.

I jump a mile in the air and whip my attention to where someone is standing on the other side of my driver's side door, tapping a flashlight against my window. The rain didn't wake me up, *he* did.

A thousand slasher-movie scenarios play through my mind in a matter of seconds. I'm in the middle of nowhere. It's still raining. There's a person dressed in all black trying to break his way into my car. At first I'm worried that he'll want to have his way with me, but then I remember I'm covered in mud, smell a little funky, and generally look like the scary girl from The Ring.

"I DON'T HAVE ANYTHING GOOD IN HERE!" I shout. "I have no money and nobody loves me, so there's no chance for a ransom!"

The flashlight clicks off, and everything goes dark.

I pinch my eyes closed and prepare for a swift death.

CHAPTER TWENTY-SIX

AFTER LEAVING MADELEINE'S apartment, I called Lucas to alert him about the situation. He got Daisy involved and within a few minutes, it seemed like everyone in town was mounting a search for Madeleine. I took Mouse back to my house and washed him off. After he had food and water and I was sure all the doors were closed and securely locked, I headed back out and joined the search myself.

The rain didn't let up for hours, and around midnight, Daisy insisted we call Carter. I was hesitant to get the police involved—after all, it wasn't as if she was a missing person—but as the minutes continued to tick by and there was no sign of Madeleine, I decided we could use all the help we could get.

I go back to her apartment around 3:30 AM. The receipt I taped to the door sits on the ground a few feet away, drenched. I call her cell phone and this time, there's no chime from inside. No doubt it's dead. How many people have tried calling her in the last few hours?

I turn and slide down to the ground, bending my knees and resting my forehead on them. I'm exhausted and drained of ideas. I know I could be out there doing more—maybe there are places we haven't thought to check yet.

Hamilton isn't large, but when you're looking for one woman among acres and acres of farmland, it feels hopeless.

She's okay.

She's not in danger.

Even repeating the sentiment to myself, it doesn't quite stick.

If she was okay, she would have come back by now. She would have come back for her phone, or to check to see if Mouse had returned, and if she had, she would have seen the note and called me, or Daisy, or Lucas.

Nothing makes sense.

I know I should lift my head and stand, head back out there and keep looking for her, but there's nowhere to go. I want to be here when she gets back, so I close my eyes and wait.

At some point I fall asleep, for a few minutes or a few hours, I can't tell.

I blink and glance down at my watch. It's barely 6:00 AM and Madeleine still isn't home. She would have woken me up on her way inside.

I call Lucas, and when there's no answer, I resist the urge to throw my phone at the wall across from me. It's useless. There's no one else I can call. I don't have Daisy or Carter's number. I try Lucas one more time, and it goes straight to voicemail.

Then a police cruiser pulls up in front of Madeleine's apartment complex. The lights are off and I can't see through the tinted windows. I assume they're here because of the missing persons calls—maybe Daisy forced them to expedite the report—but then I see someone step out, and from the passenger side, Madeleine follows.

I leap to my feet.

"Madeleine!"

She glances up and I register the exhaustion right away. She's completely disheveled. There's mud covering her legs up to her knees and her arms are just as dirty. A gray police-issue blanket rests across her shoulders and when she walks toward me barefoot, she winces as if in pain.

Carter rushes around to help her, but I'm there first, holding up most of her weight as we walk toward her apartment.

"What happened to you?" I ask, all my residual anger and fatigue gone.

I'm just so happy to see her, to know she's all right.

She smiles up at me a bit sheepishly. "Long story. Have you seen Mouse?"

"He's at my house, probably in need of a bathroom break."

She closes her eyes for a moment and sighs, as if finding peace after the longest night of her life.

"I want to go with you when you let him out."

Carter is there with us when Madeleine unlocks her door. I have so many questions I want to ask. Where's her car? Her shoes? Why did she leave her house without her cell phone? How did Mouse get out in the first place? Why did Carter drive her back home in his cruiser?

Instead of bombarding her, I swallow down each question and quietly follow her inside.

She stands in the threshold, trying to get her bearings.

"Carter, after I grab some shoes and my cell phone, I'm going to head to Adam's house. You can meet us there."

"What?" I ask, staring back and forth between them.

Madeleine puts her hand on my arm. "Carter is going to have a friend help him with my car. It's stuck in the mud out by the dog park a couple miles from here."

Pride rises inside me as if I'm a petulant sixteen-year-old boy. "I can help you get your car. I'm sure Carter is tired."

Her fingers squeeze my arm and her eyes implore me to listen. "Just let him do it. I want you to drive me to your house so I can see Mouse, and then I need some coffee and food. I'm starving."

I glance back at Carter, who's watching Madeleine like she's a china doll about to crack. "Are you sure that's okay?" I ask. "I could always come help you after I drop Madeleine off."

"No," she answers for him. "I want you to stay with me."

Carter glances away and then meets my eyes. All hints of admiration for Madeleine are gone, replaced with his cop-on-duty expression. "It's no problem. I'll pick up the other officer on my way to the park and then he can drive Madeleine's car to your house. Shouldn't take us long now that the rain has finally let up."

"Thank you, Carter," Madeleine says, releasing my arm so she can give him a quick hug. "Seriously, I owe you."

• • •

I assume Madeleine and I will have some time to talk in the car on the way to my house, but there isn't a spare second. Once she plugs in her cell phone and turns it on, she's bombarded with message after message. She spends every minute in the car and the first half hour at my house returning phone calls and assuring everyone that she and Mouse are all right.

When I come down from my shower, she glances up from the kitchen table with an exasperated expression. "Daisy and Lucas are about to arrive. I tried to tell them everything was okay, but Daisy insisted."

I nod, trying not to let my disappointment show. "I don't blame her. They were both worried about you."

She opens her mouth to say something and then shakes her head and looks down. Mouse is at her feet. He's been at her side since her arrival, when she flung her arms around him and cried. He licked her face and wagged his tail, just as happy to be reunited.

"Would it be okay if I showered really quick?"

I snap back to the present. "Of course. C'mon, I'll show you where the towels are."

She's still a mess from last night, but it's nothing a quick shower can't fix. I put together the bits and pieces of what happened from her phone calls with other people—the rain, the mud, the tires spinning until she was stuck overnight. Carter found her this morning and now here she is, in my bathroom, waiting for me to leave before she tugs her tank top overhead.

It's silly. We've had sex. I've seen her bare body from head to toe. I know she has a little freckle on her left breast, right at the top.

"Adam?" She's smiling and her cheeks, though streaked with mud, are the lightest shade of pink.

I reach down to kiss her just as a car pulls up into the driveway.

"Oh! I bet that's Daisy," she says when my mouth is barely an inch from hers.

I sigh and stand, giving us both some space.

"I'll stall them while you shower."

She bites her lip. "Are you sure? I can wait and shower later."

I laugh. "Madeleine, no offense, but you sort of stink. Now I'll go get you some small dish towels to dry off with."

She bats me out of the bathroom and closes the door. The lock clicks into the place, and then I hear her voice calling out for me.

"Adam?"

I press back against the door. "Yeah?"

"I just…Thanks for going to my apartment to check on me last night. Daisy said it was you who initiated the whole search. If you hadn't come, I'd probably still be stuck out there."

It strikes me as odd that we're having this conversation with a door between us, but then, Madeleine and I still haven't had time to put our relationship back on course. Maybe this is all she can muster. I press my forehead to the door and close my eyes, enjoying this moment for what it is.

CHAPTER TWENTY-SEVEN

THE LAST TWELVE hours have been an utter disaster, and though I'd love nothing more than to crawl into Adam's bed and sleep the day away, we seem to have initiated a full-on party.

"Hey, they don't call it a search *party* for nothing," Daisy says, clinking her coffee with mine.

I resist the urge to roll my eyes.

By the time I finished with my shower, she and Lucas were downstairs at the dining table, spreading out the food they'd picked up on the way over: donuts and kolaches, cinnamon rolls and mini muffins. Adam was filling them in on the missing details from last night, and I'd barely loaded up a cinnamon roll on my plate when Carter and a fellow officer pulled into the driveway with my car.

If possible, the hunk of junk looks even worse than it did last night, as if I had taken it mudding on some country back-roads. The duct-taped mirror on the passenger side is still somehow clinging on for dear life, but the steam rising from the hood is pretty hard to ignore.

"I hate to say it, Daisy, but this car just might be toast," Carter says, popping the hood. Plumes of steam rise up, and Adam shoots me a knowing glare.

"Yeah, I actually had plans to get it looked at this morning, but obviously I've been busy with other things."

Carter waves away the steam. "Unless you're willing to drop a couple thousand for a new engine, there's no point trying to salvage this thing. What is it, prehistoric?"

I prop my hands on my hips. "I'll have you know I've driven this car since high school and it has been dependable—"

"Not true," Adam cuts in.

"And trustworthy—"

"Nope."

"For all these years."

"Half the time it won't start," he tells Carter.

"Well I'm not just going to throw it away!"

Adam claps Carter on the shoulder and then nods to the other officer. "Thanks for getting her car, man. Do you two want to come in for some coffee? Daisy brought enough donuts to feed an army."

Carter pats his flat stomach, his friend does the same, and then the three of them disappear into the house.

"Don't worry," I whisper to my car. "I'm not getting rid of you."

The morning passes slowly as we all huddle in the kitchen, refilling our coffee and going back for donuts even though we've all been full for hours. I keep assuming everyone will eventually excuse themselves and leave, but no one's in a hurry. Apparently, we've all taken a sick day from work.

"No one wants me diagnosing patients on two hours of sleep," Daisy explains.

And like that, it's decided—no one is leaving.

Adam takes the guys around the property, and Daisy corners me in the kitchen.

"You and Adam are being really weird."

"Are we?"

"Yeah, don't play dumb. You sat next to him earlier and when he put his arm on your chair, you flinched. What was that about?"

I sigh and glance out to make sure the guys are still outside. "Olivia was at the training class last night."

She frowns. "Olivia. Olivia…"

"His ex-fiancée! Olivia!"

Her eyes nearly bulge out of her head. "Oh! *Olivia*! Oh God, I bet that was awkward. Why was she there?"

I shrug. "Actually, I'm not sure. He might have invited her. Hence the unresolved weirdness in the air."

She shakes her head. "What do you mean you aren't sure? I thought you two were dating—why would he invite Olivia to the training class?"

"I don't know…" I stare down at my coffee cup. "They might be getting back together."

She punches my arm and coffee spills down the front of the t-shirt Adam lent me. "Hey! Watch it."

She dabs halfheartedly at the stain with a paper towel. "Sorry, sorry. I need more details. How is he possibly getting back with Olivia? The last time we spoke, I thought they just went to dinner for closure or some bullshit like that."

"Well, she showed up at the YMCA last night looking like a Disney princess, and then she announced to the class that she was Adam's fiancée."

Daisy slaps her hand over her mouth in shock. "*No!*"

"Yes. So I left early and that's why I was by myself when Mouse went missing."

"You've had quite the eventful twelve hours."

I can't bring myself to laugh. "Unfortunately."

"And you and Adam haven't talked things over since?"

"Nope. For all I know, he could still be engaged at this very moment."

"Well it's a good sign that Olivia isn't here. But clearly you guys need to talk."

I snort. "Why do you think I was kicking your leg under the table during breakfast?"

"I thought that was Lucas!"

"Oh Jesus." I roll my eyes.

Now that I have Daisy on my side, I assume she'll march up to her husband and insist that they need to leave. She does try, but Lucas shakes his head.

"We'll go in a little while."

A little while turns into a few hours. Pizza is ordered for lunch, and I'm sitting in the living room, silently nursing my third cup of coffee, wondering how I can convince all of them to leave. Adam is sitting across the room, talking to Carter about cars...or vegetable gardening, I don't know. I lost track thirty minutes ago.

"Is that someone pulling up the driveway?" Daisy asks.

"*You've got to be kidding me.*"

Five pairs of eyes whip over to me and I laugh.

"I mean, you've got to be kidding me, ha ha," I repeat in a forced jovial tone. "More well-wishers for little ol' me?!"

Adam laughs, and I think he's the only one who feels my pain.

Across the room, Mouse emits a noise I've never heard

before. It's a slow-building whine that makes me think he's dying.

"Mouse? Buddy?" I rush over to him, but his attention is laser focused out the window. I follow his gaze and find Adam's mom strolling up the front path with Molly at her feet.

Mouse emits another guttural moan and then leaps off the couch. He darts to the door and jumps, scratching at it to get to this golden retriever who is apparently his one true love.

"Mouse! No! Bad dog." I try to pull him back, but he's too strong. Adam comes behind me and grabs his collar, pulling back with both hands.

"What's wrong with him?" Daisy asks.

"He's a Capulet, and his Montague is out there," I whisper.

"What?"

"Is that Molly?" asks Adam. His smile drops. "With Olivia?"

My heart breaks. "No, with your mom."

Olivia will probably be by shortly, just as soon as she finishes applying perfect winged eyeliner and brushing up on her French.

The front door opens and in what I can only describe as a lover's reunion, Mouse breaks free of Adam's hold and darts toward Molly at full speed. I cover my eyes with my hands, preparing for the worst, but when I pry them open again, Mouse is lying on his back with his paws in the air— a universal sign of submission. I've seen him do it a hundred times with other dogs, but with Molly, it looks as if he's thrown himself on the ground and is pleading with her to have him.

I love you, his eyes implore. Molly stands beside him,

peering down for only a second before she barks and licks his face. Then, they're off, tearing through the house at breakneck speeds.

"Open the back door!" Adam shouts to Lucas.

He does so just as they race past and head out into the pasture.

"They're in love," I explain to the room full of curious onlookers. "I think that's why he ran away last night. He went to look for her."

"Aw!" Daisy exclaims. "That's adorable."

We all go peer out the back window; sure enough, they're frolicking in the grass, taking turns chasing one another. It looks like a cliché dog food commercial.

"Diane, can I get you some coffee?" I ask when I turn back to the group.

Please say no, please say no.

Her eyes light up. "Actually, I'd love some. I had an early morning and I forgot to take some out on the road with me."

Of course. Why did I even dare to hope otherwise? Adam and I will never be alone. This parade of people will continue until eventually I lose my remaining grip on sanity, hoist him up against a wall by his lapels and shout, *ARE YOU STILL WITH HER?! JUST TELL ME!*

For now, I move into the kitchen like a robot, pouring Diane coffee and counting backward from ten so I don't lose my cool in front of everyone. I hear footsteps behind me and expect it to be Diane, but then I catch a whiff of Adam's body wash. Mountain-man freshness makes me straighten and pause.

"I can take that," he says, reaching around me for the mug. "You don't have to wait on everyone hand and foot. You've been doing it all morning, and you must be exhausted."

He's not exaggerating. I feel so bad that everyone spent their night searching for me that I want to make sure everyone has enough coffee and donuts and napkins to last them a lifetime.

I shrug. "I don't mind doing it."

"But you want everyone to leave."

My gaze flicks up to his. "Is it that obvious?"

He sets down his mom's mug on the kitchen counter behind me and steps closer. Our hips brush together. "I want them to leave too."

"*Adam.*"

His hand is hooked around the nape of my neck and he's tilting my head back gently so he has a perfect path to my lips. He takes advantage, placing a soft kiss there before laughter from the other room makes me jump.

He laughs. "We're allowed to kiss."

"Are we?"

He frowns. "Olivia left this morning."

It's the wrong thing to say, and he says it like it explains everything. Well, it doesn't.

"So? Will she back? Is she heading to Chicago to pack up her things so she can move here permanently?"

"No, of course not. She and I are over."

"She announced to the training class that she is your fiancée—IS, not WAS."

His eyes flare with anger. "Yeah, because she's crazy, Madeleine. I could have explained everything to you if you hadn't run off."

He seriously expected me to stay after that?

"Excuse me for leaving instead of looking like a fool in front of a room full of strangers!"

"I wouldn't have let that happen."

"It was too late! I didn't hear you say anything when she called herself your fiancée."

"What was I supposed to do? Tell everyone in the room that she was delusional? I thought it would be best to handle my personal life in private."

"Well to me it seemed like you were more worried about Olivia's feelings than mine."

He drags his hand through his hair, clearly annoyed with me. "C'mon Madeleine, you're being—just try to calm down."

"No, please, say what you were about to say. Am I being ridiculous? Well how exactly am I supposed to act right now? Polite? *Grateful*? Sorry, I'm not a fancy girl from Chicago. Down here, where I'm from, we don't shove our emotions under the rug and pretend like everything is okay."

"What's taking so long?" Diane asks from the kitchen doorway, oblivious to the full-blown argument she's just walked in on.

I tug the mug out of Adam's hold and hand it off to her. "Here you go, it's still warm. Sorry for the delay, your son and I are fighting."

Adam snorts behind me.

Diane's brows rise and her smile stretches across her face. "Do you guys want me to leave so you can keep going?"

A moment ago, I would have loved nothing more. Now? I think she should stay for dinner.

I hook my elbow through hers and lead her out to where everyone's sitting in the living room. "Nonsense, we have all day to fight. Right now, I'd like another donut."

CHAPTER TWENTY-EIGHT

MADELEINE IS AVOIDING me; she has been all afternoon. We're all sitting in my living room, and she's positioned herself in a chair across from me. She won't meet my eyes, won't look my way, won't address me when I talk to her. I'm about to call her out for it in front of everyone.

"So then I pulled up and saw Madeleine's car stuck in the mud and I figured she was in there, probably hysterical from being alone overnight…"

Carter is retelling the story of Madeleine's rescue for the hundredth time. My mother is enthralled. Madeleine is staring out through the French doors, watching Molly and Mouse play.

"Why did Olivia leave Molly here in Texas?" she asks, interrupting Carter's story. *Thank God.*

It's a good question, and one I hadn't thought to ask yet.

My mom shrugs. "I think she'd been holding her for a kind of ransom, or bait. When it became clear that she wasn't going to get Adam back, I guess Molly became worthless to her. Which is good, because Adam always loved that dog."

Madeleine's face contorts in confusion, probably because she can't imagine doing something so vicious to another human being.

"You're going to keep her, right?" Madeleine asks me.

"Of course."

There's no question. Molly is my dog, and I'm happy to have her back. The fact that she and Mouse get along so well is an added bonus.

"Good." She nods. "We'll have to set up regular playdates for them."

Everyone in the room goes silent because of what her statement implies: if we're dating, Mouse will be around Molly all the time; if we aren't, we'll have to schedule times for them to play.

Daisy gets to her feet. "Y'know, I think it's time to head out. Carter, could you walk us to our car?"

He seems confused. "It's just right down the driveway—"

"Carter, in this uncertain world, we would really feel better with a police escort," she bites out, nudging her head toward the front door. He finally picks up on her not-so-subtle hints and jumps to his feet. His fellow officer joins him, and then my mom starts to trail out after them.

Madeleine has the audacity to put her shoes on, like she's leaving as well. I thank everyone for helping with the search and promise to have them over again soon, and then as Madeleine tries to slink through the door, I hold my foot out and block her.

She nearly trips, but I take hold of her arm before she goes tumbling down.

"Excuse me," she says, calm and resolute.

"Enough. They're gone and it's time we talk."

She crosses her arms, holds her head high, and shrugs. "Fine."

We head back into the living room and I take a seat on the couch. Madeleine sits across from me, her legs crossed, her gaze right on me. I think I see a smile waiting to be unveiled, but I don't push it.

"You look cute in my shirt," I say, smirking.

She nibbles on her bottom lip, trying, *trying* to restrain that smile. "Obviously."

"Olivia is gone."

"So you've said."

"She and I are done."

"Did she come down here for closure like you assumed?"

"No. She came to Texas with plans to reignite our relationship, but that didn't happen."

She looks down at her nails, feigning indifference. "Oh? Well that's sad about you and Olivia. But that does nothing to explain what's going on between us."

"Well I'm so glad you bring that up. Because I want you to know I'm seeing someone."

A smile breeches her fortress, but I blink and it's gone.

"Huh. She must be pretty great if you walked away from the effervescent Olivia for her."

"She's..."

I glance away, trying to come up with an adjective to describe Madeleine, but nothing stacks up. Funny, amazing, great—they're weak. I've used those words to describe women in the past, and Madeleine isn't like any of them. She's in a league of her own.

I catch movement out of the corner of my eye.

Madeleine is rounding the coffee table and stalking toward me. She has on a pair of my athletic shorts and a t-shirt, both of which hang off of her.

"Extraordinary," she says, bending low and setting one of her knees down beside my hip. The other follows and then she's straddling me on the couch. I lean back against the cushions and stare up at her, tugging the loose strands of her brown hair away from her face. Her freckles are sprinkled across the bridge of her nose, and her eyes shine with mischievous intent.

"Breathtaking. Ridiculously good-looking. Smart enough to join Mensa—but she would never, because she'd probably think that's pretentious."

I laugh and tug her toward me.

"Oh no!" she gasps. "What would this mystery woman think about you holding me like this?"

I press my lips to hers and she sighs into me, finally giving me the kiss I've been after all day. It starts so innocent. She's hovering just above me, wearing loose clothes and no makeup, but then I taste her and hear her moan. She sinks lower and our hips connect. I break our kiss and wrap my hands around her back, pulling down until she's flush with my chest.

"I'm sorry about the last few days. I could have handled it better."

"Forget it, Foxe." Her breathing is labored and we've barely begun. "Believe me, I have…or at least I'm about to."

She's rolling her hips, anxious to continue, but I hold her there against me, trying to get a grip on my emotions. I close my eyes and the last twelve hours flash through me—the fear that seeped in when I arrived at Madeleine's apartment to find her missing, the elation and envy when she stepped out of Carter's cruiser, wrapped up and safe in that gray blanket. Now, I can feel her heart beat against my chest, and I have the urge to confess my love for her. It's only been a few weeks and now suddenly, I want to fast forward and ask her to move in, to convince her that Mouse needs to be here at the farmhouse, that she needs to be with me.

It's a crazy notion, so I stay silent and wait for the feeling pass.

Except it doesn't.

I take hold of her cheeks and angle her face back so I can see her eyes. She's in a dreamy state, staring up at me with unspoken words.

The emotion bubbling up inside of me is a completely new feeling. I fell in love with Olivia slowly, over years. It was a love based in comfort and routine. This thing—*Madeleine*—is a new kind of love, a scary kind of love. It feels precarious and fragile, like if I'm not careful, I could lose it as easily as I found it.

"Your hands are shaking," Madeleine says, reaching up to cup my hand against her cheek.

I laugh and glance away. "It's nothing."

"Adam."

She doesn't continue until I turn back to her.

"I'm feeling what you're feeling," she admits, leaning forward and pressing her soft lips to my jaw, my cheek, my mouth. They're short, reassuring kisses, and I pinch my eyes closed, wondering if what she said could be true. "I promise, I feel it too."

But we don't say it. Not yet.

Instead, I tug her t-shirt over her head and toss it behind the couch. The shorts go next, and there on the couch, with the sun streaming in through the window, we have the slowest, most intimate afternoon of sex. I roll her on her back and hold my weight above her, desperate to remember the bits and pieces that seem so fleeting: the feel of her fingertips skating down the backs of my arms, the delicate softness of her neck as she arches up and whispers my name, her heels digging into my lower back, her skin so flushed that she looks almost burned by our lovemaking.

"Madeleine?" I whisper her name.

She's collapsed on top of me, napping, and I don't think she's awake, but I want her to be.

"Hmmm?" she hums lazily.

I love you.

Move in with me.

Marry me.

The silence drones on and she blinks her eyes open, folds her hands, and props her chin right there on my chest.

"You know you haven't even asked me to be your girlfriend yet."

I laugh at the absurdity of it considering the thoughts spiraling through my mind. "I haven't?"

"No. You announced it to your mom, but you never asked me."

My fingers are tracing a loose pattern on her naked back. "Madeleine, c'mon. You're my girlfriend."

She smiles, and maybe for right now, this is enough.

"They're going to miss me at the singles events. I was the life of the party."

"I bet."

"And I'll have to cancel my accounts on all the dating apps."

"I want to see your profile first."

"Why?"

"So I can judge your pics and your bio. What did it

say?"

She looks away. "I don't remember."

I grin. "Yes you do."

She rolls her eyes. "Fine. *Buxom brunette bombshell seeks billionaire to fix her financial woes. Millionaires need not apply.*"

"Madeleine…"

"*Sexy real estate agent wants to show you her 1-bedroom.*"

"These are coming too easily to you."

"*Sex robot seeks first real human emotion.*"

I groan.

"Okay fine, here's the real one: *Adorably dysfunctional twenty-something seeks handsome veterinarian. Serious offers only.*"

CHAPTER TWENTY-NINE

THREE MONTHS LATER, I'm in Adam's kitchen, scrambling to leave for work on time. I have on one high heel, and my hair is still up in curlers. My coffee sits cold and forgotten on the counter.

"Here, eat this," Adam says, passing me a bowl of granola and yogurt. Fresh cut strawberries are sprinkled across the top. Life update: my granola no longer comes in bar form.

"I don't have time!"

He wraps his arm around my waist and keeps me pinned against him.

"Three bites. It's good for you."

I groan like it's really a bother that he makes me breakfast and then force-feeds me. *The struggle!*

"I even added blueberries," he says, patting me on the ass on his way to feed Molly and Mouse. The two lovers are sitting very patiently by their food bowls, waiting for their morning scoop.

I take a few massive bites of granola and then drop the bowl in the sink. "I'll wash it later, I swear!"

He laughs because he knows it's not true. In this relationship, Adam got the short straw in every arena. I'm a terrible roommate. I'm messy by nature. I don't cook very often or very well, and if I had it my way, our shoes would stay in one big pile right beside the front door. It just makes sense, in my opinion.

"What time will you be home tonight?" Adam calls from the hallway.

I'm yanking curlers out as fast as possible and then brushing out my hair so I'm left with soft, simple waves.

"Maybe five? It depends how long this showing with Mr. Boggs lasts. He might keep me out of the office all morning."

He groans. "C'mon. I thought you told me last week you were done showing him properties."

"I am! I swear, after this time, I won't let him sweet-talk me anymore!"

"Why don't I believe that?" he shouts from the other room.

Because I've said the same thing every week for the last few months. I can't help it. I have a soft spot for Mr. Boggs—a soft spot for every tough client at the agency, really. Lori is still the top-selling agent, but I've completed two sales in the last month, and they were both with clients no one else wanted. I have the patience for it, and I think it pays off.

"Don't forget," I shout. "Lucas and Daisy are coming over for dinner tonight so we can do the gender reveal for their baby!"

It's a girl. I knew as soon as Daisy knew. She called me

the second she found out, but it'll be fun to see Adam's expression when they reveal it over dinner.

He steps into the bathroom and finishes buttoning his shirt. "I'm going to make my lasagna."

I groan in pleasure. "*Yes*. How many layers?"

"Nine."

"Ohhhmahgah…" I drool.

"*Maybe even ten*," he says, lowering his voice suggestively.

"Stop it, Adam." I moan. "I don't have time to change my panties."

"Well in less-sexy news, I need you to make the salad. The vinaigrette is already done. I made it this morning."

"So basically you trust me with slicing vegetables and mixing them together?"

"Basically. Maybe we'll sign up for a cooking class when we have the time."

I lean toward the mirror and swipe on my lipstick, meeting his gaze. "Or we could just get delivery and have sex every night?"

He smiles. "Wise woman."

I smack my lips together and then dash into our shared walk-in closet (*the* closet!) to retrieve my other shoe. Molly loves to drag them around the house. She doesn't chew on them, just displaces them. The Great Displacer, we call her. Fortunately, this time my high heel is waiting for me right where it should be—a rare occurrence in this house.

"Did you talk to Mr. Hall about canceling your lease?" Adam asks.

"Yeah. He took it like I expected he would."

"Hardly concealed elation?"

I laugh. "Exactly. He didn't even enforce the need for a 60-day-notice. I think he's scared I'll change my mind and want to stay."

I slip on my shoe and head back out into the bathroom. Adam is dressed for work in gray slacks and a white button-down. Sometimes, if he's operating, he'll go in wearing scrubs, but not today. Today, I get the full Dr. Foxe effect—something I'm still not quite used to.

"What?" he asks when I can't peel my eyes away.

"Nothing."

He grins. "You have that look in your eye."

"I just like when you dress like that, that's all."

"If you get home by 4:45, I'll seduce you before we start prepping dinner."

I wink. "You have yourself a deal."

I step closer and kiss him goodbye, but I don't get too close or he'll make me late. I run out of the bathroom promising to be back at 4:45 PM on the dot then it's a mad dash to the front door. I'm supposed to meet Mr. Boggs at the first showing in fifteen minutes and I don't want him to start out in a bad mood. I pat Molly and Mouse, promise to throw them the ball later, and then I'm out the door.

"Madeleine!" Adam shouts after me as I'm running down the front path. "Love you!"

"I LOVE YOU TOO!"

Though we've been saying it for weeks, a warmth still spreads over me. I love hearing him say it, and I especially love hearing him shout it across the front yard.

There's a voicemail from Mr. Boggs waiting for me on my phone once I get my old clunker to start (yes, I'm stilling driving it) and peel out of the driveway. He wants to change up the schedule and tour a different house—a house I don't have the specs on. He includes the address, but it doesn't ring a bell and there's no time to run back inside and search the property on our database.

He's just going to have to understand that we had a list we agreed upon, and I know those houses like the back of my hand. If he wants to see a different property, I'm not going to know every detail about it.

I plug the address into my phone and follow the directions.

Fifteen minutes later, I pull up in front of what used to be Hamilton Ranch, the oldest property in the whole town. It sits out on the outskirts of Hamilton now, though it's so big, the entire town sort of wraps around its perimeter. I didn't even realize it was for sale. The rumor has always been that the owners passed it down in the family for generations.

I park outside of the front gate and sure enough, there's Mr. Boggs leaning against one of the posts.

Adam would kill me if he knew I was entertaining this showing. In the last few months, Mr. Boggs' requests have turned more and more ridiculous. I don't even tell Helen about half of them because I know she'll start pestering me to drop him as a client as well.

"Mornin' Mr. Boggs," I say as I step out of the car and settle onto the uneven terrain.

Had I known we would be touring a ranch, I would have picked more practical footwear. Like tennis shoes, or a four-wheeler.

"Morning Madeleine."

He's already working on unlocking the gate.

"How do you know the combination?"

He doesn't answer; instead, he scrolls to the last digit, tugs on the lock, and then the old gate gives way.

Before us, rolling hills stretch out as far as the eye can see. In every direction, the perimeter fence continues on as if it never ends. There's no telling how far the ranch sprawls, but it's beautiful. Oak and cedar trees are scattered across the property, and I'm not sure, but I think about a half-mile up the dirt road, there's an old farmhouse that was once used by the original owners.

"I've never been here," I admit, a bit amazed by the expansive property. The unspoiled ranch land is iconic in our old town, though I haven't heard much about it in recent years, not since it was retired from cattle raising.

"Do you know how many acres are in this property?" Mr. Boggs asks as we meander up the dirt road.

"A couple hundred? Maybe a thousand? I could have checked if you'd given me warning."

He chuckles. "No need. It's close to 13,000."

My jaw drops. "You can't be serious. Who *lives* here?"

"Well soon, I will."

I burst out laughing. "Oh yeah? So you've finally found your house, Mr. Boggs? After all this time, you've settled on a tract of land so big you can see it from space?"

My sarcasm goes right over his head. "Yes. That's why we're here."

"Well, I have to give you props. I knew when you finally picked a property, it would be something spectacular."

"Madeleine, I can't help but feel like you're mocking me."

"Mocking you?! Mr. Boggs, c'mon. 13,000 acres in this part of Texas would go for what, 30 million dollars? *40 million?*"

"Closer to 50 million."

I laugh. We might as well be talking about Monopoly money.

"Well whoever owns this ranch is going to be *very* wealthy. I didn't even know it was for sale."

He turns back to face the land and his eyes narrow. "It's not officially for sale until tomorrow, which is why I want to put in an offer today."

This is an all-time low for us. For over a year, I've put up with Mr. Boggs and his incessant demands. There's not a property in town that we haven't toured at least once. He calls every hour of the day, weekends included. I've never once lost my patience with him or pestered him to make a decision about a house, but *this*—this is too far. I have a job to do, other clients who need me.

"Mr. Boggs, I'm sorry, but I don't think this is going to work anymore. I can't afford to play games all day."

"Madeleine—"

"Now you're just abusing my patience. For a year, I've showed you houses, and if you don't intend on purchasing something, you need to tell me now so I can stop wasting my time. I've enjoyed having you as a client, but at a certain point, enough is enough."

"Madeleine, have I ever once, in all our time together, said I'd like to put an offer in on a house?"

"No." That much I know for a fact.

"So listen to me when I say, I'd like to own this ranch. I've had my eye on it for a few years, and it's finally up for sale. I wanted to have a real estate agent on hand for when it eventually came up."

For a crazy person, he sounds incredibly confident.

I decide to humor him. "So for the last year, you've worked me to the bone so I'd be 'on hand' for when you buy this ranch?"

He smiles. "I admit, I put you through the ringer, but I liked your work ethic. Now I don't have to second-guess giving you the commission from this sale."

I burst out with a laugh that's impossible to contain.

"What's the commission on a property like this?"

"I was thinking about that. A million seems fair."

"Huh," I say, humoring him. "After much consideration, I'd have to agree."

"Have I ever told you what I used to do before I moved to Hamilton?"

I shake my head, stunned into silence. This whole exchange feels like a dream.

"My father started B&G Steel, and when he retired, the company was passed down to me. I worked at that company my whole life right up until about five years ago, when I finally sold it and retired."

"B&G Steel," I repeat to myself.

Even I've heard of the company.

"What month is it, Mr. Boggs?"

"August."

Huh. So this isn't an elaborate April Fools' prank.

I'm scrambling to think of another possible explanation when the sound of tires on gravel behind us draws my attention. I turn in time to see an old Ford truck roll past the entrance gate of the property, kicking up dust and dirt with its approach.

It parks a few yards away, and then an old man slides out wearing a cowboy hat and beat-up wranglers. I know who he is right away: Steve Hamilton, a descendent of the original settlers of the town. He and his family are as good as celebrities around here.

He dips his hat in greeting to Mr. Boggs and then holds his hand out to me.

"Steve Hamilton, nice to meet you."

"Madeleine Thatcher."

He smiles and claps a second hand over mine. He has a nice handshake, sturdy and warm.

"Pleasure to meet you, Madeleine. I hear you're going to facilitate this deal for us."

What the hell is happening?

"Um, I…"

"Have you ever worked as a transactional realtor before?" Mr. Hamilton asks after he drops my hand and steps back.

I shake my head. "No. I mean, I think I can do it, but…aren't these types of deals usually handled by, y'know, big brokerage firms?"

He grins. "Call me old fashioned, but I don't need a team of vultures blowin' smoke up my ass for months. And Mr. Boggs here has already made a verbal offer that's more generous than any others I'm likely to get. So I'm happy to pay someone local to handle the nitty-gritty."

I glance back at Mr. Boggs, but he's staring out at the land as if he's not even listening at all.

"Oh, okay." I decide it's best to continue on with the charade, in case Ashton Kutcher is behind some bush with a video camera. After all, Mr. Hamilton is very convincing. "Well then yes, I would love to step in and act as the transactional realtor for the property."

"All right. Good." He nods. "I think that means your commission would increase a bit, since you'll be getting a cut from each of us."

I feel faint. I fan my face, laugh, stifle it, and then offer up a gentle, *sane* smile.

"If I email you the details, can you have the paperwork drawn up this afternoon?" he asks, very calm, so blasé. *Ha.*

I will draft the paperwork in my blood, right here in the dirt if this is legitimate. I decide not to tell him that. Instead, I nod enthusiastically and promise an expedient turnaround.

"Good. All right. I'll see you two at the title company at eight tomorrow morning. I've already scheduled an appointment to close."

Then, as quickly as he arrived, he's gone, back in his old truck, reversing on the dirt road.

"I'm assuming you believe me now?" Mr. Boggs asks with a good-natured smile.

"Can you blame me for being skeptical?" I ask with wide eyes.

He shrugs. "I have kept a pretty low profile since moving here."

We head back to our cars. In all, the showing took less than half an hour, yet I stand to make piles and piles of money, more money than I'll know what to do with.

"You know what this means, right?" I ask as we cross below the iron gate.

"You'll finally have to replace that old car."

I laugh and nod. "I'm not ready to let it go yet."

But then, as if on cue, the rearview mirror on my passenger side falls off. For months, it's been hanging in there with some duct tape, but apparently, it's had enough. It rolls unceremoniously in the dirt a foot or two away from the car.

Mr. Boggs pats my shoulder. "C'mon, I'll drive you back to the agency. I imagine I'll have some explaining to do anyway."

A laugh bubbles out of me. "They're not going to believe it when I tell them."

"You're finally going to stick it to Lori."

I can barely wait.

"How many times do you think they'll let me ring my bell for a sale this big?" I ask.

"Maybe just one big bell. Hey, we oughta just fly in one

of the bells from Big Ben."

I grin. "That's a great idea! I hope we can get it here in time."

As expected, Helen and Lori don't believe me when I explain the situation.

Lori actually turns the color of her highlights, and passes out cold. She's rushed over to Hamilton Family Practice, and Daisy texts me updates on her condition; apparently, she might have had a psychotic break. Poor thing.

When I get home that evening, I pour Adam a glass of wine and tell him to sit down. His eyes are wide with suspicion.

"I have big news."

"Are you pregnant?"

He seems excited by the prospect since we both want kids.

I try to conceal my smile. "Do you want me to be?"

"I feel like that's a trick question."

I hold up my wine glass to stop him, happy with his answer. "I'm not pregnant. My announcement actually has to do with Mr. Boggs."

"Did you finally kick him to the curb today? Is that why we're celebrating with wine?"

I laugh. "Not exactly."

I fill him in on my very long, very strange day.

He shakes his head in disbelief. He too asks what month it is.

"Not an April Fools' prank."

His eyes narrow suspiciously. "Let me get this straight: old Boggsy with his fraying clothes and nearly broken cane is going to purchase Hamilton Ranch for close to 50 million dollars, and you're going to get the commission?"

I beam and pat his shoulder, attempting to be as blasé about it now as Mr. Hamilton was a few hours ago.

"That's right. Adam Foxe, it looks like you got yourself a new hound *and* a sugar mama."

He laughs and I shrug.

"Guess I'll probably have you sign a pre-nup when we get married. I mean, you're just a *lowly* veterinarian. As of tomorrow morning at eight o'clock, I'm going to be a millionaire."

"We aren't engaged yet."

"We aren't?"

"I'll probably ask any day now."

I smile. "How will that look? Everyone will think you just want me for my money."

"I can't help but feel like this might be going to your head."

He's probably referring to the southern aristocrat accent I've adopted within the last few minutes.

I fan myself like a debutante, and lean deeper into my new drawl.

"Oh Adam, that's preposterous. I'm just a lonely heiress, lookin' to hire an animal doctor to tend to my many beasts."

I motion to Mouse and Molly snuggled in the corner.

He reaches for my waist and tugs me down until I'm sitting on his lap. His mouth finds mine and he kisses me senseless. Clearly, he's had enough of my games.

"Madeleine?"

"Yeah?" I reply, breathless.

"Do I get the job?"

I can't help but smile.

"Do that thing you did the other night, and I just might consider it."

Acknowledgements

This book was inspired by my own spoiled pooches, Ollie and Louie. Much of Madeleine's experiences with Mouse were based more in fact than in fiction, rowdy puppy moments and all. Fortunately, they have never mauled a stranger on the street—*yet!*

Thank you to my friends and family for their unwavering support. Thank you also to my fellow author friends. Thank you to my readers, especially the Little Reds!

Thank you to my editor, Caitlin, and my two proofreaders, Jennifer and Alison. You're all such a pleasure to work with and I know how fortunate I am to have you on my team.

Thank you to my agent, Kimberly Brower.

Thank you to all of the bloggers who help spread the word about my books! Vilma's Book Blog, Book Baristas, Angie's Dreamy Reads, Southern Belle Book Blog, Typical Distractions Book Blog, Natasha is a Book Junkie, Rock Stars of Romance, A Bookish Love Affair, Swept Away by Books, Library Cutie, Hopeless Book Lover, and many, many more! You all have been such cheerleaders for me and I am so grateful to each and every one of you!

Find other R.S. Grey Books on Amazon!

Behind His Lens
With This Heart
Scoring Wilder
The Duet
The Design
The Allure of Julian Lefray
The Allure of Dean Harper
Chasing Spring
The Summer Games: Settling the Score
The Summer Games: Out of Bounds
A Place in the Sun
Anything You Can Do

Made in the USA
Lexington, KY
01 July 2017